I0657913

NOT YOUR AMERICA?

*****A Novel by Dr Oliver Akamnonu*****

(Also titled as "ROMANCE WITH AMERICA")

NOT YOUR AMERICA?

Dedication

This book is dedicated to our true and most-treasured friend,

Ms. **Shelia Sullivan.**

We saw in you the face of humane, exemplary and inclusive America.

Thank you for the ideals you manifest.

Appreciation

My profound thanks go to members of my family who have been most invaluable partners in this fascinating odyssey. Chika my loving wife and best friend; our immediate family members Olisa, Chibu, Somto, Chuka, Ugo and Chioma. Brandon, Bryan, Arinze and Baby Somkene our most-loving grandchildren, you bring us the greatest joys.

My friends and numerous readers have been the source of encouragement to me to continue to write. This sport and occupation have given me the greatest joy and fulfillment. My classmate, friend and co-author, eminent surgeon and Professor, Ndubuisi Eke along with your good wife Professor Felicia Eke; with your devoted readership and book-reviews of my earlier books you greatly energized me. Dr Azubuike Ezeife, Omeiheukwu 1 of Igbo Ukwu and his amiable wife Osodieme Ndidi, unquantifiable thanks for your most-treasured encouragement. Tony Nwasokwa my childhood best friend, you were the first to acknowledge and appreciate my first book and I am very grateful. Fidelis Mkparu, Teddy Anagbogu, Tony Onuchukwu, Obiora Egbuniwe, Nwachukwu Nnoka, thanks immensely for your encouragement. Tari Benebo, my esteemed senior in that great High School that molded us, I cannot thank you enough for your immense encouragement at the early stages of this fulfilling odyssey. Paul and Diane Pellerin, friends and great neighbors, you have been most exemplary. Ophelia West and Jeanne Probst, you have remained of immeasurable assistance and encouragement. My sister Patti, my brothers and their loving wives Iso and Ugoyibo, and Omeninyo and Ebere; my kinsmen and friends, Onykaozuru CY, Akaidozuka Uche, Professor Cosmas Okoro; Topsy Nnanna Okereke classmate, brother and ace sports star of all time, mercurial Mercury David Ekwunife MD,

Onyema Njoku MD, Chris Igweatu, Garnett Harrison I appreciate and thank you all. Tony Nwafor who wrote the first review of my first book, Professors Tony and Vero Udeogalanya, Mr. and Mrs Uche and Nsomma Ogbuagu, my affable and respected in-laws and friends I am truly appreciative. Fr. John, my Parish Priest, thanks immensely for those great homilies and immeasurable spiritual upliftment and enrichment; in recent times, any Sunday without you in the pulpit makes me feel that something is amiss. Ms. Maria Pagan, Messers Matthew Jaquith, Joseph Rodio and your respective teams of fine and dedicated librarians, along with other friends, classmates, family members and readers, too numerous to mention, I am truly grateful. My special thanks go to Drs Richmond Akatue and Monique Bennerman who I have neither met nor ever communicated with. You may not know this, but your academic and professional excellence, kindness and dedication to duty are greatly appreciated by many, and especially by this author.

I thank and greatly appreciate you all. And, I hope that, along with the thousands and more world-wide, who will be reading the following pages and chapters, you will find relaxation and fulfilment, witnessing the eventual triumph of good over evil and humanity over bigotry; all told with utmost simplicity and in the context and atmosphere of our everyday lives. I hope you will all continue to read this little-known author as I 'babble' along, trying to reconcile between my native proud African background and the realities of my new-found culture and my new world. It is my hope that you share with me the experience and lessons of this new little book "**Not Your America**?" This book deliberately bears a question mark after its title. Thus, together we may continue to appreciate and promote kindness and inclusiveness, and together, spread the message of love's triumph over hate, as well as the brotherhood of all men and women, not just in America, but throughout our increasingly belligerent world.

–Oliver Akamnonu

Massachusetts, USA . April 30, 2019

Other books by Dr Oliver Akamnonu:

Suppers of Many Dishes part 1

Suppers of Many Dishes part 2

The Gods Have Not Yet Spoken

"Bature" (The Unholy War and the Forbidden Letter B)

Bature Must Make Amends**

Coming Late to America

The Trial of Monogamy

The Honorable

Nation of Dead Patriots

Taste of The West

Earth's Man of Color***

Soldier Ants of War***

Konganoga: Mauling the Polity***

Arranged Marriage and the Vanishing Roots

Comedy of Naked Vampires

A Spot to Perch

Rap to Mars

Bomb of God

The Friend is the Enemy

Big Apple to Bay State

Little Baby Lydia: Grandpa, Grandma and Student Mom

(** A new and modified edition of an earlier title.)

(*** Co-authored with Professor Ndu Eke)

Chapter Table of Contents

Prologue 1

As in every situation in life

There exist in this and every society

The good, the bad, and the ugly.

There exist the very good as well as the very bad

The very good invariably grossly outnumber the very bad

Yet, the very bad often mesmerize and drown the voices of the very good.

Yes, people of goodwill and godliness predominate in every society

They predominate but they are almost always silent

They are people who see other people as people too

Irrespective of ethnicity, tongue, color or creed

They are people who see humanity beyond our origins, our color, and our beliefs.

For most Americans in the general society,

It is not a section of Americans' exclusive America;

It is not an ethnic-oriented America

No, it is rather an All Americans' America

it is one caring America, for the ultimate good of all Americans and the world.

It is to the latter group of Americans that the message should go to:

That evil thrives when the good choose to take a back seat

God and "the gods" help those who step up and help themselves

The good must be visible and speak out else evil and the evil ones seize the mantle.

Prologue 2

THE GREATNESS OF A PEOPLE!

Her greatness and strength lie

Not in her non-surpassed military might,

Not in her unquantifiable material wealth,

But the greatness of America lies in the legendry humanity which she possesses.

And when all is done

Humanity which is the bedrock of American values

Is what really matters.

--- Oliver Akamnonu

Prologue 3

"TO FIGHT BACK OR NOT TO FIGHT"

When injustice stares the citizen in the face

When bias is made manifest and the perpetrator seems to jeer

When double standards are glorified

And a section of the society looks the other way,

And somehow believes that it is "we versus them"

When bigotry is elevated from an aberration to the norm

And the few purveyors of hate dance in the streets and jeer

And the overwhelming majority who are good men and good women choose to be silent

Or, condemn in muted tongues for fear of the "radical" label

And the scorned and marginalized lick their wounds

Or appear to tuck their tails behind their legs

And retreat to their shells and have the mauling repeat with impunity;

When the will to fight back for justice,

Is dampened or extinguished by the pious cooing of feigned piety or of religion,

And the oppressed or marginalized ask the oft-repeated rhetoric thus:

"Should I fight back and confront injustice or should I pray?

Should I trust on Karma to take vengeance on my behalf?

Should I maintain culpable silence

And mislabel silence as golden to justify my cowardice

And believe that my silence will create great opportunities

For the few haters to repent and for the many good to untie their tongues?"

"To fight back or not to fight" therefore often becomes the question;

And the choice between "Turn the other cheek" and "Two eyes for an eye", extinguishes.

To run; to stand your ground;

To go down on your knees and raise your hands

And hope that the aggressor has a change of heart;

To call on your God or beckon on Karma

Or thrust your defenseless frame against an aggressor armed to the teeth

And mimic a sling-armed biblical David against an imposing Goliath;

No, none should be an option;

The *Shinning City Upon a Hill* portends much better.

Mutual love is mostly what is required

And love in itself is not too hard to imbibe

Mutual love must prevail, and assume the highest grounds

And this is America's strength and all the values for which she stands

And the world from us will take a cue,

For, only with love and equity is our humanity true.

--- Oliver Akamnonu

The Dumb Relics

"The Dumb Relics saw, but remained silent

The practitioners stood in awe as their numbers depleted by the day

Oseburuwa must be beckoned

Lest the good gets discarded with the bad."

 – Oliver Akamnonu in the book "The Pagans' Medals"

THE GREATEST OF THEM ALL

"Faith, hope and charity persist

All three

But the greatest of them all is charity."

--- Corinthians 13

Chapter 1

ODYSSEY FOR THE PROMISE OF AMERICA

"Is it morning or evening?" Dege asked rhetorically as he opened his eyes. He had dozed off momentarily on the sofa following a rich meal of *jollof rice* and chicken which had been served as a welcome meal by his sister in-law, Oyibo. The middle-aged father of four had only a few hours earlier arrived Los Angeles airport after a long trans-Atlantic flight from a South-West African airport. It was not his first entry to the United States. But it was the first time that he flew directly without being re-routed from a European country. It was an eleven-hour flight and Dege was understandably very tired. He yawned with his mouth half open but suddenly remembered that he should close his mouth with the back of his hand. This was a habit which he was in his earlier days chided for, and which he often reminded his little son to remember. Dege had traveled with his wife Doris and his teenage son Ron. They had arrived to a warm welcome to the Rancho Cucamonga California home of Dege's younger brother and sister-in-law Isogu and Oyibo.

Dege then turned his gaze towards the exquisitely-adorned kitchen of his younger brother's beautiful house. Fresh from the relative poverty and simplicity of a middle-class background in his native home in Africa, he had rarely tasted the relative opulence of a middle-class California kitchen. The kitchen was very beautiful. It might not be said to be palatial by general American standards as Dege was to later discover after visiting many upper middle-class homes in America. Yet, it was magnificent especially for a new immigrant from Africa. For Doris, Dege's wife too, what she saw was exquisite if not palatial and the latter's amazement could not be concealed in her facial expression.

"This kitchen is certainly every woman's dream", Doris said as she walked around the very spacious kitchen which had a large centrally-placed table and kitchen-sink as well as a second kitchen-drainage located at the edge of another beautifully-sculptured set of drawers that ran in a semi-circular fashion around the kitchen.

Dege tried to pronounce the name "Cucamonga" several times so as to get used to the rather difficult name. At first, he feared for his tongue whenever he pronounced the word "Cucamonga". The beautiful mountain range was said to be an extension of the San Gabriel Mountain, one of the many mountain ranges that stretched right through the western coast of the United States and apparently guarding cities of Los Angeles and Rancho Cucamonga along the entire length from the West.

Jollof rice was essentially rice cooked together with the essential ingredients of gravy-stew mixed together. It was not a regular meal in most parts of the United States. But it was a delicacy in Dege's native South-West coast of Africa. And, Dege had only spent a couple of hours as an immigrant in the United States of America. Isogu, Dege's younger brother, had a few hours earlier graciously picked Dege up from the Los Angeles Airport along with his wife Doris and their seventeen-year-old son Ron.

Doris and Ron had partaken of the delicious meal of jollof rice. After survey of the kitchen and the meal of jollof rice mother and son got busy watching television in a smaller living room which was situated at the far end of the expansive and exquisite kitchen of Isogu's and Oyibo's beautiful new house. To watch television in one's home when one was not at work during the day was a luxury in Dege's original part of the world. That was because twenty-four-hour steady electricity power supply was still considered a luxury for most citizens who did not have stand-by electricity generating sets. Public electric power whose steady supply was taken for granted in the developed world, was, in Dege's native country, often rationed even in those early twenty first century years of human civilization. Most homes received a maximum of eight to twelve hours of intermittent electric power supply over every twenty-four-hour period most of the times. At other times, there could be total absence of electric power supply for many days at a stretch. More affluent communities who had "connections in high places" or who regularly lobbied the operators of the electric power industry could have slightly longer hours of electric power supply. And the monthly bills would still be expected to be paid by consumers whether or not they had had power supplied to them for any period of time during the month or not. The foregoing was the background from which the Dege and Doris family, legal Permanent Residents and later citizens of the United States of America, were coming from.

"Uncle, good evening!" Dege's five-year-old nephew Nathan, had greeted as he ran down the beautiful spiral staircase to greet his visiting uncle from Africa. "Nathan, good morning" Dege had replied. Dege had responded to Nathan's "good evening" greeting with a "good morning", believed that his little nephew being so young was mistaking the time of day. But Nathan was right. It was indeed almost 5pm but Dege it was, who was mistaking the time of day. Jet lag and travel fatigue had taken a toll on him and without a look at his wrist watch or the wall clock he could not immediately decipher correctly what time of day it was. The nearly half day difference in time zones between where Dege came from and Los Angeles further West of the Atlantic Ocean, had had an effect on Dege's time estimation.

"Uncle have you seen my new toys? Mommy and daddy bought them for my birthday", Nathan continued. Nathan was a very intelligent young boy. His lack of shyness and amiability greatly amazed Dege.

In a twinkle of an eye Nathan had rushed upstairs to his room and was soon back with a set of toys in a small box. They were train coaches with an engine that was very life-like. Nathan started assembling the coaches of the toy train by way of demonstration. His dexterity as he meticulously assembled the toy train was amazing. He knew where each car fitted perfectly. Where any did not quite fit he readily made adjustments until he secured a perfect fit.

Nathan's box of toys also contained even more complicated components. One was a disjointed dragon which on assemblage appeared to be spitting fire. Nathan meticulously assembled the different components correcting himself where he faltered along the way.

Dege had purchased toys for kids in the past but he had never imagined that five-year-old children would be able to operate such complicated toys as he saw Nathan successfully do on that day. He began to understand and ruminate on the possible reasons for the technological-development disparities even at such early ages between children in the developed world who grew up with modern technology and computers vis-à-vis their counterparts in the under-developed world who grew up with sticks and wooden toys. Children in the technologically-advanced world started early in life to play with fairly complicated pieces of electronics while their counterparts in the less technologically-developed world might often make do, if they were lucky, with some wooden carvings as toys. Early exposure to modern technology would obviously put the child in the western world at a big advantage in many ways. Sophisticated toys coupled with early formal education in very well-organized and excellently-staffed school systems would complete the cycle of educational excellence for the child in the West. Intellectual parity with his or her western peers or even excellence in many cases, would only begin to manifest if early intervention was instituted. Otherwise, the poor rural Third World child would grow up relishing the narrow world of nomadism with sticks, catapults and a withered wide hat as shield against the raging sun. Some tattered clothing over his waist and shoulder and a pair of make-shift slippers as protection for his trekking-withered toes would become his lot as he grows. And the developmental disparity widens by the day, exacerbated daily by unrelenting corruption-ridden socio-political leadership and a docile or severely-intimidated followership. And of course, in the midst of the corruption, capital and intellectual flights supervene and foreign interventions coalesce to complete the cycle of decline. And those who have the opportunity to escape the decay take off while the others either struggle to integrate into the social rot and decay or find themselves playing the roles of ineffectual ceaseless critics at the mercy of the emerging strongmen.

"Does your train carry passengers?" Dege asked Nathan.

"Yes, it does. But they are all asleep now inside the car" Nathan replied.

Dege did not at first understand. Nathan quickly unhooked a clip at the top of one of the coaches and displayed many seated "passengers." Some of the toy passengers were clutching toy newspapers on their hands. But the majority were seated and were "sleeping ", just as Nathan had explained.

"I can wake up some of the passengers" Nathan quietly said. "Really?" Dege asked.

Nathan immediately pressed a small button at the floor of one of the "sleeping passengers" inside the coach. Thereupon the stimulated passengers started nodding their heads in acknowledgment of some jazz music that had immediately started to play.

The ensuing excitement was not just for Nathan who giggled loudly when the "passengers" started nodding their heads. Even Dege, who had seen many battery-operated toys in the past could not hide his amazement at how far toy technology had advanced. For Nathan even as he giggled, it was no big deal. He was growing up amidst bewildering technology into which he would imperceptibly fit. For Dege, his mind could not stop wandering some 8,000 miles across the Atlantic. He remembered the wooden baby toys which he and his childhood friends played with as children in Africa half a century earlier. "Millions in Nathan's age group still play with wooden toys in my native country. Some have been lucky to graduate to fairly sophisticated plastic toys. Only a small percentage of the privileged ones can possess what Nathan was playing with. It is no wonder that people of my generation who did not grow up with modern technology will continue to struggle to fit in, into the technology-controlled world of the West", Dege said.

"These passengers are all great guys. And they are very smart too. They wake up when I tickle them. Hey, guys, wake up. Uncle wants to see you!". Nathan again said as he tickled the leg of one of the "sleeping" passengers. Thereupon the passenger immediately again went into agitated motion.

Again, even for Dege as an adult, it was all so very amazing, so very fascinating.

"If there could be so much fascination with children's toys" Dege said to Doris, "can you imagine how much more fascinating the larger society will be when we get fully settled and assimilated into the general American society". The enthusiasm was very high. The promises of America were monumental for this middle-aged couple who had applied for, and procured Permanent Residency of the United States in their desperate quest to provide the best educational opportunities for their 'Little Baby'.

"The fascination may not always be in that order of ascending crescendo, Dege." Doris said, "Children are different and simple-minded. Adults could be conniving and sometimes more withdrawn especially in company of strangers."

"True, but science and the advantages of technological inventions do not discriminate between the old and the young. It certainly will be great fun when we get better settled." Dege said.

"We will work very hard as we look forward to the fun, Dege." Doris said. "I take any promise as a mere promise. A promise is one thing. Its materialization is another. Indeed, finding of personal fulfillment in a fulfilled promise is yet another kettle of fish. All I want is the opportunity to work hard, secure a very good education for our *Little*

Baby Ron, and enjoy peace and quietness after each day's hard work. And at the end I would wish to retire quietly and to play with my grandchildren". Doris said, smiling, and with her gaze still glued at Nathan and his toys.

The to-and-fro conversation between the new immigrant couple continued unabated even as Nathan continued relentlessly with maneuvering of his toy train. The passengers still nodded as Nathan repeatedly tickled them.

"Hmmm, Doris, you are already talking of grandchildren even when your children are still in school. Why don't you pray for your children to remain level-headed, read hard, graduate, settle down and marry in the first instance?" Dege advised.

"Why won't they marry; didn't we marry? Do Ron and his siblings look to you as people who would not be level-headed enough to marry and give you lovely grand children?" Doris responded.

"Yes, Doris, we married. And we did so at the appropriate time. But don't you see that things are changing so fast. Our generation is not like these children's generation." Dege said.

"You always called me a pessimist but now it looks like you are the pessimist, Dege". Doris said, looking steadily into Dege's eyes.

For a while Dege did not say more. He merely shrugged his shoulders in apparent agreement and resignation. Finally, he softly said: "Let me live my own life first. Let everyone else live his or her own life and find and radiate happiness all around us. I believe that whatever be the promises and fascinations of America, the ultimate promise that is worth looking up to is the promise of an environment that will confer personal contentment for the individual."

Husband and wife were still naturally apprehensive about the prospects of success in their new country. They awoke each morning praying that they would not have to regret their ditching a known den of political and uniformed thieves in which they found some luxury and inclusiveness, for an unknown habitat which smacked of an Eldorado from afar but one in which they would be mere on-lookers. Amidst the many fascinations around them, they happily discussed the prospects of contentment in the fast-moving new country.

Nathan the owner of the toy trains under initial discussion, was busy assembling, dismantling and reassembling the cars of his sophisticated trains.

Meanwhile Ron the sixteen-year old "Little Baby of the house" as Dege and Doris often referred to their teenage son, was sleeping soundly in the bedroom adjoining the first-floor family living room. He had accompanied his parents on the long one-way immigrant flight from their native South-West Africa to the United States.

Chapter 2

FORAGE INTO THE GARDENS: A COMPARATIVE OVERVIEW OF THE LARGER SOCIETY

Dege soon stepped out into the flower gardens in front of the building. His brother Isogu's house was situated on a slightly-elevated section of the neighborhood. Dege was thus able to view a cross section of the houses and well-paved streets and lanes in the neighborhood. He was stunned by the beauty and orderliness.

"I marvel at what I see" Dege declared, half musing, half talking to the hearing of his equally-amazed but largely reticent wife Doris. "And I hear that this part of Rancho Cucamonga beautiful as it is, is not necessarily the most fascinating part of this city, talk less of the state of California." Dege said.

"Look at the thoroughly-manicured garden. Look at the serenity of the neighborhood. It's all so amazing, Doris."

Doris remained silent for a while and then quipped:

"The neatness of the neighborhood is stunning. Perhaps this is so because of the fact that we have just arrived from a clime where sanitation contractors often collect their payments for twice-weekly trash collections and render services only once in six or eight weeks, if ever at all." Doris said.

"You are right Doris. Of course, when sanitation workers don't get paid, the delinquency invariably leads to perpetual piling up of refuse which would block road intersections, block entire streets and attract all manner of buzzing flies and vermin. Of course, diarrheal diseases would ensue. And the money budgeted for preventive and curative health services would in turn be brazenly embezzled by conniving politicians and their cronies.

And nobody would query the defaulting contractors. The supervising officers who would have issued the query have been heavily bribed into silence by the contractors. And the Developed World would ridicule the Underdeveloped World. They would placate us by not referring to us as the Third World. And we would take offence at the derogatory language. And the Developed World would do us a favor. They would drop the term Underdeveloped. They would then elevate our status to the level of Developing World. And we will be happy at the elevation. And only God knows for how long we would remain at the level of developing." Dege said.

"Have you considered the possibility of developing in the negative direction?" Doris asked.

"Yes, Doris. Sometimes it appears that some societies are developing in the negative from the time their former colonizers left them. Perhaps the colonialists may be responsible for the problems by deliberately ensuring that the so-called developing world remains perpetually developing. This appears to be more so among African countries." Dege paused and with a heavy sigh he appeared to have a change of mind about who to blame for the lack of technological as well as socio-political development of his homeland.

"It is easy to lay blames and try to exonerate oneself. Was our native country not at one time at the same level of technological development with the so-called Asian Tigers? Our native country at

29

one time had a higher GDP than South Korea. But today, South Korea has transited to First World status while most of Africa tends to retrogress even in spite of the monumental deposits of natural resources within the African continent." Dege said.

"It is not all about natural resources, Dege. It is more of human resources. What do you expect in a situation where the best of your people migrate out of the country to the already-developed First World where they make their marks and largely refuse to repatriate some of their skills?" Doris said.

"Yes. Dege. But one can only repatriate some of the skills where there is the enabling environment. How do you replicate your skills where there is no electric power supply and no security? It is a sad chain of events which must be addressed at source. And the source is a re-orientation of the systems of values in the relevant society. A society that worships wealth and high societal status without verifying the source of the underlying wealth can never hope to rise beyond the mediocrity level." Dege said as he turned to the opposite direction, indicating a wish to end the not-very-pleasant discussions.

It did not take long for Dege to familiarize himself with the environment. He was completely new to the environment. He had no car, no house and indeed no business where he was either an owner or an employee. He quickly forced himself to accept that he was no longer the prominent and highly-respected elite that he used to be in his country of origin before he made the far-reaching decision to emigrate to the United States of America. In the latter falsely-affluent situation, Dege had people who washed his cars in the morning. Others did his cooking and many more attended to many of his everyday chores including chauffeuring him around town, and to his businesses and back. And whenever he got to his office building in the morning many "Good morning" greetings that got nothing done, would herald him from the entrance door of the building to his office door. Of course, it was all ridiculously-flawed and unrealistic. It was as unnecessary as it was ridiculous. It would have been unsustainable if people fulfilled their civic responsibilities to the underprivileged and the general society at large. But that was a different society. And Dege was quick to acknowledge the difference.

"Once educated and on a good job, we tend at home, to live well-above our means with too many redundant staff and too many hangers-on. Our productivity tends to decrease instead of increase as we go up the ladder of seniority. Accountability diminishes up the ladder and tends to vanish altogether once the top of the ladder is reached. And the magnitude of responsibility decreases exponentially as one climbs up to the level of CEO. And thus, blame and punishment for lapses and failures are borne by subordinates rather than the truly responsible chief executives. The ship of state saunters perilously and industry greatly suffers. And management absolves itself from blame. And no chief executive resigns or gets fired. And the decadence perpetuates until the state of final collapse. And that is the society of our birth!" Dege surmised, more out of personal experience and on-the-spot appraisal than from mere academic studies.

But even with Dege's apparent high position in the society of his origin, he always feared for his safety. He feared for his personal safety from government-sponsored men in uniform consequent upon his rather too vocal stances in many socio-political issues in which the powers-that-be, held opposing views. He also feared for his personal safety from men of the underworld, organized kidnapers who lived

31

among the people and who sometimes were known to the people but who would never be apprehended by law enforcement. Even when the hoodlums demanded that their dictated ransom be deposited at very open locations they might still never be successfully apprehended without some kind of inducement from the victim's end to the appropriate authorities. And even in such situations the palms of chains of security agencies might need to be greased to allow the kidnappers collect the ransom and depart without inflicting further harm or even causing death of the victim. And the state security apparatus whose duty it was to protect the citizens and apprehend the criminals would be completely hamstrung *by choice,* if not incapacitated. Credible rumors would even have it that some of the government agencies were in collusion with the perpetrators. Perhaps part of the booty might trickle down to a few unscrupulous people in other forms of uniform. And the latter were also supposed to be protecting the populace.

The foregoing was the society which Dege was escaping from. It was the highly-endowed environment where the greed of man had broken bounds and had decreed that things would not work. And things did not work! And the perpetrators of the unworkability would deposit their loot in financial institutions in the so-called Developed World and fly back and move around the same socially-depraved society and pot-hole-laden roads and corruption-ridden governance from where they had stolen the wealth. And the banks in the developed nations or the latter's agents in certain obscure locations would help to secure and safeguard the loot and shield the criminals and turn around and accuse the victim-nations of corruption. In a few isolated instances they would cry "money-laundering" and repatriate a small percentage which would again be embezzled by authorities in the originally deprived nations. And the never-ending cycle of economic official looting would continue.

Dege and Doris were thrilled at the opportunity of being part of the Developed World even when as new-comers, they were still on-lookers in the scheme of things.

As Dege and Doris stepped into the larger society they were to discover that the picture of America that they saw in movies and from story books was far different from the real America which they were trying to settle into. It was an America almost totally different from the America which they witnessed when they used to come on annual vacations. It was a society where the doctrine was work, work and more work. They found a society which took pride in repeating the gospel that there is *no free lunch in America.* Unlike in their native environment every penny mattered and every dime must be well-earned.

During the couple's earlier mostly two-week visits they did not have the opportunity of meeting or inter-acting with the much poorer and often obscure segment of the society. These were the segment of the society that inhabited the city suburbs and the down-trodden parts of the Bronx in New York City and certain areas of the cities of Chicago and Los Angeles.

As a visitor in earlier days, Dege had visited the so called Down-Town areas of the cities of New York, Dallas and Los Angeles. Those were the largely business and tourist areas bustling with dazzling lights and glamorous stores and shopping centers.

In those areas, apart from the occasional homeless man clutching a big pack of his personal belongings in big polythene bags or trolleys, the impression that the average visitor or tourist would have, was that of an America where everything was perfect and everyone was courteous. The promises of America loomed extremely large to the tourist. But the realities on the ground were not always rosy. The average visitor or tourist would see an America where poverty appeared to be non-existent and everything worked. The image thus painted was one of an Eldorado of sorts.

Yes, modern day America, the United States that is, smacked of an Eldorado of sorts as regards utilities like electric power supply, trash collection, regular pipe borne water supply and good road networks in all urban and rural communities. But perhaps that was only as far as it went. As regards the other widely-spread luxuries which would be expected to be components of a typical Eldorado it was all a fantasy for many. The Eldorado was perhaps only for1% of the top 1% of the population in the socio-economic ladder. Perhaps for the subsequent 99% of the top 1% it was a society of awesome satiety, while perhaps for the remaining 99% and more, of the general population, in differing degrees, it ranged from utter satiety and comfort to a massive public and commercial jail house where neither the jailer nor the jailed two million and more, were fully free nor fully in chains. That was even as each saw himself or herself as citizen of the freest nation on Earth who was fully-fed yet one who saw marginalization and denial of sense of belonging, staring him or her in the face.

34

Yes, this was America, God's own country, "one nation under God, indivisible, with liberty and justice for all".

This was America, planet Earth's longest lasting democracy, the world's only surviving super power.

This was America the beautiful, and by most accounts, the compassionate.

But this was America which appeared to relish the image of affluent do-gooder princes abroad while a small vocal minority of her population with little hinderance, appeared to ignore or even participate in bigotry, hate speeches or perhaps hate crimes at home and at rallies.

It was an America where, despite the great promises, gradual relapse to veiled (and sometimes overt) racism by the same small vocal minority, loomed large.

It was an America where possibility of relative abject poverty and penury, of a large percentage of her own at home, hangs by the whiskers of social security and social welfare benefits.

It was America harboring rural and urban Americans whose faces might never be seen on television or even social media but who steadily and rapidly had sunk back far below what could be imagined of any developed First World nation.

This was America the faces of a growing number of whose citizens had become so debilitated by "substances" and social disharmony that many had almost reached a point of no return.

This was the America in which an appreciable percentage of its rural populace was one pay-check away from penury and which got saddened if not angrier by the day at the uncertainty of the next day even as they daily saw many of their countrymen in high places getting wealthier at their expense.

It was an America where carefully choreographed and orchestrated chants about reclaiming of lost glory and international prestige may sensitize the unwary leading to uncharacteristic hostility to other innocent citizens.

It was an America where promises or actualization of tax cuts sounded to a large percentage of the population like fables and talks from a far-off country because it greatly favored the wealthy and really never got to the poor.

Surely it was an America where the disparity between the stupendously rich and the utterly poor widened by the day and once-friendly ordinary citizens goaded by chants or instigations of economic insecurity uncharacteristically developed hostility to migrants and other strangers whom they would begin to suspect of scheming to take over their jobs.

Yet, sullen as the picture might appear, it remained America the beautiful. It remained America the compassionate, an America where the silent majority remained God-fearing and humane. It remained an America whose "can-do spirit" and love of country were so very commendable and could always be relied upon to save it even in the worst of situations.

The latter assertion would of course stand, provided, and indeed only provided, that mutual love and mutual respect prevailed; hard work and industry remained unhindered and, most importantly, that America's upcoming generations were strongly taught love of neighbor and love of country. It would materialize the better if the upcoming generations are taught to eschew politically-motivated divisiveness and the utterly destructive drift to implosion from racial and religious hate and bigotry. The latter could only bolster disunity and mutual mistrust and had been known to wreck many once powerful nations in the past.

Chapter 3

RELOCATING TO THE CITY CENTER

It was soon time for Dege and Doris to relocate from Rancho Cucamonga to Los Angeles. For the couple, one of the original aims of immigration to America apart from the quest for security and peace of mind, was to stabilize the couple's children especially the youngest. The older two siblings were already studying and were fairly well settled in their studies. Having enjoyed the comfort of Rancho Cucamonga for a couple of weeks, it became necessary to relocate to Los Angeles to physically stay with the rest of the children.

It was akin to relocating from a palace to a ghetto, relocating from the opulence of a modern five bed-room house in a high-brow area of Rancho Cucamonga California to an old one-bed-room apartment in one of the older areas of Los Angeles. Yes, by American standards the Los Angeles apartment was certainly not a great place, being a relatively old apartment with the barest minimum in terms of furnishing: a fridge, a microwave, an old gas cooker and a standing heating unit. There was no dishwasher, and no car garage. The coin laundry that was provided was for community usage and was on the expensive side. The few free street parking spots along Alexandria Avenue had alternate day street sweeping and most of the metered parking spots were for maximum of 2 hours. The latter made for residents being perpetually in danger of getting parking tickets. There was hardly peace of mind for car owners in that part of the city. None was at mind's ease if they parked their cars along the roadside from

7am to 6pm all week days. Perhaps it was not expected that people who lived in that part of the city would own cars. True to that expectation Dege and Doris did not own a car for the first two months of their stay in Alexandria Avenue Los Angeles. They later came to own one, courtesy of one of their older sons who was relocating to New York City.

As would be expected, with the owning of a car came the many added burdens of car ownership in Los Angeles. All in all, the fascinations for Dege, Doris and Ron were truly immense.

"I too will like to be a doctor, Mom." Ron had repeated to his mother Doris as the two walked leisurely home from a 9AM Sunday service in the Catholic Church in their Downtown Los Angeles neighborhood. Ron was looking forward to entry into college. Doris was a Catholic and was quite a committed one too. Ron being the youngest of Dori's four children, was usually the latter's companion during her attendance at Sunday morning church services right from Ron's much younger years. This was even when other members of the family who were around, might choose to attend latter Sunday Masses or even skip attendance all together.

"Yes, you too will be a doctor. But that will be if you study very hard to make the right GPA and score high marks in the MCAT or relevant prescribed exams. You must work hard to score very high marks in case your other credentials are deemed insufficient." Doris told her "baby".

"You and dad may have to help find out from some of your friends whose sons are in Colleges here what pathways they followed to make their children succeed." Ron said. Ron was coming from a clime where his friends often narrated the sometimes-unwholesome pathways their friends' parents had to explore before their children and wards could secure College admissions. Ron was fearful that his parents might as usual choose to "let events play out their normal courses." Dege in particular had often manifested stolid aversion to having to "lobby" someone in high places in governance or in the academic institutions for the purposes of securing admission for any of his children into college.

"Success is dependent more on hard work and less on prayers and public relations, Ron." Doris said. "You have to study hard for the TOEFL and other exams, check out what others who had succeeded did, what they read, what hours and dedication they put in, and what they concentrated on. You need to study past questions, time yourself and work hard to improve on your scores. Above all you must pray hard for divine guidance because you cannot do it all on your own."

As she spoke, Doris cast a quick glance at her son who was busy with the key board of his cell phone as he walked alongside her. Feeling that his son ought to be deep in thought about working and praying for success instead of habitually playing with a cell phone, Doris chided:

"You don't appear to be listening to what I am telling you, Ron. Success is a product of hard work and dedication to your books not to your cell phone. Those numerous text messages and chats with friends can wait for now."

"Yes mom, I know. But I also need to network and communicate with friends so as to know what others in similar situations are doing. I have already applied to three institutions among which, as you and dad suggested is the State University here in Los Angeles as well as The University of California here in LA. I enclosed all my CV and the other documents and academic transcripts which they required. But you know how these things work, at least in our home country. I don't know about this place, whether you also have to know somebody before you are admitted."

The rest of the quarter mile trek to the rented family's apartment went without further discussions as neither mother nor son would wish to sour the Sunday morning any further.

.

Chapter 4

FACING THE REALITIES AND CHALLENGES OF COLLEGE WORK

Ron had secured admission into University of California Los Angeles, UCLA, for medical sciences. He had just completed his high school prior to relocation to the United States and had scored high marks in the Test of English as a Foreign Language (TOEFL) and other college-entry required exams.

It was a thoroughly challenging, yet exciting moment for Ron on the day that he received the admission letter from the college. It was very exciting seeing the smoothness of college admission process once the student qualified and scored highly enough to be among the most outstanding. It was exciting seeing the cordiality in communication between prospective students and the admission officers. It was even more exciting seeing the patience and understanding of the admission officers, the attention to details notwithstanding. As Ron observed, he marveled at the orderliness and the mutual respect that existed between the college staff and the prospective students and the peace of mind and reassurance that the care and environment gave to the parents.

"I marvel at the orderliness and the courtesy extended to prospective students." Ron said. It is as if old friends are discussing. I had the opportunity of personally meeting the admissions officer. Even when he had never met me before he was so courteous and even called me by my first name. I felt I was already part of the University community." Ron emphasized, smiling broadly as he narrated his experience on a visit to the University's Admissions office to his mother.

"I am very happy for you Ron. Your dad and I have decided that you will live in-campus or at least one of the Students' Halls of Residence for easier access to the Lecture Halls and for easier bonding with other students." Doris told Ron.

"But I understand that it is quite expensive, Mom," Ron said.

"Yes, we will shoulder the financial burdens as much as we can, and with time, you will inevitably have to apply for students' loan." Doris further stated.

"I understand mom, I have assured dad that I will ensure that I am as prudent as possible financially. I also understand that there are a few part time job opportunities like working in the University's security Department on a part time basis."

"That's my boy!" Dege shouted. "I was about to suggest to you that you need to occasionally combine studies with work, realizing our very tight financial situation. I am happy the decision emanated from you." Dege said, feeling obviously relieved.

On the first day that Ron moved into residence as a college student it was a mixture of joy and apprehension for Doris. After Dege and Doris had driven their son to his college residence they helped him convey his bags into the room that he shared with another student. It was a "studio apartment". The scanty furniture consisted essentially of a small bed, a reading table and chair, and a small refrigerator for each room occupant. Doris sat on the chair. Dege stood for the length of time that the couple spent in the room with their son. Ron's room mate was not in the room when Ron moved in.

"We should now be on our way, Doris", Dege said after a while. There was no response from Doris. The wish to go home was repeated after a further ten minutes. The muteness was indicative that Doris was reluctant to go home. She appeared very relaxed in the scantily-furnished room. She repeatedly brought up another topic for discussion to while away the time. But at last it was time to depart. The "baby" of the house must be allowed to mature and live with a roommate away from home for the first time. On his own part, Ron appeared indifferent to whether the parents stayed longer in the room or not. His roommate a very amiable sophomore student soon came back and the freshman appeared eager to get around and survey the college environment.

Mid-way on the drive back to their Los Angeles Alexandria Avenue apartment, Doris turned sideways and looked at the floor of the back seat. She saw that Ron's bathroom slippers was forgotten inside the car.

"Gosh! Ron forgot his bathroom slippers in the car". Doris exclaimed. Her exclamation was reminiscent of someone who had narrowly missed a fortune.

"That's no big deal Doris. Ron is a big boy now and he can easily procure another pair of bathroom slippers". Dege said, almost disinterestedly.

"This is terrible, how is the poor boy going to manage without his slippers after a shower?"

"This pair of slippers is only one dollar in Dollar Store. Ron can readily buy another one in any nearby store."

"No, we need to drive back to drop it for him. He will be greatly inconvenienced without it".

"But he needs to start learning to improvise."

"No, not at these early stages Dege. I don't want the poor boy to suffer."

And the argument went on for, and against, the couple having to drive back to drop a pair of slippers for Ron.

"Ha, ha, Doris, could it be that we purposely forgot the slippers?"

"Not at all. Why would anyone do such a thing?"

"One might want to have a reason for going back to check out on one's little baby."

"Or the baby might want a reason to make mom and dad drive back to check on him?"

It appeared as if neither dad nor mom would want to lose the argument.

But at the end, as was usually the case, Dege conceded.

"You win, Doris. Let's drive back to the college campus. We will go to drop off the one-dollar worth of bathroom slippers".

Doris heaved a sigh of apparent relief.

"These are sacrificing that parents have sometimes to make for their children." She said.

"Hey Ron, your parents are back!" one of the students was overheard shouting out to Ron as the former sighted Doris clutching a small packet wrapped in polythene bag and walking briskly towards her son's allocated room.

Ron had already made new friends. He was fully relaxed in the dormitory and was laughing and joking around with three other students when the anxious Doris came into the room.

"All the anxiety is completely misplaced. But it is at the least reassuring to me that my baby is not lonely or in distress." Doris whispered to Dege.

"I told you that Ron would be all right. There would be many more things that he would need to purchase from the stores, and he would have managed very well without the slippers." Dege said.

"Yes, indeed. I agree completely with you but at least Dege, we have satisfied our curiosity." Doris replied.

"I hope Ron did not also forget his tooth paste or his comb. Perhaps we might discover that either or these was forgotten in the trunk of the car when we start parking the car at a difficult-to-secure parking space along Alexandria Avenue. That would be a more cogent reason to drive back. Lucky Ron! He certainly is very lucky to be doing well academically even as mommy's handbag. Not many handbags make such successes."

Doris, cast a passing glance at her husband as the latter spoke sarcastically. She was already very used to Dege's sarcasm and jokes. She therefore merely smiled wryly and said: "You call Ron a handbag when he is already taller than each of us, Dege. I am yet to see any handbags that tall. Very soon too he will equal or surpass each of us in the academics. That way he would have become a master-handbag."

"Sure, Doris, that is what every parent prays for, isn't it? Doctor-handbag will even be better."

"And that is why we should drive back to deliver his tooth paste for him if we discover that he forgot this in the trunk of the car!" As if to assuage her fears, Doris immediately walked to the rear of the car and opened the trunk.

"I want to convince myself that no tooth brush or tooth paste was also forgotten in the trunk", Doris said, as she smiled wryly. Dege cast a furtive glance at his wife but said nothing. He was obviously relieved that he did not have to argue about driving back to the college campus to drop a tooth brush or a tooth paste.

After parking the car Dege and Doris walked into a nearby grocery store to buy a gallon of milk.

As they walked into the living room of the one-bedroom apartment a mildly-unexpected sight awaited them: there on the center table in the living room, was a small transparent bag containing among other things, Ron's hair comb, his electric shaver and his toothbrush and toothpaste!

Doris picked up the transparent bag and displayed it before Dege as the couple simultaneously burst out laughing.

"I told you so, Doris! So, now shall we drive back to the college campus to drop the toothpaste? Certainly, his electric-shaver is costlier and perhaps more important to him than the pair of slippers!"

"You win, Dege!" Doris said in reciprocity.

There was no further mention of driving back to the University campus.

Chapter 5

THE FRUITS OF HARDWORK AND PERSISTENCE

Three years had gone by very quickly. Ron had been very dedicated in his studies aided by constant reminders from his parents that he needed to score very highly in his college grades if he wished to fulfil his ambition of getting into the medical school.

"Shoot for the moon in your GPA, Ron, and if you miss, you will land on the stars". Dege again reminded Ron in a text message. This admonition was so often repeated to Ron that it literally became his watchword. In keeping with the constant prodding, Ron had studied very hard and did not disappoint. He regularly came home with A's and A+ in most of his courses to the great joy of his parents.

Semester after semester, year after year, Ron, the tall lanky black student from South-West Africa greatly impressed his teachers academically, and made his parents proud. He was a household name in almost all his classes, bagging honors as he went. Student loans, scholarships, grants and regular small financial input from his parents had ensured that Ron's college education was well funded.

It was again that time of the year when prospective medical students, college seniors who had the intention of studying medicine, would need to sit for the Medical College Admission Tests, the so-called

MCAT. Those were the highly competitive standardized tests administered by the Association of American Medical Colleges AAMC.

Ron had never relented in his oft-repeated desire to follow the family tradition to become a medical doctor.

"It is like a family tradition and I must not be the one to break the trend" he often said.

"I have worked very hard and have made A's in most of my classes. But I understand that some of these MCAT exams could be treacherous. I understand that success in them is not based purely on how much academic stuff that one knows. I understand that a lot also depends on how much of the examination technique that one has". Ron had told his mother.

"Yes, Ron, but the fundamental fact is that hard work and fundamental good grips of the academic stuff make most of the difference". Doris had replied.

"Yes, I know mom. I know that I now have to work very hard to make good grades in the MCAT."

Ron was not disappointed. He always had his eyes on gaining admission into Columbia University New York, University of California Los Angeles or to one of the historically Black Medical Colleges in that order. His first room-mate in college who had gained admission into the historically Black Medical College in Nashville Tennessee, had talked so highly of his experience in his school vis-à-vis what his other friends in some other medical schools narrated. He had told Ron of how friendly and hardworking the students were and how cooperative and caring the faculty and other staff of his medical school were. He spoke particularly highly of one of the Program Directors in the college.

"The medical school here is so very different from college work, Ron. The senior students make you feel so much at home. And the teachers treat you as family. They treat you with courtesy and respect as the adult which you are. It is a completely new world in the academics." Tim, Ron's former roommate who was in the renowned medical school at Meharry Medical College had written to Ron. The latter's enthusiasm about entering the medical school was greatly enhanced after reading Tim's letter.

Even in spite of his skepticism after the exams, Ron's aggregate result in the MCAT was very good. It was no surprise that he secured interviews into seventeen of the eighteen Medical Schools which he applied to. Most of the institutions that he applied to were situated in the East Coast of the United States.

"I have spent all my college years in the West Coast. I would now want to survey the East Coast, especially the North East". Ron told his parents. He was in very high spirits during attendance at the numerous interviews. His college GPA of 3.98 made him even more confident.

"It is my ambition to match at Harvard. If this fails, I would be glad to be accepted into one of the other Ivy League Institutions." Ron said.

Even though he did not match to the school of his first choice he matched into one of his best choices, Columbia University Medical School.

"Finally, mom and dad, the path has been cleared for the fulfillment of my long dream of becoming a medical student preparatory to becoming a medical doctor." Ron gleefully told his dad and mom when he called the latter on first receiving the good news that he had matched to Columbia University Medical School.

Dege and Doris had accompanied Ron to the airport in Los Angeles on the latter's departure to New York. Even though Ron had done a lot of travels during his interview period, the journey to New York for the commencement of his medical school training was to be the first time that he would be far away from home for any extended period of time. While Ron was in residence in University of California Los Angeles, Doris could readily visit and see her "baby" within half an hour drive.

"I could not sleep very well last night, Ron; we are certainly going to miss you". Doris told Ron as the latter did his final packing on the morning of his departure to New York.
"But I am an adult, mom. I will miss the family, but I will certainly cope very well and will stay in constant communication", Ron said.

It was an emotional farewell at the Los Angeles Airport as Doris and Dege hugged their son repeatedly prior to the latter's checking-in for the flight to New York.

The enthusiastic and highly-determined first year medical student of Columbia University had arrived the campus in New York. In a detailed first mail to his parents soon after arrival on campus in New York had stated thus:

"It's even a more beautiful place than I thought after the interviews, dad and mom. The apartment though less spacious and may be a little older than in L.A, is very good and literally within the campus. There is quite some congestion, but New York City rocks. But this is not what I am here for. I am here to study and to become a doctor. The housing rent is high but It is a very good price for the installed amenities. There may be extremes of weather conditions but there are no earthquakes or periodic forest fires.

"There are as many, if not more tourist attractions and amusement parks as I used to see in Los Angeles. But again, these are not what I am here for. Even with the congestion and the noise, there is tremendous physical and economic development with great relaxation amenities. All races and all creeds mill along the busy streets. I find New York very rich in culture and music, especially in this Manhattan area. And I am sure that Dad will find so much to write about when you visit."

Strands of tears of joy flowed down Doris's cheeks as she read her son's first mail from New York along with her husband. Even though mother and son had spoken many times on phone, the physical written mail from Ron made more impact on Doris than the calls.

"My little baby is now a man, very soon to be a doctor. I cannot wait to see him wearing the white coat with his name tag and MD attached to his name", Doris said as she read the mail again from the beginning.

"Hey, Doris, that is vanity if an MD tag is all we are looking forward to. I look forward to what difference Ron will make in other people's lives with his medical education." Dege said.

"Yes, but he will have to have the degree first and an MD tag is emblematic of the degree. Thereafter he can make the difference." Doris responded, as if to justify the vanity.

Periodic mails from Ron narrating his progress and experience in New York were always looked out for, by Doris and Dege.

Eight months after Ron's departure to New York, Dege and Doris too had to relocate to New York in quest of Doris's attendance of the mandatory Advanced Standing Program for International Dentists course in New York University. There in New York the couple too started feeling the initial turmoil that came with relocating to a North East city from the West Coast of America. It was colder and certainly more traditional in the North East of the vast and highly-diverse and very sophisticated country.

More traditional North East? Yes, Dege and Doris had relocated to New York City, but it was not quite as traditional as one would imagine when compared with the other states and cities of the North East like the states of Maine, Vermont and New Hampshire. Though some cities in *Up-state New York* were relatively more traditional, New York City itself was indeed more cosmopolitan and more culturally diversified than Los Angeles as Dege and Doris were to later find out.

Chapter 6

DR DORIS: 2ND MISSIONARY JOURNEY AS A STUDENT

Doris had to go back to school in New York. She had to train again to practice as a dentist in the United States. That was more than two decades after she graduated as a Doctor of Dental Surgery from a renowned College of Dentistry in his native country. She was back in New York as a student at the same time when her last son Ron was also a medical student in Columbia University New York. In effect, she and her last son became students at the same time, one in Columbia University, New York, the other in New York University, New York.

Doris and her husband Dege had rented one tiny one-bedroom apartment in Astoria Queens New York. The total surface area of the apartment for which the couple paid $1,350 per month was no larger than the total surface area of a standard living room less the kitchen and bathroom in Los Angeles or other parts of Queens New York. And it was in the same New York City. Manhattan Apartments would indeed have cost them much more.

Every morning for three straight years, except for Sundays, some Saturdays and the official public holidays, Doris would get up by 4.30 am to rush through her morning chores. She would then have a hurried breakfast and rush out of the house to catch the 6 o'clock N-train or Q-train to Manhattan New York where her school was located. Invariably the train would be filled to capacity, even at those early morning hours. Many passengers would be standing as would be sitting. Many would be having their breakfast standing up or sitting in the trains. The take-away-breakfast often consisted of sandwiches, beagle and cheese, or some cereal-based meal which would be gulped with speed before the passenger's destination.

Each morning after entering the train from Astoria Queens to Manhattan In New York City, Doris would remember her first day in her brother-in-law's house in Rancho Cucamonga when young Nathan was demonstrating the sleeping passengers in his toy trains. True to the scene in Nathan's toy trains, there were always passengers sleeping or nodding their heads in the Manhattan-bound N and Q Trains from Astoria to Manhattan New York. Some of those passengers actually slept in transit while many more clutched newspapers just like the periodically-agitated passengers in Nathan's toy trains. It was obvious that the creators of the toy trains did quite some good study of the scenes in the New York trains. Nathan would be very fascinated to see the actual passengers who were replicated in his toys in Rancho Cucamonga many decades earlier.

"This is the Manhattan-bound N train. The next stop is Ditmars Boulevard."

The characteristic train-announcer's voice would bellow.

"Stay away from the closing doors please!" The characteristically-sonorous voice would again ring out loud and clear to warn the passengers before take-off.

And the train would jerk into action.

New York was almost always filled with tourists every season of the year. And the trains were always teeming with passengers. A number of first time riders or people who were not paying enough attention to the announcement as they stood would hit their nearest neighbors on the shoulders at the first jerk of the train. There were usually no apologies for such light human collisions. It was taken for granted that strangers who would ordinarily not shake hands with one another would hit one another on the shoulders at the invariable turbulent jerk of the train. Nobody would complain. It was "no place for a gentleman" even when there were adequate warnings pasted at strategic places inside the train. "There must be no indecent touching under the guise of inadvertent turbulence". But the indecent jerking of the train on take-off would overrule that warning sign. And it was a good thing that people bumped on one another. If it were otherwise, some people taken completely unawares would fall face down or on their backs if there were no other standing passengers to act as wedges.

The massive moving machines did not seem to be regulated as regards the total number of passengers who could board it at any one time. There appeared to be an unwritten rule that as many people as could be accommodated sitting or standing, within the coaches, would be carried. Dege's original part of the world had adequate train services under British colonial rule. But many of those instituted infrastructures appeared to have rapidly evaporated a few decades after the exit of the colonialists. The younger generation would not know the difference as they see the nascent Chinese trains replacing the English trains!

As early as 5 o'clock in the mornings, on weekdays and weekends alike, Manhattan was already a beehive of activity. Irrespective of the time of the year, winter or summer, but more so during the summer months, the human traffic was usually overwhelming. New York "the City that never sleeps", in all respects truly deserved that name.

By the time Doris reached the 1st avenue location of her school, Ajayi her classmate from her original country was already seated in the classroom. Ajayi drove all week days from New Jersey. And, on his school laboratory days, he would have been busy trimming dentures for a patient by 8 o'clock in the morning. Many of the Professors/Attendings and Supervisors who resided in Long Island would also already have arrived and would be busy at work as early as 8 o'clock. They would arrive home late from work and arrive early back to work the very next morning. The unending rat race was so very characteristic of no other place but New York City.

Doris saw the daily rat race every day at her Manhattan school.

"Did these people ever sleep? Did they have time enough for their families? Or were they perpetually married to their work?" Doris asked herself.

Even when nobody else was there early in the classroom or the lab, Professor David was sure to be there. Professor David was the indefatigable Group Practice Director of NYU Residency Program. He was a middle-aged man bubbling with enthusiasm and experience. He was already going from specimen to specimen of the crowns and bridges fabricated by his students on the previous lab day. With his very sharp eyes for details he was already busy making notes and comments on the different specimens.

"Good morning Prof. D" Doris greeted from the distance as soon as she entered the classroom. "Good morning Duureez. I hope you have come ready to improve on the last crown that you cut yesterday." Prof. D bellowed. His voice sounded as sharp and as distinct as he regularly mispronounced Doris as "Duureez". Professor David knew every one of the 116 students in the class by name. But he would invariably mispronounce most of the names even after repeated corrections. He was particularly fond of mispronouncing the name of Doris's best friend Ugoye. He would invariably pronounce Ugoye as "Yugoyeye." In that particular case, Prof David's pronunciation of "Yugoyeye" for Ugoye was a great improvement on how some of the other teachers and classmates would pronounce the name of the amiable lady. Ugoye was in her mid-forties and was very mildly-mannered. She was ever so polite and ever so ready to help. She was a renowned professor of pediatric dentistry in her home country in Africa before she came in to do the "Advanced Standing Program" in order to be fully licensed to practice dentistry in the United States. The majority of Ugoye's classmates had devised the name of "U.G" for the relatively simple name Ugoye. Despite her gentility, Ugoye would usually taunt those who encountered difficulty with pronouncing her name.

"You guys readily pronounce the name of the actor Arnold Schwarzenegger. And you can correctly pronounce the jaw-breaking name of the country Czechoslovakia. But you find difficulty pronouncing my name Ugoye. There must therefore be something really amiss somewhere", Ugoye would taunt her classmates. "I would not want you to bite your tongues in an effort to pronounce my name. So, here's how you can get about it. If you can pronounce Ukraine and Eugene, and you can say the words "Oh Yes" then you should have no problem pronouncing my name. It is equivalent to linking the U of Ukraine with the "Oh Ye" of "Oh Yes." Just remove the "S" of "Oh Yes" and you are home."

Many of Ugoye's friends tried her recommended *recipe* for pronouncing her name but the majority still ended up pronouncing the name as "Yugoyeye" just as Prof D often did. A shortening of the name to "UG" often saved the day.

Ugoye had relatively stronger words for one of her discussion group mates Kate. The latter was very loud and like Prof D, often also mispronounced Ugoye as Yugoyeye.

"And you Kate, I probably will start calling you by the name of that popular bird in my country of origin. You probably have not seen those wide-winged big birds here in New York City. They are called by a name which sounds very much like Kate. They are called kites and even though they fly really high in the skies they can be very menacing when they swoop on little chickens on the ground. And so, Kate, how about calling you kite?"

"Sorry Ugoyeye, so sorry, U.G. I have to learn fast because I certainly cannot fly as high as the kite and I certainly cannot be a predator to little chickens." Kate apologized, smilingly.

Ugoye and Doris had struck some friendship not just on account of both coming from Africa, but also because both of them were about the same age group. They never discussed anything relating to religion because while Doris was a devoted Catholic, Ugoye was a devout Muslim who however did not wear the distinguishing headgear. Both friends respected each other's religious beliefs.

Members of Ugoye's class worked as one large family even when they had small discussion groups of between 6 and 8 students per group. Study groups met one or two times every week in question-and-answer sessions and to simulate exam situations.

Members of the discussion groups were particularly close to one another. Tricia, a 24-year-old from Peru was exceptionally smart and particularly talented with cutting crowns and preparing bridges. She was ever ready to help out any member of the group who was in academic difficulty. She always volunteered her time to practice with Doris and Ugoye or indeed any other member of the group after normal office hours.

"You are so very smart, Tricia. You certainly are an all-round 'A' student" Doris told Tricia.

"Thanks Doris. We are all 'A' students to be able to get in here in the first instance. It only requires some little extra diligence." Tricia said.

Prof. D, as Professor David was generally known by his students, was the longest-serving member of the faculty. He was the Group Practice Director or GPD for short. He was very dedicated to his students and to his work in the faculty. All kinds of gossips circulated about Prof. D, even when it was not supposed to be anybody's business. But the students appeared to lessen the stresses of their class work by gossiping about Dr David.

"I understand Dr D had been married five times and that each marriage had ended in divorce after a year or two. I am very surprised at how he finds time to be so punctual to work and so dedicated to his duties." Tricia said.

"Yes, nobody knows whether he had any children." Ugoye replied.

"Dr D is a giant of a man. He must be more than six feet eight inches tall. I used to hear that such big people are often tender-hearted." Another female student chipped in from behind the class."

"Yes, I hear that despite his great height and huge stature Prof. D is very kind-hearted outside of the class room. He is very soft spoken. His other name perhaps should be Mr. Perfect," another female student added.

"But he is so very meticulous. He will not manage with any half measures or imperfections. I learnt that he hates to see students fail in exams. But they said that he will not accept substandard work." Ajayi said as he listened to the otherwise all-girl gossip from the side.

Doris merely listened and occasionally grinned as the gossip progressed.

Heavy footsteps were soon heard along the hallway and Prof David's entry into the class abruptly ended the early morning gossips.

Chapter 7

AND THE CROWN FRACTURED!

Doris had prepared diligently for the Dental Board Licensing Exams. Often on the first Monday of every month she would, along with other students in her class, read and work in the lab through the night only catching a few hours of sleep on class room desks before the 7.30 A.M 1st Tuesday steeple chase tests. These tests were often held on the morning of the first Tuesday of every month provided the Tuesday was not a public holiday.

Early on such Tuesday mornings after hurried freshening up, the tired and almost dazed students would troop out to the nearest fast food joints which were scattered around Manhattan New York as if in readiness for such night crawlers. A particular spot that was patronized by members of Doris' class was called "The Luckiest Chicken" That particular fast food spot served particularly delicious and affordable chicken, potato-fries and coke at very affordable rates. On one occasion Dege had taken the very early train to Manhattan to bring some dental instruments which Doris needed for her tests but which she had forgotten in the house. Dege therefore had the opportunity of accompanying Doris to "The Luckiest Chicken" fast food.

Two plates of steaming hot chicken-breast complete with wings, along with mashed potato, and gravy with the option of a cup of tea or soda cost Dege and Doris only a little more than nine dollars. That was a great price for such treat in Manhattan New York City. Dege was thoroughly amazed. It was no wonder that there were scarcely any vacant seats left in the store after Dege and Doris had taken their seats. The "Luckiest Chicken" staff were very busy. And they were very polite.

Dege could not resist wishing that he was a student again, just like Doris. Student life appeared exciting, simple and straightforward. "I can see what you guys enjoy often here Doris; two plates of *luckiest chicken* for only nine dollars!" Dege exclaimed.

"Yes, you enjoyed it because you are not here every day. If you were to have supervisors and the Professors virtually on your neck watching every little move you make, with these lab works in conjunction with the daily tests, you would see it differently. Perhaps you would enjoy only as much as the truly-lucky chickens. These ones that are steaming-hot and ready for human consumption are obviously not so lucky." Doris said.

"Yes, I believe you. I could easily see the stress on the faces of the students even as they ate the "luckiest chickens". Every one of them was gulping the cup of coffee as if they were about to miss a departing train." Dege said.

Even Doris who previously did not tolerate a hot cup of coffee had also learnt to gulp her hot coffee along with the other students.

Dege was still meticulously sipping his own coffee when Doris got up and was ready to go. She flung her back-pack behind her back and bid Dege good-bye. In a moment, she was off, back to the labs.

Dege sat back and sipped his coffee for another fifteen to twenty minutes before heading back to take the N-train to Astoria New York.

As the months rolled on it was soon time for the Professional exams for Doris' class. The candidates were required to arrange for their own patients for the various branches of the

exams. The required sets of patients ranged from those for periodontology, to those for restorative dentistry. It was not an easy task finding the patients who readily fitted the different ailments which the student dentists would want. Whichever patients that were available to any students were therefore greatly treasured and pampered. They were booked well in advance of the examination periods. Their transport and feeding costs were paid for. And, in some instances where such patients came from out-of-state, their hotel bills would need to be paid for by the students. This was to ensure that the patients were comfortable and cooperative with every stage of the examination. An uncooperative patient in the examinations could spell doom for the candidate. It was the duty of the candidate to ensure cooperation, not by overt bribery, but "by persuasion and other means possible."

Doris had arranged for the transport and hotel accommodation for Lizzy who was one of her long-time patients for prosthodontics.

Lizzy had arrived on schedule for the exam treatment and had cooperated very well through the procedure. She was well educated and she knew the full implications for the student-dentist, regarding the treatment that she was taking.

"I hope you will do very well in the exam because you are so very good, Dr. Doris" Lizzy kept telling Doris at every stage of the exams. Lizzy often called Doris by the name Dr. D, sometimes unwittingly embarrassing Doris with that name in the presence of Professor David who was also called by the name of "Prof. D" or "Dr. D".

Doris was quite confident as the procedure progressed. Lizzy would open her mouth quite widely ever before Doris would complete the request. She wanted her student-doctor to do well. Even when she felt any discomfort she would not complain lest the supervisors would count it against Doris. It was all so smooth-sailing until the final stage of fitting of the prepared denture.

As Doris was fitting in the denture to sit properly in place, she noticed that the meticulously-crafted little object still needed some little trimming. Lo and behold as Doris tried to do the little final trimming the denture snapped and broke into two pieces on Ugoye's hands! It was a disaster!

The time remaining was so minimal. Doris stood speechless for a few seconds holding the fractured little object in her hands. She knew she could patch up the damage if she were to have the time. But she could not do so adequately because of time constraints.

Lizzy had been a frequent visitor to the dental clinic for quite some time. She had been at the exam situation two times in the past. She was always very happy when her student-doctor was making good progress. She could guess when there was problem. When Doris' denture broke, Lizzy was so very upset that she wept openly even when she was not the candidate. Lizzy wept, not for her denture, but for her student-doctor's fate. She could not be consoled.

"We will be fine, Lizzy", Doris had tried to console Lizzy. She tried to put up a courageous countenance about the misfortune that had befallen her.

"I am more saddened because of the pains that you have taken to make this succeed, Lizzy." Doris said.

"No, Doctor D, I feel so guilty that this has happened. I have been at a couple of these exams and this is the first time that this has happened to my doctor." Lizzy bemoaned.

"But it is not your fault Lizzy. You have been such a wonderful and cooperative patient. It is entirely my fault that I did not handle the denture well." Doris said amidst her hurried efforts to fix the broken denture.

Doris hurriedly tried to patch the broken denture with sealants. Her hands were trembling as she tried to hurry through the procedure. She just succeeded in joining the two broken pieces and the time was up. Doris had not done any further trimming that she planned to do. And she had not fully cleaning up any spilled sealants. But she was confident that her denture was perfect otherwise. The bell sounded for all procedures to be stopped.

"All procedures must stop now." The Chief Examiner bellowed.

"All candidates must move away from the tables." The authoritative voice of the Chief Examiner again sounded.

It was all over! Holding the hurriedly apposed denture in her hands Doris gently dropped the hastily sealed object on the examination table as required and moved out according the instructions. At first, she wondered whether the apposed pieces did give way or whether they still held together. She was tempted to move back to the table to take a quick look.

"Should I risk disregarding the "time-up" warning bell and fully clean up the sealants for a further minute or two?" Doris soliloquized. Of course, that would call for instant disqualification of her job. And so, as the other candidates moved away from their benches, Doris had no other options than to also move away.

"Nobody needs to inform me of the result". Doris muttered to herself.

"I think I already am sure that the result will be bad. Three years of preparation that needed to be demonstrated today have just fizzled away in a twinkle of an eye." Doris lamented as her legs trembled. She nearly collapsed but for her holding firmly to the edge of a table. She took in a series of deep breaths. She said a prayer or two. It was not for a miracle to happen to make her pass. No, she only prayed for the courage to remain strong in failure.

But no, it was not all over. Doris had been an excellent student throughout the course. And she was very good with dentures. The particular denture that had snapped had been beautifully prepared, though hurriedly patched-up, yet, perfectly so. And the technicians had done a very beautiful work too. And Doris had managed to seal the broken pieces so well that only a fine, almost microscopic line, could be visualized, certainly not readily visible with the naked eye. And the candidate's other works were excellent. And so, even when the candidate felt disappointed that she had not satisfied herself, the examiners felt quite satisfied and accepted the job for grading. If the job was very bad it would have been rejected outright. It was almost incredible to Doris and to her husband Dege to whom the story was later narrated.

As Lizzy left the dental chair after Doris' seemingly failed procedure, she was in deep remorse. She felt that she was part of the problem even when she had cooperated fully throughout the procedure. She prayed the result of the exams would be different. Little did she realize that a different result would have meant a disappointing result. Before she left the building, Lizzy sent a text message to Doris:

"Dear Dr D,

I feel so very sorry for the outcome of today's procedure. It is saddening that despite my full cooperation, the denture fractured in the end. I want you to know that in spite of the accident, I still hold you with the highest regards. You remain my great dentist. I will mail back the stipend that you had given me for transportation and it is all in good faith. I will always call back any time you need me. I know you will always do an excellent job. I hold you with the highest esteem. With thanks, Lizzy."

Doris was moved to tears after reading Lizzy's text message. She had known the successful acceptance of her job even though the detailed grading was not yet available to her. But at least the job was successfully accepted and given the nod of the examiners.

Doris immediately contacted Lizzy after reading the latter's text message.

"Thank you very much Lizzy, the results turned out well. It was accepted for grading which means that it has passed the preliminary stage and only awaits the final grading. Your cooperation made it all possible. You remain my angel in this exam. You are not just my patient.

You are my good friend,

 Doris"

Lizzy could not contain her joy when she received the message. She called back immediately and was shouting in the phone out of excitement.

"The examiners must have a way of knowing who the good student-doctors are, Dr. D", Lizzy said.

"I was so very worried, but I still had a glimmer of hope that your excellence would bear you witness in other ways. I thank God for you, Dr. D, and I rejoice with you."

Doris was very close to tears; tears of joy and gratitude to a friend to whom indeed she should be very grateful instead of the other way around.

Doris while narrating the full story to Dege later that evening solemnly said: "I see Lizzy and the tenets and friendship which she represents, not just as the kind gestures of a single individual who wishes to see others succeed. No, I see her as a representation of that great promise which this great country truly represents. A number of the patients would be condescending to me because of the color of my skin. Even when you are treating some with due diligence and dignity, they will make it obvious to you that they are doing you a favor by allowing you, a black student-doctor, to treat them. Lizzy is the best of America. She is the America that I love. She is truly the epitome of my America." Doris said aloud.

When Doris came back to the house from the school on the evening of the following day, a big and beautiful bunch of well wrapped fresh roses was waiting for her from the mail man. And the tag simply read: "A present from your grateful patient, Lizzy"."

The sight of the beautiful present brought some strands of tears of joy and appreciation to Doris' eyes.

Dege seeing the emotion on her wife's eyes, even as taciturn as he was, he could not help breaking into an unusual statement. Slowly and with measured words he said to his wife.

"You have a great friend in Lizzy, Doris. Such individuals abound in large numbers in this society. But since they are mostly silent, the few rancorous bigots that abound here and there tend to overshadow them and thus present the false face of a bigoted and non-inclusive America which we often see."

Dege paused for a while and still looking steadily in the direction of the beautiful bunch of roses which was being firmly clutched by his wife, he continued: "Even in spite of unguarded rants and bigotry that one occasionally comes across from irresponsible individuals, our American society is replete with great and responsible individuals who indeed form the vast majority of the population. These fine men and women are in overwhelming majority in the population. But often the latter are the silent majority. It is the very small vocal minority who are, to a large extent, societal failure, or individuals with instinctive feelings of social insecurity, who tend to exaggerate racial differences. They have little else but their favored skin color to fall back on. They thus find solace in the melanin content of their skins or the disdain for the melanin abundance of their neighbors' skins and use the latter to claim superiority or to claim certain privileges. These latter bigoted individuals use the difference conferred by nature for protective purposes, as their yardstick for judgment or assessment of the individual. It is the latter who habitually judge people based on the color of their skins rather than on *the content of their character,* to quote Martin Luther King Jnr. The latter are essentially *losers* in the main. And they need to be either totally ignored or better still, vigorously called out and strongly challenged. I totally agree with you, Doris. Lizzy your friend is indeed the true face of my America too. The bigots that appear to dot the landscape will attempt to make you feel inferior. They will show you disrespect in every possible way. They will literally put it to you that this not your America as much as it is theirs. But they are wrong! At the end of the day, for every bigot that sneers, there are a thousand Lizzys that may choose to be silent. And, for every one thousand racially intolerant small men and women who strive hard to put it to you that this is not your America, there are ten million open-minded and welcoming men and women who are the best of American values. The latter strongly hold those great values which this great nation stands for." Dege stated emphatically. He was almost sounding emotional. He appeared to have used the opportunity of Lizzy's flower present to Doris, to pour out his long-held opinion on race and race relations in America.

Chapter 8

"CAN I HAVE A WORD WITH THE AUTHOR?"

Dege had mentioned to Doris that he was planning to visit the Astoria Library in New York. He wanted to see the Librarian for a possible book reading exercise there. "That will be great. But ensure you dress well and present your proposed project well. This is because there must be many such requests on the library and so, the first impression presented by the author will matter a lot." Doris had advised.

"I will be going to present a great book and not a great sartorial display." Dege joked. It was summer time and so Dege donned his mid-summer T-shirt and jeans and headed to the Astoria Library. The T-shirt and jeans mode of dressing was what almost everyone else appeared in, at that season of the year. Dege was very optimistic that he could readily arrange to do a book reading of his newly-published book especially since he had seen a number of other authors occasionally do such events in that library. The Astoria library was very close to the apartment in which Dege and his wife Doris lived. The Library was not a very big one but it was very well stocked with books. It was also very conveniently located and presumably, efficiently managed.

"I have come to request a book reading event in your library", Dege told the front desk officer of the library.

"For all such requests, you may need to speak with the Chief Librarian of this branch" The front desk staff politely answered. The middle aged immigrant from Africa who had been residing in Astoria New York for nearly a year was thus directed to the office of the Chief Librarian.

"Good afternoon ma'am. My name is Dege and I am an author living here in Astoria. I have been directed to see you in connection with my desire to do a book reading event in your library."

"Oh, that's awesome. We are always so excited to have local authors do events in our library. Tell the author to do us a small email detailing the book title, the ISBN, publisher, and the time and date that he or she would like to do the event. This is so that we can check with our events calendar for availability. We always like our authors to book well in advance so that we can check out on the book and plan our calendars appropriately. A short description of the book will also be helpful. But first get the author to formally write to us, OK?".

"OK, ma'am, and can I submit this formal request later today?" Dege asked.

"Yes of course, he can. Get him or her to apply formally as soon as possible because we get similar requests almost on a weekly basis and we are often fully booked."

"Thank you, ma'am, I will make the formal application right away".

Dege moved quickly from the Library chief's office straight to one of the available public computers in the library. He immediately wrote and printed out a brief application introducing himself and formally applying for a date to do a public reading of his new book in the library. He thereafter signed the application and went back again to the office of the Chief Librarian.

"I have brought the formal application, ma'am." Dege enthusiastically stated.

"Oh, good, the author must be around then. Why don't I speak with him? Or is it a she?" The Librarian politely stated.

"It's me, ma'am, it is a he".

"Ok, tell him to just give me ten minutes and I will be with him right away." Dege did not at first give much thought to the repeated use of "he or him and she or her" instead of "you" in the Librarian's address.

"Ok, ma'am" Dege again greeted the librarian and walked out of the room.

After about fifteen minutes of waiting in the general reading room, Dege again went in to see the librarian.

"I am back again ma'am. I hope I am not unduly disturbing you."

"No, not at all. I am actually free now. Please tell the author that he can come see me right away."

Dege was a little confused. "Here I am, coming in for the third time into the librarian's office and being given one excuse or another almost repeatedly." Dege mused.

"Did you say I should wait, ma'am?"

"No, I said that you should tell the author to come in now. I am sorry I kept him waiting this long, but he can come in now."

It was only then that it became obvious to Dege that the librarian thought that he was merely booking the appointment for audience with the librarian on behalf of another person, probably his author boss. Dege did not know whether to be amused or to feel offended.

"Could it be that I did not make myself clear enough? Could it be that I dressed so shabbily in conformity with my poor sartorial choices and I was mistaken for one of the many unfortunate newly-homeless people who often spent the day inside some libraries for warmth and company? But I have seen many other white and Asian people dress like me and they were recognized for who they were and not for how they dressed. Or, could it be that the librarian was not used to seeing authors of my skin color in this part of New York City? Or could it be that my accent made it difficult for the lady to understand me? But our discussions were smooth and both of us appeared to fully understand each other. Even then I always spoke in the first person when talking about the author even when the librarian appeared to repeatedly speak about the author in the third person. He kept referring to "the author" while he spoke to me." Dege mused.

Dege did not wish that his surprise should display on his countenance. He had learnt to smile rather than frown even in situations of uncertainty. After all, it could be a simple mistake.

"Looks like there is some little identity mix-up here, ma'am. I am the author of this title *A Friend is the New Enemy*. Presenting this book here first, is of much significance to me. This is because this book was actually written over the last five months from inside this library."

As Dege spoke, the librarian's lips went agape. She then instantaneously covered her open lips with the palm of her right hand in undisguised surprise.

76

A mild scream of "Wow!" accidentally escaped from the librarian's lips. She then appeared to summon courage and looked up to Dege and said:

"I am sorry for the mix-up. You will see the Adult Librarian. She is in-charge of scheduling these events."

Dege stood for a while. He was beginning to get a little concerned. "But I was told that the Chief Librarian was in charge of these events. And the chief had at one time asked to see the author! Was she expecting to see a different face?"

For some five to ten seconds Dege stood speechless but deep in thought. Meanwhile the Chief Librarian's face was glued to her cell phone which was by the right-hand side of her office table.

"I do not wish to be paranoid, but I have often heard of profiling and all kinds of discrimination being meted out to people of my skin color. Could this be one of such situations?" Dege muttered silently.

The Chief Librarian then briskly picked up the intercom:

"Hi Nancy, there is a guy here who says he has written a book. He says he would like to do a book reading here and I am referring him across to you. His name is-s, ..." Turning sharply to Dege she asked 'what's your name?'"

"Dege!" Dege replied.

Dege was thus directed back to the front desk to be redirected to Miss Nancy the Adult Librarian. His being introduced with the sentence "He says that he an author" did not sound to him as the best of compliments. But he brushed off the obvious allusion of doubt.

The Adult Librarian was a little more welcoming. She was most likely of Hispanic descent, judging from her accent.

"Congratulations, I understand you have written a book. We are usually excited to see new authors who use our library. Do you live in this vicinity or are you visiting?" Nancy asked excitedly.

"Yes, I live in that big block of apartments which lies across the street."

"That's great. My boss is particularly welcoming to local authors. She advises we schedule them at the earliest opportunity. Indeed, often she schedules them by herself. That's how welcoming we are to local authors. Of what genre is your book?" Nancy asked.

Most times I write fiction. Two or my titles are based on real-life events." Dege replied.

He then reached for a copy of the book which he had in his brief case and handed it over to Nancy the Adult Librarian. Just at that moment, the Chief Librarian walked into the room. She appeared to have thought that Dege had left. Perhaps she came in to do some little gossip on *the guy who says he has written a book.*

The expression on the face of the Librarian on seeing Dege holding a copy of his book was one of complete surprise if not of disbelief. She involuntarily stretched out her hand to receive the book from Dege, in place of Nancy. Her gaze was cast completely on the face of the lean and gaunt casually-dressed greying middle-aged African American man whose very athletic features almost always belied his age. Even Dege who always said that he did not know the meaning of blushing, saw one on the face of the hitherto amiable lady who earlier sat dignified behind the modest Librarian's office table.

Ms. Theresa Wilkinson had been the Librarian at that Astoria Library in New York for four straight years. She was known to be very polite and very diligent with her work. She obviously was never racially or ethnically-biased in her dealings with patrons of the library most of who were white Americans of Greek origin. Persons of various other nationalities and ethnic backgrounds, especially, Mexicans, Central and South Americans, Asian and African Americans, also abounded in varying numbers in Ms. Wilkinson's Library.

Ms. Wilkinson had obviously seen and associated with a couple of authors of color, especially because of the highly-mixed demography of Astoria. But on that particular day that she was receiving a copy of "The Friend is The Enemy", Ms. Wilkinson knew that she had miscalculated. She obviously did not expect that the lean and gaunt-looking African American man who had come to her office to schedule a book presentation event was the author of the book himself.

Dege on his part was perhaps a little too critical or too sensitive. Perhaps he had begun to hold very high race-relations expectations of his society based on the very cordial relations between Doris and his patient Lizzy.

"I had believed after the association between Doris and Lizzy that this society held great promises in excellent race relations. Events like this with this Chief Librarian make me to begin to doubt the reality of this promise. Maybe I am over-reacting. Maybe I am expecting too much. But certainly, I was worried why any doubts would still exist about the identity of the author after repeated corrections, if the skin of the applicant contained less melanin, perhaps there might have been no more doubts about him being capable of writing a book." Dege said. He was probably over-reacting. But certainly, his misgivings were well warranted.

Ms. Wilkinson soon appeared to regain her composure: As she received the book from Dege she momentarily turned to, and quickly read the back cover and exclaimed:

"Oh my God, I had been referring to the author in the third person, not realizing that the author was standing before me. I am truly sorry for the mix-up."

She then again turned to the front cover of the book and read aloud the title before returning to the back cover. She then steadied her gaze at the author photo. Perhaps she wished to reconfirm before apologizing further. Then, looking up to Dege, she slowly said:

"Again, I am so very sorry. I, …. I, I never thought it was you. You …, you could see I always asked whether the author was a he or a she." Ms. Wilkinson stammered.

"No problem, Ma'am. Many people make the same mistake whenever I go for book exhibition with my many books." Dege said, trying to down-play the situation in the face of the profuse apologies.

"Certainly, the apologies are genuine even when the mistake appears to be a product of some form of profiling. Perhaps it was initially assumed that someone of my skin color in this part of the city is not likely to be able to write a worthwhile book." Dege mused. "It is perhaps one of the many wrong assumptions that one has to initially cope with, in this society. Too many socially-disenfranchised people of my skin-color have, perhaps erroneously, come to regard this great country as *Their America*. Unfortunately, certain utterances and actions of people in power unwittingly tend to lend credence to these abhorrible situations. But it is not exclusively *Their America*! As a bona fide citizen of the United States I must not simply eat the humble pie and accept to play second fiddle. I must not accept or associate myself with this non-inclusive and utterly discriminatory characterization. I must strive to, demand and insist that I belong. Even against any, and all obvious odds, as a citizen of this great country, it is also *My America*, as much as it is any one else's." Dege said. He smiled at, and thanked Ms. Nancy the Adult Librarian. The latter stared at Dege in a rather hawkish manner as if the latter was up to some mischief. But Dege readily shrugged off the incident, thanked Ms. Nancy again, straightened himself up and proudly left the Adult Librarian's office. He had gotten a date for his Book Reading event. That was what mattered the most at that moment. "All's well that ends well." Dege said, smiling broadly as he left.

Chapter 9

IS THE AUTHOR THE RIGHT SKIN COLOR?

Four weeks after the Astoria Library experience Dege had travelled to Saratoga Springs New York to participate in a Book Exhibition. Some one hundred and fifty authors and Author Representatives as well as Publishers and Publishing-materials Representatives were in attendance. Dege's exhibition table was sandwiched between two other exhibitors each of who was exhibiting one book title. Dege was exhibiting a total of eight titles of books on various genre. He had a very colorful display which consequently attracted many visitors to his stand.

Most visitors to Dege's stand who purchased books invariably asked about the author. "We would like to have the purchased books autographed by the author. Can you call the author so that we can chat with him?" One of the visitors to Dege's stand said. Indeed, she had specifically insisted on seeing the author before she would pay for the book which she purchased. "I can easily buy books online or in the bookshops, but I come to book exhibitions to physically see and discuss with authors," the lady said. Dege was standing behind the table with his assistant Tim, who happened to be a white guy. "I will gladly autograph the book for you Ma'am" Dege said as he brought out his pen to autograph the book. But the lady's countenance changed immediately Dege readied his pen to autograph the book. In a most surprising move, the lady quickly snatched back the book from

Dege and said: "I want original autographing of the book by the author himself not by any surrogate."

Dege all along maintained a smiling face. But for the first time he felt very humiliated. He had felt a little profiled in the Astoria New York Library when he was innocently mistaken for a canvasser for an author some months back. The Librarian had apologized and the mistake was amicably settled. On this other occasion he was again apparently not deemed capable of producing a book. And so, even in spite of repeated attempts at maintaining equanimity, the middle-aged immigrant who came from a background where everyone else looked like him and where he indeed was very highly respected, could not help muttering to himself: "Have race relations always been like this over the years; or is this all a new development in the society? Is this going to be the new face of America? Is this indeed *My America*, the America of my dreams?"

But Dege again picked up courage and forced a sustained smile to the great surprise of Tim his Assistant.

The lady paused for a while and then handed the book to Tim, Dege's Caucasian Assistant. Tim was standing by Dege's side. Obviously, the lady had believed that Tim, was the author. She had believed that Dege was probably the paid Assistant. Tim was hesitant to accept the book being handed over to him. He turned in Dege's direction and motioned on the lady to hand the book to Dege. "Receive the book Tim. The customer is always right. At least she must be assumed to be right. And she is our customer!" Dege said, smiling politely and motioning on the lady to proceed with delivery of the book for autographing to Tim. Tim thereupon received the book and handed it over to Dege. As Tim was handing the book over to Dege, he turned the back and showed the author photo to the lady. "That's the author, Ma'am. I am his Sales Assistant." The lady almost froze with regrets for the obvious bias. In a flash she apologized profusely:

"I am so very sorry, Sir. I feel like evaporating. Please don't get me wrong. 99% of the authors here are white. There are a few Hispanics and an occasional Asian or African-American author as you can see here today." The regret for the identity error was very genuine. The embarrassment was unmistakable and the apology was very profuse.

"No problem, Ma'am" Dege said smiling. "Anybody can make this kind of mistake because of the demographic composition of the people at this exhibition." Dege continued, trying to dampen the mix up. He then autographed the book and handed it over to the lady.

"I did not mean any bias Sir. And I will purchase three more books to give to my friends as a way of compensating for my mistake." The lady said smiling as she pulled out her credit card to pay for her purchases. "I will also ensure that I advertise the book in my work place and let my friends laugh at my mistake. Again, I did not mean to be rude, but we do not get to see many authors of color in these parts" the lady further apologized.

"It's no problem Ma'am. I can understand, Saratoga Springs may not be a very attractive place for authors of color. I believe that the same thing can also be said of horse-racing. I saw a lot of molded horses and horse-riders in front of the houses. It was the first thing that I noticed as the taxi took me to my hotel yesterday. This place may also not hold much attraction for people of color for horse racing, even though I love watching horse-racing." Dege further said, trying to make light of the situation and lighten the mood.

"You are very right, we do not witness many jockeys of color, during the horse racing competitions either." The lady said.

The drift from black authors to black jockeys and horse-riding was a welcome relief to all concerned parties especially for Dege.

Many book-lovers buy what others are reading. They therefore tend to congregate to bookstands which appear very busy with visitors. They do not mind waiting in the queue where others are already lined up. The prolonged discussions had therefore attracted many more visitors to Dege's stand with consequent increased publicity for the latter's books during the Saratoga Springs Book Exhibition events.

As people queued up at his stand, Dege turned to the lady and jokingly said: "You see, Ma'am your mistake has attracted many more visitors to my stand".   The lady who had by then regained her composure happily replied: "Yes, I am happy for you. And besides, we need much more diversity in these events. I hope you will be here again during next year's events".

Dege had narrated his Saratoga Springs experience to the Chief Librarian Ms. Wilkinson and her Adult Librarian Ms. Nancy when he went for the earlier-scheduled Book-Reading event in the Astoria New York Public Library. Both officers had graciously taken off time to be present at the Book-Reading event. It was a great compensation for the misunderstanding that had trailed Dege's first meeting with the Library's Principal Officers some weeks earlier.

The narration of the Saratoga Springs events obviously put the Astoria Librarian at greater composure. She came to realize that she was not the only person who could make such a mistake. She obviously was a very dedicated staff who made an initial honest mistake. And she went to great extents to correct and compensate for the mistake.

Dege's book presentation at the Astoria New York Library was very well attended. It had very good publicity at no appreciable cost to Dege who only provided a few posters and book marks which were reproduced by the library for circulation to the library users.

The library had indeed gone out of its way to provide a few snacks for participants in the book presentation. Dege on his part had a handful of printed excerpts from the book. He read the passages and took questions from the enthusiastic audience.

The Chief Librarian who breezed in shortly after the start of the presentation had retold the story of how she had mistaken the Author for the Author's Assistant to the assembled audience at the Book Reading event. There was much laughter from the participants as Dege made funny grimaces depicting a frightened under-dog Author's Assistant during the narration by the Chief Librarian.

"Yes indeed, I did not mean to be rude or to be disdainful, discriminatory or condescending or anything of that sort. But this author was so simply-dressed. He put up such a meek and humble appearance when he entered my office that I easily mistook him with all due respects, for an Author's Assistant who was helping to project someone else's book. And I kept requesting to see the author of the book while the author was standing there in front of me. That was indeed a true manifestation of the old saying that looks could be deceptive. It reminded me of the old saying that *the hood does not make the monk.* It was akin to the *abracadabra* or *mumbo-jumbo* of magicians portraying the saying by magicians in my original part of the world: *the more you look the less you see.*"

Participants in the event roared with laughter when the Chief Librarian finally stated thus: "When next in the library I am addressing a casually-dressed stranger who bows as he greets me, and who clasps his palms together in front of him as he addresses me about a book, I must not take him for granted; I must first assume that such an individual could be an accomplished Author and not an Author's Assistant. If I end up addressing the Author's Assistant as the Author, the mistake will be a compliment and therefore will not require much apologies." The Librarian said.

 Dege had scheduled many book exhibitions both within New York City as well as in many other cities in and out of New York State. On every occasion, thereafter, he always remembered the episode which he encountered at the Astoria New York Library.

"I would not wish to further embarrass any more librarians by being mistaken for an Author's Assistant. I would hate to be mistaken for a magician's abracadabra during subsequent encounters with library staff" Dege said. "But my gaunt and hungry looks and my often-disheveled hair are features which I found difficulty with overcoming. I will probably have to grow a short beard and wear some thick-rimmed eye-glasses so as to resemble some deep-thinker and writer of old." Dege told Doris when he got home.

But then, Dege again remembered the old statement about the monk and the hood. "Thick-rimmed glasses with gaunt looks on a bearded disheveled dark-skinned man from afar in Astoria New York could paint the picture of an irredeemable homeless drug addict." Dege said to himself. "Even with modest denial of racial profiling, I know that, that would be the case. It's not that it bothers me whatever any bigot might think, but first impressions greatly matter. Decency, whether sartorial or behavioral, should take the front burner when one is threading along very readily-profiled and competitive paths." Dege concluded.

Dege did not have business cards. He noticed that he was the only exhibitor at the Saratoga Springs events who did not issue business cards to visitors to his stand. As a first measure therefore, Dege decided to stop over at a nearby business center to order for 100 business cards. I will readily hand over one of these to any receptionist that I seek to do business with before I introduce myself. Even when it is not always the norm here, I will make it my personal habit. Perhaps the sight of the business card pulled from my breast pocket ahead of my introducing myself would have prepared the mind of the receptionist that the gaunt-looking visitor is the Author and not a hired Assistant." Dege said.

Elated by the success of the Astoria New York book-reading event, Dege proudly said to Doris on the latter's return from the practical class that evening: "The Astoria event ended as a comedy of errors".

"Comedy of errors? Did you make some errors during the reading, or were some major errors detected in the book?" Doris asked.

"Doris, Doris, when will you begin to understand English?"

"But I passed all my exams and they were not in Spanish language. They were all in the English language."

"But those are dental and medical English, Doris. I mean English as in Queen's English."

"Or do you mean English as in American English? I know that Comedy of Errors is some Shakespearean comedy. I wish I could be as literary inclined as you, Dege. But I am not. And so, what was the comedy and what were the errors?" Doris asked, eager to get back to her General Practice Residency documents which she had been compiling for the previous two days.

Having successfully completed her clinical requirements for her Doctorate in Dental Surgery and passed the necessary Board Exams, Doris was often busy searching for a spot where she could do a two-year residency in New York State.

"And so, what was the comedy of errors?" Doris again asked.

"Well, I earlier told you how I was mistaken for an Author's Assistant. The converse was the case this evening during the introductions for the book-reading event. My Assistant took the floor to introduce me. I had requested him to make a short speech before introducing me. He gave a beautiful short speech listing some of my earlier literary works and how funny and entertaining they were."

"But those were no errors, Dege", Doris interjected, rather impatient for the full story.

"No, but a few members of the audience who had read one of the books believing that Tim was the author gave series of thunderous applause. Tim was in truth, very articulate in his introduction. Indeed, I felt proud to join in the applause for that hard-working young man who definitely would make a great writer with time. When I eventually took the stand the enthusiasm and applause had completely waned. The usual dictum was that the good actor should leave the stage when the ovation was loudest. But I entered the stage when the ovation had died down. It was some kind of antithesis. That was the error in the comedy. Of course, Tim and I savored the moment with hilarious winks as we exchanged places in the podium. The comedy and the errors notwithstanding, I enthusiastically read two chapters of the book before the initially-cynical audience came to recognize that the Author and his Assistant had not permanently switched places." Dege said, beaming with smiles.

"Happy for you, Dege. You are getting a good dose of entertainment in your new profession." Doris said.

"Yes indeed, Doris, but there is no guarantee that any subsequent errors will be as pleasant or as positive in the end. I am happy though that a very good first impression has been made." Dege said, still flashing his characteristic grin.

Chapter 10

LIFE IN BEAMING-GRIN MEDICAL CLINICS

Doris had completed his mandatory one-year residency in New York City. She and Dege had always wished to live in a small city a little removed from the hustle and bustle of New York City. Dege had craved for a quiet environment from where he would write his books. Unfortunately, such small cities were not likely to have group dental practices where Doris would practice her own profession. Two opportunities however came up suddenly and simultaneously. But none of the two practices was in New York City, not even anywhere in New York State. One was in a city called Chicopee in western Massachusetts. The other was in Miami Florida some one thousand and three hundred miles away from New York City. "This name Chicopee sounds weird, Dege. But I have Goggled it and it looks like it has historical origin from the Native Americans."

"Yes, I too had Googled the name when you first mentioned it to me. I guess it will be fun relocating from a city that never sleeps to one that may go to bed by eight in the evening, even in summer."

Although the offer in Massachusetts was closer to family and friends in New York City, the conditions of service were better in the offer from Miami Florida. Doris had therefore decided to join the Miami Florida practice.

The Miami dental practice was a franchise called Beaming-Grin Medical Clinics or BGMC for short. It had medical and dental sections under the same roof. A six-dentist team along with five hygienists and a handful of Dental Assistants ran the dental clinic. Doris was very excited that the clinic had nationwide franchise. The particular branch where Doris worked was said to have over the years developed a good reputation with children's oral health. It was very exciting for Doris who had always loved children.

"I always feel very fulfilled after attending to every child that attends my clinic. Perhaps I should have insisted on specializing in pediatric dentistry". Doris said.

"When a child proves uncooperative and refuses to open his or her mouth even after prolonged pleadings and enticements, I can understand. I see my own children at their ages in every child that I attend to. But the moment you earn a child's trust, it becomes a most fulfilling journey all the way" Doris said.

"And in the rare situations where we are compelled to literally coerce a child to render a much-needed intra-oral treatment, and the child cries, it hurts at first, but the joy still comes at the end when the procedure is done. The child comes to realize that the little hurt from a small needle was not deliberate or intended action after all. In many such situations the child, back in the warm and endearing grips of the parent, often gives you a much-appreciated smile at the end of the procedure." Doris said.

Dr. Johnson was the youngest team member in Beaming-Grin Dental Clinic. He was not just the youngest by chronological age. He was also the youngest in the team. Dr Johnson joined Beaming-Grin practice three months after Doris' arrival. He was a very jovial and hardworking young man. He almost always wore a smiling face and his entry into the clinic every morning made the environment boisterous.

"Dr. J is here" Dr. Johnson would always announce to everybody's hearing anytime he arrived for work. He was quite tall, about six feet five inches without shoes, lanky and boisterous. He would jokingly sway from side to side with a kind of a deliberate swagger as he entered the clinic. He would often walk as if he was being blown around by the wind.

"I hope no strong winds will come soon to Miami. The very tall ones like me can be blown off balance since our centers of gravity are much higher up." Dr. Johnson would jovially say any day there was weather forecast of strong winds.

Dr. Johnson was neither a citizen nor a permanent resident of the United States. He was working as a contract "limited license" employee. He trained as a dentist in his native Jamaica and had specialized in prosthodontics. He entered the United States on a visa which would enable him work in a specialized area with yearly renewal of his license and contract. Since he had not sat for the Board exams to be licensed to practice dentistry independently in the United States, he still needed to be supervised even though he was already a specialist.

Dr. Johnson had his work permit papers prepared for him by Beaming-Grin Dental Clinic and was employed by them. As a result of his immigration status, Dr. Johnson appeared to live in perpetual fear of losing his job and being out of status. The latter status would make the individual liable to being expelled from the country unless another clinic did his papers and absorbed him. Being on Temporary work permit was not the most comfortable situation to be in. It was akin to subtle bondage.

"You know I have to work extra hard and not get into any form of trouble, or get fired, otherwise I am off. And I want to remain in this your beautiful country where I can always be sure of the big burgers." Dr. Johnson would always joke around at break times with the other members of staff.

Yes, Dr. Johnson knew what he was talking about. He knew that he needed to be in the good books of the management of Beaming-Grin Dental Clinics. It was certainly not the best situation for a boisterous young man to be in, constantly watching every step that he took, especially for a twenty-nine-year-old who occasionally might make ordinary mistakes.

Because Beaming-Grin Medical Clinics had a target revenue for each of its practitioners, Dr. Johnson found that he occasionally had to take on high revenue-yielding cases which he was not very conversant with by virtue of his age in the profession, even with his specialization in prosthodontics. This he needed to do if only not to continuously lag behind in his expected revenue generation target. The alternative would be to falsify procedures performed, or to perform unnecessary procedures or to unprofessionally exaggerate diagnosis, for instance labeling simple extractions as surgical extractions which latter procedure would attract higher bills.

"I am fully aware of my limitations. I will be true to my conscience and to the tenets of the profession which I have sworn to practice with dignity and honor. But I have to muster courage and take on cases as best as I can" Dr. Johnson would say. Still, the young doctor never failed to seek for help whenever he got stuck with very difficult cases. And he was always humble enough to apologize to his patients whenever he took too long to work on them.

"Ms. Jane, how are you feeling today?" Dr. Johnson would call across to the elderly patient with complete dentures who had come to check on her loose dentures.

The very senior patients almost always preferred to see their old dentists. But a number of them liked to see the funny young dentist who made them laugh with his jokes.

"I will add a fantastic glamor to your grin today, Ms. Jane. And you would love to show-case the grin for a long time"

"Yes, that is why I have come to Beaming-Grin Dental Clinic. And that is why I would like to see the young dentist with strong hands that will readily yank off any intruding calculus in my teeth, no, in the teeth that you gave me, ha, ha, ha! And I will tell my friends in the seniors' home about the tall young dentist. Perhaps, you will soon inform us, the shorter people, what the temperature is like, up there, in the sky and nearer to God." Ms. Jane the elderly lady said.

"Ha, Ha, it is not yet my wish to go to God. I still love this part of the great divide." Ms. Jane replied as she displayed a gleaning set of dentures delivered some months earlier and fitted into her mouth by Dr. Johnson. Ms. Jane even in spite of her years was meticulously neat. She always readily told any and, all who were ready to converse with her: "I was a teacher and later a head teacher for many years. And my constant advice to my younger teachers was thus: be clean in your habits and in your heart; do your best always and laugh over those things which you have tried to achieve and failed to; smile always and give a boisterous laughter where you can and when appropriate, that way, all burdens will exit your soul and lighten your brain with the explosion of your laughter." Ms. Jane, though with occasional trembling voice, appeared to be living every aspect of her admonition with her jokes and smiles at eighty-six years of age.

Chapter 11

"THANK YOU FOR YOUR SERVICE"

"Good morning, Dr Glen, how are you today?" Dr. Johnson had shouted across the corridor to Dr. Glen who was about to enter the waiting section of the operating room. Dr Glen was the Medical Director of Beaming-Grin Medical Center, BGMC. He was a veteran of the US Navy. He was in private dental practice for many years before he joined the Navy. And after he retired from the Navy, he had joined a Group Practice of private dental practitioners in Miami Florida. He was reputed to have rash and impatient temperament and allegedly could not last long in private practice. He was said to have changed practice partners a number of times and had unsuccessfully worked with two or three other private practices before he finally joined Beaming-Grin Dental Center as Dental Director. His exit from his immediate past work place in Tampa Florida was facilitated by Debbie who was a Dental Assistant and Dr. Glen's erstwhile friend at work back in Tampa Florida.

Dr. Glen's rashness and impatience with other staff as well as with his patients had made him very unpopular in his last work place before he joined Beaming-Grin Medical Center. The final straw that broke the camel's back in Dr. Glen's last working place before Beaming-Grin, was a scandal linking Dr. Glen with Jessica a female subordinate staff in the office. Allegedly Debbie, the Dental Assistant friend of Dr. Glen and Jessica the subordinate staff in question, were each vying for Dr. Glen's attention. Debbie had lost out in the bid for Dr. Glen's

97

attention and had hurriedly resigned from the Tampa Group Practice. She thereafter relocated to Miami and was hired by Beaming-Grin Medical Clinics.

After Debbie joined Beaming-Grin, the scandal involving Dr. Glen in Tampa broke into the open forcing Dr. Glen to exit from the Group Practice. Dr. Glen turned again to Debbie who was only too happy to help Dr. Glen apply to, and join Beaming-Grin Clinics in Miami. That way Debbie became the ultimate winner in the contest between her and Jessica, the other Dental Assistant, for the love of Dr. Glen.

The romance between Dr. Glen and Debbie thus continued unabated in Beaming-Grin. This was especially so, as Dr. Glen had assumed the post of the Clinical Director of the Center.

Like sixty-three-year-old Dr. Glen, thirty-eight-year old Debbie was a divorcee. She had however remarried barely two months before Dr. Glen joined Beaming-Grin. However, unlike Dr. Glen who was rash, impatient, uncaring and often consumed by bigotry, Debbie was a very pleasant, humane and down-to-earth individual. She was naturally pleasant, very generous and was ever so ready to give useful advice to any of her work colleagues who was in difficulty.

Although she came from a very wealthy family, Debbie was never boastful or cocky. She always wore a pleasant smile and radiated empathy and confidence to everyone when these were needed. She often brought joy and relaxation to the room especially in the usually boring Beaming Grin environment. In the absence of Dr. Johnson who was also a source of warmth and laughter Debbie brought fun and relaxation to the otherwise tense Beaming Grin environment. When there were no patients around and the environment appeared moody, Debbie was always a source of cheer and sweet stories. A lot of times she would bring fruits from her orchard for her colleagues at work to take home. At other times, she would bring assorted cookies and at lunch time she would unveil whatever she brought with a smiling face and invite the other members of staff to partake.

"Dr. D, you don't seem to enjoy the strawberries; why don't you try my apples. They are all products of my little orchard", Debbie told Doris when she noticed that the latter was hesitant to partake of the fruits. Debbie was a bundle of good nature and humanity. She did not appear to mind the regular gossip among the rank and file in Beaming Grin about her romance with Dr. Glen. She rarely mentioned her family members during general conversations which bordered on domestic matters. Once in a while she would make references to the emotional pains that she went through during her earlier dissolved marriage. But she would never make references to her subsisting family especially when Dr Glen was around.

"My former husband was so rash. He did not like fruits and vegetable and almost always made me feel ill-at-ease in public gatherings whenever he saw me packing fruits and vegetables into my plate." Debbie would say jokingly as her colleagues enjoyed the fruits which she brought from her orchard.

On one occasion during lunch break, Dr Johnson had made a statement about a movie titled "work-place romances." Everybody in the room showed enthusiasm about listening to the story; everybody but Debbie. The latter got up and briefly left the room. She did not want to listen to the story but she did not attempt to interrupt Dr Johnson or show aversion to a discussion in that direction. *Her man* Dr Glen was not in the Common Room and so there was nobody who would share Debbie's disgust with her if the story got ugly. And so, rather than stay in to be embarrassed, Debbie momentarily vacated the room. When she later came back wearing a rather unusual countenance. When Dr Johnson discovered that Debbie appeared hurt by the movie that he was discussing he had to apologize to the latter. Debbie obviously thought that the Dr Johnson had sinister motives for telling the story.

"I hope you do not misunderstand my purpose for narrating the movie, Debbie. It was a new movie that aired last night and I had nobody in mind for narrating it." Dr Johnson had said. Debbie smiled broadly and said: "Not at all Dr. J. If there is any gossip about me, I know it cannot emanate from you. I know there is always something and somebody to be talked about amongst co-workers. Something or somebody has to be the subject of discussions. I know that I happen to be the subject of discussions most of the time. But I do not really mind. As long as people are happy and relaxed, I am fine."

Debbie smiled again and went off back again to the Doctors' Room to hand some more bunches of grapes to Dr. Glen. She was such an amiable lady. She appeared to disarm her critics and any and all detractors with her love and kindness.

"Debbie is simply being her good self, Dr. J." One of the Dental Assistants who was sitting close-by said to Dr Johnson.

"Yes, it is the roving eyes of Dr. Glen who has been twice divorced consequent upon unrepentant infidelities, which are in fact taking advantage of Debbie's good nature in the friendship." Another co-worker a front-desk staff who was also sitting out the break period, said.

It was general break time and a number of the staff of Beaming Grin were as usual gathered around a central table in the staff room of Beaming Grin clinic. Dr. Glen was munching a bunch of grapes which Debbie had brought for the staff members from her orchard. Yes, it was not unusual for members of staff to bring snacks and fruits for other members of staff to enjoy as a team. Debbie of course was the biggest and most regular donor in the camaraderie.

Dr Glen soon walked leisurely into the Staff Common Room where the other members of staff were gathered. As he plucked off and threw grapes into his mouth, he munched slowly and said: "While I was in the Navy as a Navy Captain, I used to have my boys procure me the finest grapes fresh from any base that we were stationed at. It used to be great and I greatly miss my days in service", Dr. Glen said as he loudly tapped his feet on the floor and hurled more grapes into his mouth. Nothing pleased him as much as having younger female subordinate staff surround him while he glibly narrated his escapades and alleged heroism in the Navy. Later that afternoon, after he had completed a difficult dental procedure, Dr. Glen appeared to stagger into the Doctors' Office where he deliberately slumped into one of the office chairs faking panting. Thereupon Debbie who exclusively assisted him in almost all procedures, followed him. She pulled up another chair and sat behind him. She then proceeded to repeatedly rub his back as would a loving mother to a hurting small son. And the *Big Boy* was deliberately heaving heavily and panting as would an unpracticed athlete who had just completed a 100 yards sprint.

Dr Seene another dentist in the facility, was sitting nearby and observed for a while but could no longer contain herself and her disgust.

"This open display of affection is not necessary" Dr. Seene muttered from where she sat at the other end of the central table in the Doctors' Office. Dr. Seene was the taciturn middle-aged Associate Dentist of Indian ancestry who rarely stayed in the Doctors' Office. She often preferred to stay in the larger general common room instead of in the adjacent smaller Doctors' Room. As she muttered her disgust, Dr. Seene made her way out of the room. As soon as Dr Seene left the room Debbie started to rub the back of Dr. Glen more vigorously as if to mock the disgust of Dr Seene. Dr Glen did not appear to care about whoever was watching. He leaned forwards on the table as would a physically exhausted little child.

Dr. Seene was perhaps the only staff of Beaming Grin who uncharacteristically often voiced her disapproval of the open display of affection between the Clinical Director and Ms. Debbie. Most of the other staff would either gossip in slow tones about the shenanigans or remain silent altogether even if the *love birds* fell forward against their feet as they practiced their play.

"Why would this nonsense be taking place in full glare of the other staff in an open office?" Dr. Seene muttered. She was a Hindu who had converted to Christianity. She was very religious and sometimes openly complained to the other doctors about her dislike of Dr. Glen's improprieties.

"I don't know what these guys think they are doing. To me this is disgusting and should not be happening here." Dr. Seene complained loudly on her way out of the general office into the doctors' Common Room. She had just completed a *root canal therapy* on a patient and had walked into the Doctors' Room to write her notes. Sighing loudly and donning a long face she quickly exited the room at the sight of Debbie rubbing Dr. Glen's back in the open office.

"What is more disgusting is the fact that Dr. Glen who should be showing good examples allows Debbie to stick her palm under his theater gown to rub her bare palm against his bare back. It should not be my business, but the venue is not right." Dr Seene said with a prolonged sigh.

Even though Dr. Seene's expression of disgust about Dr. Glen and Ms. Debbie was made on the corridor on her way out of the Doctors' Common Room, both Dr. Glen and Ms. Debbie had heard Dr. Seene. Dr. Glen, on hearing Dr. Seene's statement was livid with anger. He turned towards Debbie, all red, and the two had made brief hateful eye contacts. The other two doctors who were in the room writing their notes on their computers had also heard Dr. Seene but were not inclined to say anything.

Dr. Doris was still in the surgery battling with a badly-carious tooth which she was extracting. With her many years of experience in the profession, there were not many types of dental extraction that Dr. Doris could not handle. But Dr. Glen had always wanted to handle all extractions which deviated even slightly from the ordinary. He always told the front desk and scheduling staff to direct all cases that might require dental extractions to him. That way he would handle almost all cases that he did as if they were extra-ordinary cases. Invariably he would label the cases as "surgical extractions". Surgical extractions were billed almost three times as much as "simple extractions".

The irrepressible Dr. Seene had on many occasions complained openly and loudly before the other doctors:

"Dr Glen is wittingly and unwittingly damaging the long-term integrity of this institution and indeed of this profession. By labeling all extractions done by him as *surgical extraction* he is not only depriving us, the other dentists in the team, of patients, he is also heavily bloating his revenue production and defrauding the paying patients or the insuring bodies, government agencies or insurance companies. He is doing great damage to all of us by his actions because ultimately his misrepresentations will be discovered and the ripple effect will consume all of us. Our integrity and that of this institution will be in jeopardy when eventually these misrepresentations are discovered. It will be wrongly assumed that we are all guilty of the same wrongdoings, even when I know that neither I nor Dr Doris will ever contemplate any of these misdeeds. Dr Glen, aided by Debbie his partner in workplace romance, bloats and massages his ego as the only dentist in the facility who could handle all extractions, and this is wrong and unacceptable."

Most staff members of the facility agreed that Dr Seene was very right in her statement. Dr. Glen's wrong designation of simple extractions as *surgical extractions* would attract higher revenue by the self-acclaimed *god-sent Oral Surgeon* who was adored by the management. But the adoration stemmed from the Clinical Director's padding of cases. And the unsuspecting management eulogized the Clinical Director for heavily boosting the revenue of Beaming Grin Medical Center since his arrival to the Center.

Many of his other colleagues did not like what Dr. Glen was doing but since the latter was the Clinical Director of Beaming Grin, he always had his way. In any case, there was no formal complaint of any wrong-doing against the Clinical Director and the Management could not be held culpable for what it did not know about and what could not be substantiated in the absence of complainants.

Dr. Johnson had no problems being turned to an exclusive clearing house for cases which the boss did not wish to handle. The Clinical Director's yearly assessment determined his (Dr. Johnson) being retained in the US practice since Dr Johnson was on a Temporary Work Visa. And the visa renewal was dependent on Dr. Glen's whims and caprices. With the other US citizens like Dr Doris and Dr Seene, and US-trained doctors, who did not require Dr. Glen's assent to continue to practice in the USA, it was a little more difficult for the self-styled dental Czar, to always have his way. These other ones could always find other practices or set up shop if their contracts were not renewed and if they had the courage and confidence to go into private practice.

Yes, Dr. Seene had made some unsavory statement about a sight which was offensive to her sense of morality. And yes, both Dr. Glen and Ms. Debbie had heard Dr. Seene's statement. The backlash was spontaneous.

"Was she talking about us?" Dr. Glen had asked Ms. Debbie. The incipient anger was palpable on Dr. Glen's deeply reddened face as he turned towards Debbie on hearing Dr. Seene.

"Yes, isn't she silly?" Debbie said.

"Dr. Seene needs to be curbed. I think she is getting wild. There doesn't appear to be any more respect and discipline left in this office", Dr. Glen barked as he sprang up from his seat and walked towards the corridor in the direction of Dr. Seene. Even though Dr. Glen was not known to be a violent man, the speed with which he sprang up from his seat and the anger that manifested on his face, made Debbie fear for the worst.

"No, Dr. G, no! Come back!" Debbie shouted as she ran after Dr. Glen pulling him back by the left hand and dragging him back.

Like a small child who had been restrained from an imminent fight, Dr. Glen followed Debbie back to his seat. A few whispered exchanges followed between the two love birds and Debbie quickly left the Doctors' Room. As soon as she left Dr. Glen reached for his cell phone and was overhead calling Mr. Clifford the Chief Executive Officer of the Center. Mr. Clifford's office was in another building a little detached from the main building housing the Dental Clinic.

As the drama played out three of the four Doctors who were also in the adjoining Doctors' Office writing their notes heard the exchanges and exchanged glances in silence. Those were colleagues who had mostly been cowed into submission by a combination of boastful narratives, subtle intimidation and downright blackmail as in the case of young Dr. Johnson. The fourth doctor was Dr. Doris. The latter had come into the room at a later stage but was not interested in what she always considered as child-like behavior by Dr. Glen and Ms. Debbie. Unlike the other dentists in the team, Dr Doris always preferred to read her medical journals when she was not busy writing her notes or seeing patients.

"Did I hear Dr. Glen mention respect and discipline?" Dr. Burd. one of the three doctors whispered to Dr. Johnson. The latter only nodded in the affirmative. He did not want whatever he would say to be heard by his boss, *a bull in a China shop,* who had the power to refuse to sign him up for a renewal of his license to continue to practice in the United States.

Within one hour of Dr. Glen's phone call to Mr. Clifford, the CEO was seen walking into the Dental Director's small and over-crowded private/administrative office. Dr. Glen followed the CEO into the Clinical Director's office and both men shut the door behind them.

It was obvious that the fate of Dr. Seene as a staff of the private non-profit, grant-aided medical facility, was hanging in the balance.

After about fifteen minutes of private discussions between Dr. Glen and Mr. Clifford, the two men were again seen walking out of the Clinical Director's office.

"Thank you for your prompt response to my call, Cliff".

"No problem, Dr. Glen, and thank you for your service".

Of course, everybody in the room knew that nothing delighted and excited Dr. Glen as much as being thanked for his service in the Navy of the United States. Yes, that was even when his service which deserved always to be appreciated anyway, had absolutely no relevance to the indiscreet behavior which he had exhibited at that particular occasion.

Chapter 12

SUBDUED RANCOR IN THE HOUSE

"What do you think of Dr. Glen's improprieties and his designation of all extractions as surgical extractions, Dr. D?" Dr. Seene asked Dr. Doris as soon as the latter walked into the Doctors' Office on the morning after the visit of the CEO on invitation by Dr. Glen. It was obvious to all staff that the visit of the CEO following the back-rubbing incident and comment by Dr. Seene would not go without repercussions. Following that incident, both Dr. Glen and Dr. Seene each appeared to be gathering allies in preparation for an inevitable show-down in the clinic. The other staff of the clinic who had not witnessed the events had heard the details both from Debbie and from Dr. Seene. Even members of the medical teams learnt of the impending show-down. Many were greatly interested in what was about to happen next.

"I am not usually bothered by how people choose to carry on with their private lives, Dr. S." Doris said in reply to Dr. Seene.

"As long as their actions do not impact on my person, people can carry on with bed-room talk or whatever they want wherever they want. It is only the obvious professional improprieties which will bear the imprimatur of this clinic and taint all of us as forgers, which borders me. But even at that, I am not the policeman of the system. We all know that the Assistants here are the eyes and ears of the management, and so, they will report what they see." Dr. Doris said with an air of indifference.

"But where one of the so-called policemen is one of the culprits do you think that the necessary report will be launched?" Dr. Seene asked, almost with the tone and anxiety of a desperate conspirator.

"No, Dr S, the system will, in good time, definitely fish out any, and all bad eggs, and deal with them appropriately." Doris said grinning. She was being careful not to be dragged unnecessarily into a work-place camp-formation.

"I wish I could share your optimism, Dr. D, but things are not likely to change where nobody guards the guards." Dr. Seene said.

The inevitable gossips had hit the roofs. The atmosphere was riddled with suppressed anxiety. Ordinarily the atmosphere in BGMC, since the arrival of Dr. Glen as Clinical Director, was at best one of subdued tension. Dr. Glen's immediate predecessor in office was also a retired military man. But unlike Dr. Glen the latter was a very affable, very responsible and very humane senior citizen who cared very deeply about how his every statement and action would impact on the establishment which was entrusted to his care. Again, unlike Dr. Glen who not only always derided family life, Dr. Kenwood who was Dr. Glen's predecessor was a very devout Christian and family man and he managed Beaming Grin as family. He had the greatest respect for even the most junior staff of the Center. He had earned the admiration and respect of all staff right from inception up to the day that he handed the mantle of office over to his successor, Dr. Glen.

Dr. Kenwood had participated in the interview that employed Dr. Glen as Dental Director. As a retired Captain in the US Navy, on the day that he was saying goodbye to the staff of Beaming Grin he had stated inter alia: "I leave you in the hands of another retired officer and gentleman. I leave you in the able hands of another man who has passed through the crucible of fire of military and professional discipline. I leave you in the able hands of my brother in service, Dr. Bob Glen."

In spite of the glowing encomiums heaped in advance on Dr Glen by Dr Kenwood, the disparity in management capabilities and professional integrity between the two gentlemen was not lost on any member of staff of BGMC. Least of all was Dr. Seene. After her initial discussions with Dr Doris, Dr Seene quietly turned to Dr Doris and said:

"I cannot stop missing Dr. Kenwood as opposed to this current braggard of a Clinical Director. Dr. Kenwood meant well for every staff and for the center. But this Dr. Bob Glen is a moral and administrative disaster. His taciturnity and apparent gentle mien are mere smokescreens for ethical and professional irresponsibility. He is vain and boastful. And under the guise of making money for the institution, for which he always boasts, we all know that he embarks on procedures which are not fully essential for the health of the patient. He sees each patient as a vehicle for advancing his ego and career rather than as a fellow human who has a soul and feeling and whose good should be paramount in whatever we do here."

Dr. Seene paused for a while. She and Dr. Doris each turned their ears in the direction of the door where someone was talking loudly. They heard the familiar self-adulations:

"I did sixty-four surgical extractions in the past three days, and all of them turned out perfect! Two of those patients were awful. But trust me, I yanked off the goddam things almost with my eyes closed. Tons of money for Little Cliff and his Admin people to spend. I guess it's high time I compelled them to include me in those wasteful official tours that they undertake. I make the money and they spend it."

That must be Dr. Glen talking. No one else would talk in such a boastful manner." Dr Seene whispered to Dr. Doris. The former thereafter continued:

"Some visitor or some junior members of staff must be around. There must be some audience listening and being entertained. It always looks as if this Clinical Director always thirsts for some audience for him to narrate his apparent surgical prowess to." Dr. Seene said to Dr. Doris. The latter merely listened. She had learnt not to be too quick in joining any unnecessary criticism or condemnation of constituted authority even when she did not approve of their behavior. This was especially so, since she knew that conspiratorial and behind-the-scene criticisms would not produce any positive changes.

On the Wednesday morning following his Monday morning near-show-down with Dr. Seene, Dr. Glen had seen some nurses and assistants gathered near the changing room. The Assistants were discussing among themselves and Dr. Glen as usual wanted to impress them. Immediately upon his arrival the ladies were all but falling over each other in loud greetings, each angling to be noticed by the "King of the jungle" as Dr. Seene regularly called Dr. Glen behind the latter's back. Everybody had expected to hear some statements about the previous Monday's elephant-on-the-grass fight between Dr. Glen and

Dr. Seene. But it looked like better reasoning had prevailed consequent upon the intervention of the CEO, Mr. Clifford. The latter had seen no merit in the complaint by Dr. Glen against Dr Seene. Besides, the CEO had on several occasions learnt of the *roving eyes* of the Clinical Director.

"Good morning Dr. Glen. And how are you today?" The chorus of greetings was spontaneous and almost thunderous emanating from a dozen female voices most prominent among which was that of Ms. Andrea Wilson. Ms. Andrea Wilson was a young blonde Dental Assistant who coincidentally bore the same first name as a nurse in Dr Glen's former place of work.

Ms. Andrea Wilson had always seen herself as next in succession to Debbie in Dr. Glen's favor in BGMC. So fierce, albeit unhealthy, was the competition between Debbie and Andrea for Dr. Glen's favor that Andrea had once openly and carelessly stated thus: "Whatever Debbie can offer, in this job and for Dr. Glen's attention, I too can offer and even better". Andrea certainly was not Debbie's best friend in the presence of Dr. Glen. But the *King of the jungle* appeared to be savoring the competition for his attention. None in the house except Dr. Johnson and more so, Dr. Seene appeared particularly embarrassed by the on-going cat and mouse games between Debbie and Ms. Andrea Wilson. But while Dr. Johnson always turned the other way while the open display of affections lasted, Dr. Seene never failed to show her disgust either by sighing audibly or by immediately leaving the Doctors' room and relocating to the surgery even when she was not seeing any patient. Dr. Doris on her own part appeared less concerned about what she always considered as "silly adult indiscipline" in work place. She always turned to her copy of JADA, the

Journal of American Dental Association when she was not very busy at work.

"Very well, Andrea, fired up and ready to go?" Dr. Glen shouted as he surreptitiously visually searched for Debbie from among the gathering of Assistants, nurses, hygienists and other staff who were signing in for the morning duty. "That's the way we used to say it in the military. Oh, my God! I miss the military". Dr. Glen continued. His large eyeballs rolled anxiously behind his thick-rimmed glasses apparently searching for Debbie or other praise-singers who would extoll his military and extra-ordinary surgical accomplishments.

Dr. Glen was not to be disappointed in his search for his soul-mate. Debbie soon emerged from the changing room and hurried towards the group of nurses and Assistants. It was as if Debbie wanted to make sure that Dr. Glen did not get into any conversation, no matter how briefly with any other member of staff all of who, but for Dr. Johnson and a security man named Jimmy, were females.

"Hi Bob!" Debbie shouted from a distance as soon as she was within sight from where the *King of the jungle* was standing.

Dr Johnson was around the corner. Although usually funny, he was not used to talking too much or being sarcastic. But seeing Dr. Glen gyrating from side to side in the midst of a multitude of nurses and Assistants he could not but involuntarily mutter to Dr Seene's hearing: "This fellow reminds me of one deposed African military dictator who once got some European merchants in his country to carry him shoulder high on a hammock. I think he was called General Idi Amin. They said he thereafter had declared himself as 'the white man's burden'. Wow! What do we call this one?" Dr Johnson quickly recollected himself. He immediately wiped his face with the palm of his hands as if to wipe away the statement which he had unwittingly, but silently, made. None of the other people in the room appeared conversant with the activities of the former Ugandan strongman, and so none of them commented on Dr Johnson's unsavory statement against someone who was a one-time Head of State. Yet, Dr Johnson was quick enough to try to vitiate his uncomplimentary remarks. And so, he sighed and quickly said: "I just said something about General Idi Amin of Uganda! I mis-spoke. He might have been said to have been a brutal dictator and a tyrant. But, who am I to judge someone who served for some time as a Head of Government be it in Africa or elsewhere? After all, history is replete with many crazy or near crazy Heads of Government in diverse countries in Asia, Europe, other African Countries and the Americas. It should be left for history and their people to judge them not me, poor embattled Dr Johnson!"

Dr Glen was not listening to Dr Johnson. As the latter soliloquized and contemplated on an appropriate *mea culpa* for his flippancy, Dr Glen was busy looking out for his soul-mate.

"Hi Debbie. I was wondering whether you were off-duty today". Dr Glen had whispered.

"I couldn't be off duty without your knowing, Bob." Debbie said. She deliberately spoke loudly-enough so Ms. Andrea Wilson would hear. Anything that would make her rival jealous was fair game. Ms. Andrea Wilson, the target of Debbie's statement, was rinsing her sippy-cup in the wash hand basin at the far end of the room.

Dr Johnson's earlier Idi Amin comparison was made very quietly, almost inaudibly. But it was not without somebody hearing it. Dr.

Seene heard it. And, it was the kind of comparison that Dr Seene always wanted to hear about Dr. Glen.

"It looks like Debbie always wishes to establish ownership of the Clinical Director. It appears she would want to make all else, especially Andrea, jealous of her good fortune." Dr. Seene muttered mockingly to the hearing of Dr. Johnson.

"This overt display of affection is reprehensible." Dr. Seene continued. "It is a very unhealthy situation where a Clinical Director had all but completely compromised his position before one of his subordinates."

It was the Thursday following the Monday morning episode that necessitated the invitation of the CEO. The latter's visit as of then had had no known sequalae. There was little or no love lost between Dr Glen and Dr. Seene. Every little incident amplified the disharmony.

As Dr. Glen and the nurses and Assistants were exchanging banters in the lobby near the changing room, Dr. Seene walked past them and in her usual polite way greeted the staff as a group. Uncharacteristically she extended special greetings to Dr. Glen.

"Good morning everybody. I hope you all had lovely nights. And good morning Dr. Glen. And how was the traffic from your end this morning? There was an accident along my route, but it appeared to have occurred just before I got to the spot and so the traffic had not built up by the time I passed. It certainly will build up with time because one of the cars involved was a write-off. Happily, nobody appeared seriously hurt".

As the mention of the accident was made, all the staff crouched just before Dr. Seene stated that there were no fatalities.

Dr. Glen who maintained a straight face glanced from one staff to the other and snared at Dr. Seene as the latter walked off briskly towards the Doctors' Common Room. Then, fixing his gaze on Debbie, *the King of the jungle* blurted out in apparent disgust and with veiled reference to Dr. Seene: "Looks like someone always likes to spoil the morning's fun. I have told Janet that this Center needs to start weeding out sadistic dead-woods and fun-spoilers from here."

Janet was the newly-employed Office Manager at BGMC. She was for many years a Receptionist at the Center before she took a protracted Study Leave to study Office Management. Upon graduation Janet, had called back at BGMC and was lucky to meet the retirement of the long-serving amiable Office Manager Ms. Bloomberg under whom she had served as Receptionist. Janet had promptly applied for the post of Office Manager for which she had become academically qualified. She did not have the requisite experience but because of her long association with BGMC and upon recommendation of the ubiquitous but highly-friendly Ms. Debbie, and the latter's connection with the Clinical Director, Janet was given the job of Office Manager at BGMC.

Debbie cast a glance of disapproval on Dr. Glen immediately after the latter made his statement about "sadistic dead-woods". She was ordinarily a friendly individual who would not wish by action or words to hurt anyone. Much as she was considered too close to Dr. Glen, and would take sides with the latter in the event of a showdown, Debbie would not wish to antagonize Dr. Seene. She indeed would not wish to antagonize any other staff member, except perhaps her perceived rival Ms. Andrea Wilson. Debbie would always oppose Andrea in any argument or discussion in the presence of Dr. Glen.

"No, Bob, it is a beautiful morning and the issue of the accident does not spoil our day." Debbie said trying to obviate Dr. Glen's adverse comments about Dr. Seene. She knew that Dr. Bob Glen was thrice divorced and could be as rash and unpredictable as anyone could imagine. And she had always told her friends who had suggested to her to actualize a formal divorce from her marriage and formalize a marriage to Dr. Glen instead of pussy-footing around with him at work place.

"I would love to marry Dr. Glen," Debbie had once told Dr. Johnson whom she occasionally confided in, "but I would not wish to drastically hurt my present husband and father of my son. Besides, I would not wish to live in constant fear of being counted as Dr. Glen's fourth divorced wife. I would rather remain his first surviving girlfriend."

Between Debbie, Janet and Dr. Glen, a power-brokerage triumvirate was formed in BGMC. All major decisions about the institution were discussed and agreed to well in advance between members of the triumvirate. This was usually before any such proposal was presented to Mr. Clifford the CEO, who Dr. Glen always privately referred mockingly before his nurse-admirers as "Little Cliff". The derogatory reference to Mr. Clifford as "Little Cliff" was on account of the latter's rather diminutive stature. As far as Dr. Glen and Debbie were concerned, the pleasantly-natured CEO was a mere figure head.

Indeed, the CEO appeared to have become so thoroughly bamboozled by Dr. Glen's boastfulness that he had relinquished all authority, even in matters of administration to the overbearing Clinical Director. Mr. Cliff had become more of a rubber-stamp to Dr. Glen in all matters relating to the administration of BGMC.

"Why hasn't Mr. Cliff taken action against Dr. Seene two weeks after your complaint?" Debbie had asked Dr. Glen.

"You know I did not specifically request that the impudent lady be fired. I merely asked Little Cliff over here to brief him on the disruptive behavior of Dr. Seene. If I chose to ask for her firing, Little Cliff would have had no choice but to fire her immediately." Dr Glen told her mistress.

"But the impudence is not likely to abet. We saw a manifestation of its worsening in the General Office this morning. Dr Seene is certainly not likely to back down. She even appears to be gaining the subtle support of Dr. Doris". Debbie said in an apparent uncharacteristic desire to expand the enmity list.

"Are you inferring that Dr. Doris is also bothering us?" Dr Glen inquired.

"Not exactly, but her silence in the face of rampant display of impudence from her friend and colleague, speaks louder than words?"

"I do not reckon much with Dr. Doris. It does not really matter very much what she and her people think."

"What do you mean by her people? You mean people of her color or people of her creed? She is an American and she is a Christian just like you and me."

"I mean people like her in both categories and more!"

"Or do you mean people in her professional cadre; she is a senior staff, next in rank to you and certainly senior to Dr Seene."

118

Categorize it however you wish Debbie, all I know is that I just can't stand her and her people."

"I already know your skewed views on racial matters, Bob, but the fact remains that Dr Doris is a highly-respected senior staff of this center."

 "Says who?"

"I understand she became a doctor before Dr. S. She trained and did her residency in highly-respected centers in New York City, and she joined BGMC well before Dr, S. Or how else does one calculate seniority? And of course, she is obviously older in age than Dr. S. She is a quiet friendly lady with a very affable family background. You obviously just don't like her because of the color of her skin, and you must admit this Bob!" Debbie said, looking enquiringly at Dr, Glen.

"I don't know when you became a spokeswoman for the NAACP, Debbie. And as regards seniority, there is no question of seniority here, Debbie. After the Board of Management there is the CEO, then there is the Clinical Director and then there is the rest. This is a service-oriented Non-Profit, and Dr. Glen essentially makes most of the internally-generated revenue that sustains this place", Dr glen said dismissively. He had referred to himself in the third person as he was wont to do whenever he was planning some mischief.

"What is this NAACP that you often refer to and seem to loath so much?" Debbie asked looking askance at Dr Glen.

"Hmmm! Then you don't deserve to be the spokeswoman for the National Association for the Advancement of Colored People if you don't know the abbreviation of their name, Debbie."

"Then the hate is deeper than I ever imagined. This is our America, Bob, not just your America. And we must realize that for us to be truly happy, we must begin to be tolerant of, and accommodate our fellow Americans. Skin color, creed and ethnicity have little or no place in our Americanness. What makes us truly great is our diversity. As a distinguished military man, you know more about this than I do."

"Wow! Debbie, I didn't know that you could be such a wonderful preacher. I begin to see that with you by anybody's side, the person would not need an ordained preacher. But you may do well to also preach to this silly and sinful Dr Seene and her silent supporter that conniving bitch called Dr Doris, to stop bothering us or get kicked out." Dr Glen said, intermittently smiling and frowning.

Chapter 13

THE PLOT THICKENS

Even though she had great affection for Dr Glen, Debbie knew within her that the Clinical Director harbored deep racist tendencies which he sometimes found difficulty to conceal. Unlike Debbie, Dr Glen could not control his tongue when it came to inter-personal relations with colleagues and other staff members. Debbie often tried to moderate Dr Glen's statements and comments. She indeed often persuaded the latter to speak little. But for a man who was boastful and bossy it was not the easiest thing in the world to comply with.

"I have observed that you seem quite interested in Dr Doris. Nothing that she does ever seems to offend you. What is it that really fascinates you in that dumb show? She is so nauseating. Honestly, she sucks!" Dr Glen asked Debbie.

Debbie's reaction surprised Dr Glen.

"Why do you speak in such strongly-negative terms about Dr D? She is such an amiable lady and she is very professional in her dealings with her patients." Debbie said.

"Well, Debbie, it is good to be amiable. But it is another thing to belong, and to make the money for the institution. In these regards your Dr D does not measure up. She is way, way down in the scheme of things." Dr Glen said almost dismissively.

"I had always known that Dr. Doris is the most professionally-senior provider in the Institution next to Dr Kenwood your predecessor. I am not aware that anybody senior to her has joined us here since you assumed the post of Clinical Director. Or, have you demoted her for some reasons since your arrival, Bob?" Debbie asked, half-jokingly and half-seriously.

"You urge me to talk little on one hand and you make me say things that you often consider offensive on the other hand, Debbie." Dr. Glen heaved heavily and continued.

"As far as management of this Center is concerned, your friend Dr Doris is a nobody. These aliens descend on our institutions like vultures. They are parasites who flock to this country to take away our jobs and resources. They want to impose their dark ages on our modernity. They are doing more harm than good to our very decent and cherished ways of life."

Dr Glen paused for a short while and looked at Debbie as if in quest of approval or disapproval for his vitriolic against Dr Doris who was not anywhere within sight. He then continued.

"I know you will as usual label me as a racist or ethnic bigot, but this is my view Debbie. And, luckily, we still have the First Amendment to protect people like me. Luckily, we still have freedom of speech which these latter-day Americans who would like to displace the real Americans would like to dispense with. We can't even express our opinions freely any more. We live in perpetual fear of being branded as racists by these guys. We have become virtual prisoners in our own country. It's so very sad!" Dr Glen said, sounding almost emotional. His usual smile whenever he was with Debbie had rapidly turned into a permanent frown. Debbie immediately understood better than to continue with the unpleasant discussion. She tried to change the topic to something more pleasant to Dr. Glen.

"You have done so much surgery in this place, Bob. A wing of this building ought to be named after you to encourage hard work on the part of your successors."

But Dr. Glen's unprovoked anger did not appear to have ebbed. Debbie's effort to massage his ego did not appear to have doused his deep-seated revulsion against "these latter-day Americans" who masquerade as "real Americans". He did not ever seem to recognize that people like Dr. Seene, an American of Indian father and Irish mother, were born in the United States as much as he was. The fact that others like Dr. Doris had naturalized and sworn allegiance to The Star-Spangled Banner and were bona fide citizens of the United States was apparently not recognized to any extent by Dr. Glen. Some of his colleagues like Dr Doris had previously trained in some of the best institutions in the world overseas and in the United States. But these facts appeared to be of little or no significance to Dr Glen. Bigotry had taken the center stage.

Happily, Dr. Glen's opinion was not widely shared at BGMC. Most of the other members of staff were very friendly with one another. Indeed, Debbie, even with her overt romance with Dr. Glen, was one of the friendliest and non-racially biased individuals in the institution. That was notwithstanding the fact that as the Clinical Director, Dr. Glen's opinion carried a lot of weight in professional and even administrative matters in BGMC.

It was time for another set of surgical procedures. The Operating Room had been prepared, the surgical equipment set out and the patient was wheeled in, waiting for administration of full anesthesia. As usual, Debbie was assisting Dr. Glen and the two chatted along as the procedure progressed.

"Little Cliff will be visiting this office tomorrow" Dr. Glen had whispered to Debbie as the latter was about to hand him the final swab after an oral surgical procedure that took a little longer than usual to close up.

"Oh, what for? He does not usually come here on the last Friday of the month when you guys hold your monthly meetings in his office."

"Yes, you remember the incident of two weeks ago that necessitated my inviting the CEO here. After his visit he wanted to take some drastic measures but I had to prevail on him to give that lady another chance. Since then there has been no improvement in Dr. Seene's behavior and work ethics. I am not quite sure now that I can continue to tolerate all this rubbish. I specifically invited Cliff to come and witness what I had been complaining about this Seene fellow. This rubbish cannot just continue this way." Dr. Glen stated with an air of absolute authority and finality.

"I can now see why you were so pensive during most of the cases since today. You should not allow these things to disturb you. You have already had enough of women's problems to contend with."

"No, no, no, nothing of the sort disturbs me, Debbie. It's just that a stop needs to be put to this lady's intransigence. It is either she goes or I go".

"No, no, Bob, you both can coexist here. I thought that the CEO had brokered peace between the two of you. Honestly, I don't see anything wrong with Dr. Seene as a person. Same goes for Dr Doris who you often seem to dismiss as an outsider even when she is such a mild-mannered and respectful lady and an American citizen just like us. Again, as regards Dr. Doris she may be feeling offended by our open friendship. She may be keeping too much to herself and may keep aloof in the social activities of the Center. But this may simply be her nature. We all have our different shortcomings. We all have certain areas where we may feel unreasonably prejudiced against other people's activities. And back to Dr. Seene, yes, I know that she had not been fully minding her business about our friendship. But that is no reason why she should go." Debbie stated, looking Dr. Glen straight in the face, half assertively, half beseechingly.

"But you were the person complaining about Dr Seene's meddlesomeness, Debbie. And you seem to concentrate on Dr. Seene. You seem to largely make light of the reticent but still meddlesome Dr. Doris who pretends to be reading journals but subtly and silently lends support to Dr. Seene by not cautioning her. Dr Seene would not be so bold against us if she does not have the subtle support of Dr Doris. Therefore, Dr Doris who acts as a support pillar for Dr Seene must be brought down first. You can bring down a solid target most successfully by first eroding its pillars of support." Dr. Glen interjected.

"Yes, but there are no sufficient justified reasons to work against their stay, Bob. I never suggested that their employment in the Center be terminated." Debbie said.

"You appear to be ascribing too much powers to me, Debbie. I do not own the place to fire Dr. Seene or even Dr. Doris, you know." Dr Glen said.

"But you do have the power to recommend any of them being fired, I know." Debbie said in a rather beseeching voice.

"But I am not doing that!" Dr Glen replied.

"Yes, you are, Bob. You just said it. Otherwise why is the CEO, Mr. Cliff coming here today?" Debbie said cutting the fierce image of a lioness protecting her threatened cubs.

"Little Cliff is coming to witness things for himself. He is coming to personally interview some of the staff members regarding their opinion about Dr. Seene and Dr. Doris. Then he can form his own opinion." Dr. Glen said, sounding defensive.

"But then even the CEO cannot fire Dr. Seene or Dr Doris without cause." Debbie said

"Yes, he can! Their contracts said that any of them can resign and that their appointments can be terminated with, or without cause. And so, any or both of them can also be fired with, or without cause. They only need to be paid some months' salary in lieu of notice, just as they can quit by payment of three months salaries in lieu of three months' notice." Dr Glen said.

"Yes, I know all that, Bob, but in this particular case what particular reasons will you give to the CEO for recommending Dr. Seene's or Dr Doris' firing?"

"Come on, Debbie, who told you that I am recommending the firing of Dr. Doris? Have you become a mind-reader over night?"

"Come off it, Bob! I have known you for more than a decade, you know. Remember that we started being friends from the other hospital in Tampa! I can always tell with ninety nine percent certainty when you are disturbed and when you are planning something, good or evil"

"Good or evil, Debbie? That's why I said that you are becoming a mind-reader. But the truth is that I don't have the power to fire Dr. Doris or Dr Seene. And I am not plotting their exit. By the way, what gives you the impression that I am planning such a thing? Or could it be you, Debbie, who are plotting their exit? It is said that out of the abundance of the heart, the mouth *speaks.* Or, could it be the parable of the pot calling the kettle black? Little Cliff is coming only to conduct some investigative interviews."

"Well and good Bob, but I hope the CEO is not going to interview that intrusive lady Ms. Andrea, otherwise you may be biting more than you can chew. Andrea is a naughty and intriguing little fellow. She can say things that you may not like, if only to hurt me. It looks like all that go by the name of Andrea are conniving boy-friend snatchers!"

"You and Andrea, Debbie! What is it in that name that makes you so jealous? You know we are not in the state of Utah!"

"And what has this got to do with the state of Utah? I will not be party to your denigration or ridicule of any people not the least, of a good and devoted highly-religious and pious Americans." Debbie said, believing that Dr Glen was attempting to cast aspersions on a religion.

"Even in Utah, polygamy is against the law. They say there may be sister-wives, but polygamy is still against the law in our America. And I mean the America that we know, before these millions of intruders from all sorts of failed countries swoop on us like black falcons and denude our treasured values". Dr Glen said with apparent grief-stricken tone.

"What are all these parables about black falcons and white falcons, Bob?" Debbie asked.

"What I mean is that there is no rivalry between you and Andrea for my affection, Debbie. There should not be one. And as regards falcons, I never mentioned white falcons. It looks like you are perpetually deliberately looking for reasons to paint me as a racist. Not that I care very much about any appellation. Thank God, there is still the First Amendment."

"Oh, come off it, Bob. The fact that you are saying these things means that you are thinking about them. Come off it! We have the First Amendment and we also have the Civil Rights Laws. Neither exonerates hate speech. It's still about mid-day, Bob; too early for frivolities. Please let me have a can of Pepsi from your fridge if you have any!"

"Yes, perhaps that's what you may need Debbie. A chilled can of Pepsi or Coke will certainly cool you down and perhaps replenish the lost energy and hypoglycemia that are making you cranky. Looks like you are doing too much exercise at those early morning gyms, Debbie. You may need to slow down a bit lest you hand me the wrong instruments during surgery!"

"Yes, I think I need to slow down a bit. Even my husband is beginning to complain about my weight loss."

"Your husband?"

"Yes, my husband says I am getting too skinny from those daily walk-outs on the treadmill. I guess I may have to slow down tremendously."

For a while there was no further response from Dr. Glen. It was not often that he heard Debbie mention her husband. It looked that the Clinical Director had forgotten that Debbie was married.

Dr. Glen had invited Janet the Office Manager to be present during his meeting with the CEO, in the Clinical Director's office. The meeting was expected to last for no longer than one hour.

The CEO arrived quite on schedule and had waited for a while in front of Dr. Glen's office before the latter arrived by 8.30 am and both entered the office together. Janet soon emerged from her small office at the far end of the hallway and walked briskly into the Clinical Director's office. The CEO and Dr. Glen were already seated and were exchanging banters when Janet walked in.

"Hi, Janet, please sit down. Little Cliff ..., I beg your pardon, Cliff here, appeared to have arrived before us even in our own territory."

Dr. Glen was so used to referring to the CEO as "Little Cliff" in his discussions with Debbie that he inadvertently addressed the CEO as "Little Cliff" even in front of the latter and in the presence of Janet, the Office Manager. Janet understood. He had heard Dr Glen use that derogatory term for the CEO more than once. He simply beamed a gentle smile.

"It's no problem, Dr. Glen. It is not unusual for people who live closest the church to arrive late to church services, later than people who come from farther away. The church-goer who lives further away from the church sets out from home much earlier. He or she is therefore not likely to be late for the service. But the guy who lives next to the church dilly-dallies at home and invariably arrives late." The CEO said, smiling. He always held and addressed the retired military dentist with the greatest respect. That was in spite of the fact that Dr. Glen often appeared cocky and overbearing and persistently referred to the CEO as "Little Cliff" in the latter's absence.

"We will always be grateful to you Dr. Glen. You generate the greatest revenue for this Center in addition to your many other services even when we are not paying you as much as you deserve. And so, even when you are late for any appointment, we can always excuse you." The CEO said. He sounded apologetic and almost revering, and oblivious of the derisive nick name that the Clinical Director had used to address him.

Dr. Glen smiled and nodded his head in appreciation. Janet smiled wryly. She too, was always intimidated by Dr. Glen and so, she turned a blind eye to the obvious indecencies that she witnessed in the Center. She was a very ambitious yet subtle operator. She was infinitely calculating. And, she would appear to be very friendly especially when she was plotting her way into the warmth of the members of the Board of Directors of the Center, at the expense of the other staff.

To Janet's credit and great advantage were her dynamism and robust energy. And she used the latter two qualities to introduce innovations that attracted more grants to the Center than had hitherto ever been witnessed in the Center prior to her arrival. In view of her ability to attract more federal grants to BGMC, the CEO and Board of Management of the Center were very appreciative of Janet's services. She had introduced School Visitations and Free Dental Assessment Services as part of services to the remotest parts of Miami-Dade County in the state of Florida. She had thus elevated the status of BGMC as a federally-recognized champion of healthcare services for all. Her innovations physically stretched the provider-staff of the center to the utmost. And while she took the glory for the success of the innovations, hardly any credit went to the providers like Drs Doris, Seene and Johnson. Janet was almost always on the move. She attended all available conferences and workshops. She invariably had free lunch and other accruing benefits while the rest of the working staff were left at the mercy of, and were literally bullied and harassed daily by an egotistic Clinical Director.

In all that involved increased work-load the meek and reticent Dr. Doris was placed at the front burner. There was hardly any commendation for the ever-increasing work load. But in the event of anything going wrong, there would be none to blame but Dr. Doris.

"Dr Doris has practiced long enough to know that this is not good enough revenue yield for the month." The Clinical Director would say whenever there was some shortfall in the expected revenue for any month. But if there was greater-than-expected revenue for any month the CEO would call the Clinical Director to congratulate him. The latter would shout "I did it!" He would beat his chest and would recount how many badly-carious teeth that he *surgically extracted.*

In the event of the undeserved blame that would be heaped on her for any short-comings of the other staff, Dr Doris would never complain or raise her voice. Where, for any reason, she escaped being the scapegoat, then somehow, Dr. Seene would be next in line of maleficent succession for bullying, verbal pummeling or fault-finding during providers' meetings. The one person who patients often called "a butcher" and, or loudly complained about, was the one person who would never ever be officially blamed for any surgical or outpatient case going awry. And that person who attracted the greatest bad public image but got the most commendations from the Board of Management of the Center, was Dr Bob Glen.

"Cliff, I am happy that you are here so early in the day to witness the remarkable punctuality to work which I have achieved with our team since my arrival here. Even the doctors who are not required to clock in by 8.00AM are all here before 7.45AM. You have also seen the peaking of our internal revenue generation as well as our government grant awards over the past eight months since my arrival. You must also have observed the reduction in providers' demand for supplies. We succeeded in reducing waste and frivolous requests for supplies to the barest minimum. Also, …" Cliff cut in ever before Janet concluded her litany of self-adulations. He did not want the Clinical Director to be left out of the eulogies:

"As long as quality of service is not compromised, cost-cutting measures are very commendable. Yes, we have observed the spike in revenue over the past one year since Dr. Glen's arrival. The management is certainly very grateful to Dr. Glen."

Cliff had interjected at the middle of Janet's speech. Janet's countenance immediately soured at the double mention of Dr. Glen and the apparent ascribing of the improving fortunes of the Center to Dr. Glen alone instead of largely to her. She was aiming at taking credit for whatever improvement in punctuality and increased revenue generation that there were at the Center.

Disappointed at her apparent ignominy Janet still managed to feign a smile and said: "Yes, Dr. Glen is trying very hard. Everybody is talking about how hard he works."

"Well, thank you very much, Janet. I was about to follow your lead in heaping more encomiums on you for the success of the place over the past eight months" Dr. Glen said in reciprocity. As he spoke, he smiled sarcastically.

"Did you say eight months? I thought Janet joined you here only four months ago," Cliff quipped in.

"No, Janet was improving BGMC by remote control from college even when Ms. Bloomberg was the Office Manager here. Just joking!" Dr. Glen said. But the latter was not joking. He was aware of the overbearing nature of the former office receptionist who was appointed office manager straight from Community College only four months earlier. He easily remembered the receptionist who had ambitions of becoming a dentist but who could not make the grades to be a hygienist. He remembered the *ubiquitous petit young lady* who ultimately settled for training as a Dental Assistant. He remembered the *not-so-smart* receptionist who he had interviewed for the post of office manager. He immediately remembered how the latter who he had hoped to control, had settled in as office manager and was already eavesdropping into conversations between him and his "best friend" Debbie. He knew that Janet would like to ascribe all the same things which he claimed credit for, all to herself. The subdued rivalry between the two individuals was very evident.

"Well, Dr. Glen we will always remain grateful to you." The CEO interjected with the obvious intention of halting a possible brickbat from either of the two parties. A verbal exchange between a pompous Clinical Director and a contriving Office Manager would not be a good thing for an early morning meeting.

"And so", the CEO continued, "Dr. Glen, and Ms. Janet, you both know why we are here this morning. Reports have reached me that one or two of the Doctors here are gradually making the smooth running of the Center almost impossible by their intransigence. And since management would not wish this to continue, I have come to seek your individual opinions again before I proceed to interview a few of the other staff about the goings-on."

The CEO paused for a while and turned first to Dr. Glen and then to the Office Manager, Janet.

Dr. Glen, smiled briefly and kept looking at the ceiling as if the news was strange to him.

Janet adjusted her seat and then asked: "Which of the Doctors are the objects of the complaint Sir? Is it Dr. Doris, Dr. Johnson, Dr. Seene or some others? Or, is it a combination of two or more of the doctors?" She asked.

"No, it is Dr. Doris and Dr. Seene, Janet. Were you not aware of this" The CEO asked. He appeared surprised that the Office Manager was not aware of the reportedly-recalcitrant doctors who were said to be giving *the major revenue-generator of the Center* a hard time.

"The Clinical Director had lodged a complaint to me that the recalcitrance of the two doctors was known by almost all the other staff. He had reported that the two doctors were causing disharmony in the Center. Were you not aware of these, Janet." The CEO asked.

"The complaint about Dr. Doris is news to me. I am only aware that Dr Seene and Dr Glen had occasional brushes in the past week or two. No, I don't really have complaints about any of the doctors, but sometimes Dr. Glen doesn't appear to get on well with them. And some patients also sometimes complain about some of the doctors", Janet said feigning ignorance of the details. She sounded a little apologetic that she appeared to be reporting something that the Clinical Director himself should be reporting about.

Janet, of course knew well before, that Dr. Seene was at logger heads with Dr. Glen over the latter's indecent behavior. Inclusion of the docile and reticent Dr Doris as one of the "trouble makers" was another grand plan by the Clinical Director who had indeed concluded plans to edge out Dr Doris from the Center purely out of his xenophobic inclinations and also to make way for the hiring of the young dentist-wife of his golf-club pal in BGMC.

"Dr. Seene is more likely to make more trouble if she is terminated unceremoniously." Dr Glen mused. "But she will inevitably be frustrated out of the Center especially if Dr. Doris her ally, is forced to leave. Dr. Seene is so unhinged and so volatile that it would be better to let her fall out under her own weight. But a case, no matter how flimsy, needs to be built strongly against Dr. Doris who, is an immigrant, who is older, and who is less likely to challenge an assault on her career." Dr Glen again mused.

There was mutual desire on the parts of Dr. Glen and Debbie for the exit of Dr. Seene. But Debbie bore no grudges against Dr. Doris. The latter never posed any threats to her romance with Dr. Glen. Dr Doris rarely commented on matters that were outside her professional circles at work. And even when she did not socialize much, she participated in all official social events and routinely brought cookies and soda as snack for the general staff. She was indeed friendlier with Debbie than with any of the other Dental Assistants. This was more so, since both she and Debbie shared the same Christian religious denomination. Debbie however did not believe in making the sign of the cross before lunch meals as Dr. Doris would always do. Both ladies however believed in generosity to the poor and they shared mutual desire to visit *The Holy Land* sometime, on pilgrimage. On other matters of morality however, the two ladies were as far apart as the North and South Poles.

Chapter 14

COALESCING OF THE PLOTS

There was silence in the Clinical Director's Office venue of the meeting between the CEO, the Clinical Director and the Office Manager Janet. For a while it appeared that each person wanted another person to raise more points for discussion. There did not appear to be any very specific issue that would form the bedrock for renewed discussions. There was no drawn-up agenda for the impromptu meeting. The CEO turned through the notes in his file preparatory for a follow-up on the already-tabled topic for discussions. At every passing second, he expected Dr Glen at whose instance the meeting was scheduled to initiate definite discussions. But Dr Glen remained silent and only repeatedly and rhythmically tapped his thumbs on the table. It was an idiosyncrasy which he exhibited anytime he was badly agitated with a situation.

Then the CEO stepped in: "Janet, you stated that there were complaints about the doctors. I assume that that is part of the objectives for this meeting. Which particular doctors did you receive complaints about and what were the complaints, so we can start with specifics." At the conclusion of the CEO's question Dr Glen appeared to see the non-specific characterization of doctors to include himself. For a while he feared that Janet might be secretly attempting to rope him in. He knew that his surgical records had not been without blemish. Debbie had on many occasions told him that patients were complaining about him for carrying out unnecessary procedures for purposes of increased revenue generation. Debbie had even informed him that some patients were referring to him as "the butcher of BGMC." Could this be a manifestation of the fabled three fingers of a clenched fist pointing back at the accuser while only the index finger pointed at the accused and the thumb remained neutral? Dr Glen's face immediately turned red. He could no longer hold his revulsion about what he saw as utter pretense on the part of Janet. He managed to control his rage and in an uncharacteristic subdued voice, said:

"Janet, why don't you come clean. You know fully well the intransigence that has been going on here. You have witnessed some, and I have discussed others with you. I get p**sed off when people try to be foxy or evasive. The truth is that Dr. Seene challenges my authority here. I don't see both of us continuing to work as team members here for much longer."

Dr Glen paused for a short while as if to allow his verbal attacks to take some effect. Then looking straight at Mr. Cliff, he continued in a slow measured tone: "Dr. Doris for her part is one pious sycophant who sits passively without condemning Dr. Seene as the insults fly at me. And as regards the young Dr. Johnson who throws his height about the whole place, I think I can easily handle his situation in my annual reports on him. There seems to be a gathering ring of conspiracy against authority in this Center. My worry is that if nothing is done about the ring leader, the other doctors will take a cue. The other staff members will see the intransigence as the new normal. Discipline will plummet and the system will collapse". Dr. Glen said in an undisguised display of anger.

"Did you say that the system will collapse? No way, Dr. Glen, not under my watch". the CEO interjected feeling sidelined or diminished by Dr. Glen's air of finality.

"Well I mean that there will be collapse of discipline in the system" Dr. Glen said, raising his voice a little and trying hard to steady his fingers that were already shaking in his anger and agitation.

"I spent a good deal of time in the military and I have learnt that you cannot have two captains simultaneously in control in the same ship!" Dr. Glen said, once again pointing to his military background. He never lost any opportunity to remind anyone who cared to listen about his military service even when there were other more distinguished veterans around.

The CEO looked on apologetically and then said: "Again Dr. Glen we thank you for your service. I assure you that I will specifically step into this issue and address it with dispatch". The CEO appealingly told Dr. Glen.

Then turning again to Janet, the CEO said:

"Now Janet, I am right now giving you this task: compile all the indiscretions and complaints about Dr. Doris and Dr. Seene and indeed any other doctor or other member of staff who is making Dr. Glen's work difficult. This should be done irrespective of seniority. Dr. Glen is in charge of clinical practice here. He is, as you well know, the pillar of our revenue generation here. He single-handedly generates what three or four doctors put together generate every month. Even with the grants which we receive from the Federal Government for operating in an underserved area, there is no way that we can sustain this Center without the enormous revenue generated monthly by Dr.

Glen. I therefore cannot tolerate anyone who keeps him uncomfortable here. You remember that we had to plead with him to withdraw his resignation the last time that he threw in his resignation notice. But for our appeals and the kind sustained persuasion to him from Dental Assistant Debbie, we might have lost his services. We cannot afford to have a repeat of this. And I want to receive your detailed report within forty-eight hours".

Having read what was akin to a riot act, the CEO quickly assembled his files and then turning to Dr. Glen as if in a bowing position, he said;

"Please be patient with us while we sort this issue out doctor. And for the umpteenth time, thank you for your service".

The radiance on the beaming face of Dr. Glen consequent upon what he enjoyed the most, praise and adoration, could be visualized from two dozen feet away. Unfortunately, "Thank you for your service", the well-merited acknowledgment and appreciation of great and dedicated service to the nation which should be treated with well-deserved reverence was almost being bastardized and dishonored by inappropriate use by one who perhaps should know better.

But Dr. Glen could not care less about the tarnishing of this otherwise treasured acknowledgment when it is overused in situations where it was uncalled for. The encomiums were being unnecessarily poured on the middle-aged retired navy Captain and Dentist, for completely unrelated matters in a little office hidden away from view of even the other members of the twenty-two-member staff of the Medical Center. The encomiums were being repeatedly poured simply because it was known that the recipient relished them.

Janet did not wish to be left out of the adoration.

"Thank you for your service, Dr. Glen." She said, rather dryly and without much enthusiasm.

Whether the gratitude was being genuinely rendered to Dr. Glen for his service in defense of country or whether Janet was simply aping the CEO, did not really matter to Dr. Glen. As long as his ego was appropriately massaged by the salutation: "Thank you for your service", everything else was acceptable to Dr. Glen. Of course, in either situation he thoroughly deserved the gratitude for service to country. His craving for the compliment was of little consequence.

The CEO assembled his papers and momentarily left the room to use the bathroom. He came back after about five minutes and was about to declare the meeting closed. Immediately after the CEO's reentry into the meeting however, Dr Glen who had also stood up ready to leave, turned to Janet and in an uncharacteristic low voice said:

"Janet, you told us that some patients had complaints about some of our doctors regarding procedures carried out on them, right?"

"Yes, Dr. Glen, there were periodic complaints from patients after procedures, but you know these are to be expected. I remember that as a receptionist here a number of years back, we used to have lots of flimsy complaints from some patients especially the fee-paying patients. The complaints after procedures were more in situations where the patients felt that their bills were on the high side. After settling such seemingly high bills nothing would seem to satisfy the affected patients. It would either be that the shade of the denture was too white or that it was too dark. It was either that the doctor explained too much and frightened them or that he or she did not talk at all to them and went ahead and extracted the carious tooth. It would either be that the doctor did not attempt to save a badly-carious tooth or that he went ahead to attempt to save a very bad tooth which should have been extracted. Nothing seemed to please them." Janet surmised.

"Who did they complain most about? You see if we must make changes for the better in this Center, we need to start weeding from the worst among us."

Dr Glen had asked the last question, obviously trying to pin down Janet to specific names.

"As a matter of fact, Dr. Glen, most complaints from patients emanated from surgical procedures carried out on them by the Clinical Director. One of the patients who you had carried out some difficult and extensive procedures on, had reported as an emergency and had referred to you as a butcher. She had stated thus to my hearing when she came for a follow-up visit: 'the butcher who called himself a specialist had unnecessarily removed all my teeth. He deliberately removed both the good ones and the bad ones to make more money. If I had money for the lawyers I would have sued the hell out of him'. Those were the patient's exact words. I tried unsuccessfully to appease her but she went on telling everyone who cared to listen that her doctor was 'a careless and heartless butcher'. Indeed, she said that she would rather change clinics than come to see you again. We had to placate and oblige her. We had to ask her to choose the doctor that she would like to see and she had chosen to go back to Dr. Doris who had initially referred her to you. We tried to convince her to see you and explain the situation, but she insisted on changing clinics if we did not change her back to her old doctor. And her old doctor as I told you is Dr. Doris. We consequently assigned her back to Dr. Doris. We did not even mention this issue to you. I knew how hurtful you might feel after a very diligent procedure which yielded quite some good revenue to the Center. Such complaints about you had been coming in for some time even before I became the Manager according to some of the older-serving staff."

As Janet spoke, Dr. Glen could be seen to turn suddenly pink as he was wont to appear whenever unsavory statements about him filtered into his ears.

"I am not talking of what happened many years back Janet. I am asking for complaints that have recently occurred since you assumed duties as manager. You have had complaints about our doctors, right?" Dr Glen emphatically asked.

"Yes, of course, there have been complaints. You can't please all the patients, can you?" Janet said.

The affirmative response to a question which was expected to implicate one or two of his targets was a welcome diversion from an earlier deeply-implicating question about *the surgeon with the golden scalpel,* one who was obviously not exonerated from the nomenclature of *the butcher of BGMG.*

"No of course not." Dr Glen replied. "I was informed that there were occasional complaints about Dr. Doris. Haven't you been getting such complaints?"

"Hmmm, not really! Indeed, there have been more commendations from our patients than complaints about Dr. Doris, even though I find her occasionally aloof and apparently disdainful about management."

"Then if she had been aloof and disdainful about management that's not the kind of person you would wish to work with. That's even worse than patients' complaints about anyone yanking off their teeth. That's what I wish to hear about, not petty gossips about butchers and abattoirs. Certainly, we have no abattoirs around here." Dr Glen said dismissively, trying to make light about Janet's subtle report of complaints about a Clinical Director who painted the image of an infallible surgeon.

Even as he tried to make light of Janet's veiled complaints about him, Dr. Glen's reddened face gave away his intense anger at being called "a butcher" by a patient. He suddenly appeared very agitated. He then suddenly turned towards the door and appeared to wish to leave the room. But he again changed his mind as he pressed his trembling fingers firmly on the table. His lips quibbled and beads of sweat were noticed on his brow even in the fully-air-conditioned room. It appeared that the hunter had suddenly turned to be the hunted. It was as if Janet's brief report of a patient's disapproval of him was too hurtful. His ego appeared to have been momentarily deflated. He strode towards the door and suddenly walked back to his writing table. He perched halfway on the edge of the table and took a deep and audible breath. Though watched by only a small audience, it was a drama that had never been rehearsed in the long history of BGMC.

Cliff the CEO watched in utter surprise. The man who invited him to witness the carpeting of other staff members was right there before him being inadvertently carpeted by a subordinate staff. He held his jaw with the palm of his right hand for a while and then unsuccessfully tried to say something.

Dr Glen soon regained his composure. "Now, Janet," Dr. Glen said in a lower voice as he got off the edge of the table and pulled his chair towards Janet. "Let's get things straight. I was talking about Dr. Doris, right? You mentioned nastiness and disdainful attitude towards management as traits that you observed from Dr. Doris, right? Now, go do a detailed memo about this nastiness and disdainful attitude. Do more research with dates and instances and have this ready in the next two days with the main memo to the CEO as he requested, and do a copy to me. We need to start sanitizing this place. Things cannot continue this way. There has to be sanity and respect for constituted authority." Dr. Glen concluded with an air of finality.

"I did not actually use the word nastiness in describing Dr Doris, Dr. Glen. I actually said aloofness. "

"OK! What is aloof when it should be down to Earth is obviously nasty, Janet. Let's not get into further semantics. Whether it is nastiness or aloofness, do a memo to me as instructed and copy the CEO." The obviously-rattled but recovering Dr. Glen said.

Janet apparently not wanting to let the opportunity of also exposing the *sins* of his boss during the rare opportunity that she had to do so, then said in a low but clear voice:

"Should I include the case of the lady who alluded to "the Butcher of BGMC" with complaints of all her teeth being wrongly yanked off?"

At this statement from Janet, the CEO who had returned and was speechlessly observing the drama, suddenly turned in the direction of Dr Glen. His gaze seemed to ask the question: *how now, Mr. Integrity?*

Dr Glen's response was spontaneous and brisk:

"Janet, I instructed you to limit yourself to recent complaints! Is that instruction not unambiguous enough?"

"I asked this just in case the aggrieved lady suddenly turns up some day long after we may have forgotten about her case."

"You are bordering on intransigence and insubordination, Janet. Please go and do as I said!"

Janet having successfully agitated Dr. Glen, decided to mend fences. A punching bag must be found. Dr. Doris was the natural victim. The latter was without doubt the line of least resistance. She was the one senior member of staff who would not be expected to punch back if punched. She was the one expected to turn the other cheek. She was more likely than Dr Seene or even Dr Johnson, to fight back if attacked. She was expected to "hand everything over to God." The latter was a phrase which she was often known to use when offended by people. Unlike Dr Seene who would vigorously fight back if attacked, Dr Doris would either retreat or remain meek. She was therefore the natural punching bag for any, and all bullies like Dr Glen or even the office Manager Janet. Even Ron, Dr Doris' youngest son knew very well that her mom was so meek and humble that he once bought her a copy of the book "Two Eyes for an Eye" for her birthday.

Even in spite of her audacity against Dr Glen because of the presence of the CEO, Janet knew her limits. She knew that the retired Navy Officer could fight back big time. She did not want to jeopardize her own job in defense of Dr Doris or Dr Seene. There was not much besides being common employees of BGMC that bound her to either lady. She would rather ally with the strong man. And so, she readily blinked.

"Yes, Dr. Glen, I completely I agree with you." Janet said. "We need to bring sanity back to this place. When I was the receptionist here, I observed a lot of inadequacies. But I was in no position to initiate corrective measures. Now I must confess to you that I don't like Dr. Doris. She doesn't belong to this place. BGMC is a Community Hospital. Dr. Doris doesn't live here. He contributes very little to this community even when she draws her pay check from here. But you know this equal opportunity thing. One has to be very careful not to fall foul of the law. At the smallest provocation now, they will shout racism and discrimination. And everybody will start staring at one as if one is the greatest racist of modern times. And the next thing, everybody will start searching for the "N-word" or where they will label you a racist. And the condemnation will descend from everywhere and from all racial groupings, Black, White, Asian, Hispanic and all. And one will start wondering where one has gone wrong. I certainly would not wish to be associated with that kind of tar brush. That is why I try to keep my feelings about some of these intruders to myself." Janet said, sighing audibly. She wore the look of the innocent and oppressed rather than the oppressor, as she tried to warm herself back into Dr. Glen's good books. Everything must be done to please the Clinical Czar of BGMC.

Dr. Glen appeared less penitent and more aggressive. He listened to Janet with rapt attention and interest. It looked like someone was about to help him do the nasty job which he had been contemplating silently for some time: the job of dispensing with the services of Dr. Seene or preferably Dr. Doris. The excision of either of the two "troublesome" doctors would enable the Clinical Director to hire someone else of his choice. He had earlier promised his golf club friend that he would ensure that the latter's dentist-wife was employed in BGMC. But there was no budget for an extra dentist in the Center, and therefore a serving staff must be fired, with or without cause, to make space for the favored staff.

Dr Glen left the edge of the table and moved back to his seat. He purposely brushed against the seat of Mr. Cliff as he walked towards his seat. He wanted to ensure the latter's attentiveness.

Having ensured that the CEO was listening he raised his voice and in apparent response to Janet's equal opportunity statement he said:

"Equal opportunity my foot, Janet! This country was built and nurtured by some people. Other people can't just come in from nowhere and hijack it. All this talk about equal opportunity, unequal opportunity and all that bulls**t mean very little to me. Just do me the memo and let me take it on from there, right? I am happy that you seem to see these things as I see them. It is one area where I strongly disagree with Debbie. She seems to be too liberal about this equal opportunity thing. Even when her very job is threatened, she still feels that she should see about the interest of others before her own. But this is your America, not theirs. The General Elections are coming up fast and we have to affirm it at the pooling booths. But first we have to start playing our parts from here in BGMC. They should all get back to the failed jungle societies whence they came. And when I say they, I mean they and their offspring, American-born or not." Dr. Glen said. The unmistakable hate was written all over the latter's face as he spoke. He painted the image of a wounded strong man in mortal distress. Even the CEO looked at him and was very surprised that such a highly-educated and highly-placed doctor, a veteran for that matter, would allow himself to be so worked up to be so consumed with bigotry and hate against fellow Americans. He was so unjustifiably vindictive.

"But these *foreign Americans* do not in any way threaten your job, Dr G. It is people like me, the junior and intermediate staff who are actually often threatened." Janet said. She felt she was being more realistic, even as she characterized some bona fide American citizens as "foreign Americans". She did not see any discrimination in the latter characterization.

"Everybody is in danger, Janet. Everybody is threatened when one of us is threatened. They are aspiring towards the top positions too. When they finish taking over your lower-paying jobs, they will start aspiring towards my higher-paying job. Look at this Dr Doris. Go look at her background, she and her folks. I tell ya, nobody's job is safe anymore. But it is time to let them know that this is not their America. It is our America. Our forefathers built it and we have to fight to keep it ours."

As Dr Glen spoke his face again turned rapidly deep pink. His neck veins appeared to be bulging, and he presented the look of someone who was being emotionally tormented.

Even Janet was a little surprised at how strongly Dr Glen appeared to feel about what she felt was a relatively inconsequential matter. But she needed to appear sympathetic to her boss' feelings.

"You are right, Dr Glen. Sometimes when I see Dr Seene or this Dr Doris behaving as if they are co-owners of the place, I seem to hear a voice urging me to speak out and say to them, *this is not your America*. This is more so when I hear any of them arguing forcefully about their rights and all such nonsense. Sometimes when I hear this Dr Doris in her rare moments of outspokenness talk about "this our country" I am tempted to ask her which country she is referring to whether she is referring to our America or her real jungle origin."

"There you are Janet! You too have experienced it. So, go now and do the needful. Go and do me an appropriate report." Dr Glen said.

"OK, Dr. Glen. I will oblige as quickly as possible. The only thing is that I don't want the trouble of these equal-opportunity and anti-discrimination activists. There is this one that I see on National TV which calls itself NAACP or whatever. You know I am new on this job and this Dr. Doris fella appears to read and write so much. Whenever she is not seeing patients, I see her reading or writing one article or another. She appears to occasionally visit these activists' websites. She doesn't speak much but she writes a lot, and ..., and ...."

Dr. Glen did not allow Janet to conclude her statement before he cut in: "Well, if she has been reading activist articles at work when she is supposed to be working for her pay, that in itself is a serious violation of the terms of her employment. That must be one reason behind her relatively low revenue yield which is reason enough for firing her!"

"No, Dr. Glen. As a matter of fact, Dr. Doris' revenue yield is the highest after yours. As a matter of fact, some patients that you had treated had come back later and requested to be sent back to be attended to by Dr Doris." Janet corrected.

"I mean her revenue yield is very small relative to mine. She has not been measuring up as much as expected. She is a senior staff of many years' experience. Her revenue yield is expected to be higher than whatever she currently makes. By the terms of her employment contract Dr. Doris is expected to generate on the average at least four times her monthly income every month. From my records, she has not always been doing that. In the past eighteen months of her employment here she has missed that target twice. From what I heard you say a short while ago, she has been busier visiting civil rights websites and keeping mute except when she is talking equal opportunity."

Janet was silent briefly but looking down as if in difficulty about what to say, she slowly said: "Yes indeed, Dr G, but in truth, Dr D's revenue yield has in recent months been clocking six to eight times her expected mark. And, her patients seem very satisfied with her work and have often highly commended her."

Dr Glen's hitherto boisterous countenance soured at Janet's apparent commendation of Dr Doris and he immediately cut in:

"Whatever be the case, Janet, you have just told me that Dr. Doris reads and writes on activist websites at work. And you also said that she is nasty and disdainful. If she is nasty and disdainful to you then you obviously don't like her. And you obviously cannot work amicably with her. Do a memo on these to the CEO, copy me and leave the rest to me." Dr. Glen talked with so much venom and presented the picture of one who had bottled-up anger against someone. Even Janet was a little surprised that Dr Glen's anger was channeled more against Dr. Doris and not Dr. Seene.

"Ok, Dr. Glen as long as you leave me out of the whole mess, I am not strong enough to handle any controversies. It was a tough job rising from being a receptionist to my present position as Manager, and I don't want to jeopardize it with unnecessary controversies." Janet said. She apparently was trying to distance herself from the budding conspiracy.

"There is no mess, Janet. And there are no controversies, only statements of fact. Somebody that is nasty and disdainful is not the right choice for this Center, and that's it! As for the intrusive and vociferous Dr Seene, leave her to me. She is sure to walk into her own trap. When her buddy Dr Doris goes, she will be so lonely that she will opt to leave on her own.

Dr. Glen appeared completely unhinged. He did not seem to mind the presence of the CEO in all his rant. He and Janet had dominated the meeting and Mr. Cliff who was supposed to moderate the discussions had once again abdicated his position to the Clinical Director. He stared into the emptiness and neither cautioned nor even moderated the unhinged Dr. Glen.

When Dr Glen took back his seat, he started gathering his papers. The CEO Mr. Cliff witnessed the drama and knew it was time to adjourn the meeting. He had seen and heard more vituperations than he bargained for. He had never believed that so much hate existed in the system.

"Looks like you guys have many unsettled internal problems here. I only hope that you get these quickly resolved Dr. Glen. I also hope that the revenue of the Center doesn't get diminished as a result of your internal wrangling. I will like to work on facts and not emotions. Sort out your internal problems and let me have the factual summary. We will meet again after Janet has compiled and circulated her reports and findings. But I would request you, Dr. Glen, not to be discouraged by whatever difficulties you experience pending the time we set things right. BGMC needs every cent that can be generated and we greatly rely on your continued dedication to revenue generation, Dr. Glen."

Dr. Glen brightened up. He smiled wryly and muttered: "As we say in the military, Duty calls! It is my duty!"

Once more the towering image of Dr Glen had succeeded in cowing down and silencing the CEO who ordinarily would have raised eyebrows from what he had seen and heard Dr Glen and the Office Manager discussing. No, Mr. Cliff did not intervene while Dr Glen was making what were obviously discriminatory if not outright racist comments against his colleagues even in the presence of the CEO. The latter merely gazed at the ceiling in a show of absolute indifference.

As Janet walked back to her small side-room office she pondered over the instruction Dr. Glen had just given her about Dr. Doris. She and Dr. Doris had not been the best of friends. Their principles and attitudes to life could not be any more varied than between the sizes of the African elephant and the bumblebee bat, both mammals but both at extreme ends of enormity in size. Dr. Doris was principled, highly educated, deeply religious, modest, taciturn, hardworking and humane while Janet, though occasionally reasonable, largely lacked empathy, was vain, and was often prepared to indulge in any business that would enhance her position at work. As long as such indulgence would not get her into trouble either domestically or with her employers, she would move along.

As she quietly walked into her office after her discussions with Dr. Glen, Janet tried to remember any issues or complaints that had involved Dr. Doris. Attention had shifted from the more loquacious and more belligerent Dr. Seene to the more taciturn and more principled Dr. Doris. Janet did not definitely want Dr. Doris to be fired. But at the same time, she wanted anything that she could do to please Dr. Glen. To facilitate the latter's desire to get rid of Dr. Doris could be one such thing. She was cognizant of Dr. Glen's less-than-concealed romance with the Dental Assistant Debbie. She was also aware of Dr. Doris' tacit but obvious aversion to the whole sordid behavior playing out in public, worse still in the workplace. She (Janet) was a happily married mother of two and had no reasons to be in romantic competition with Debbie as regards the so-called *king of the jungle*, Dr. Glen. Even if she, Janet, ever entertained the idea of warming herself into Dr. Glen's attention, Debbie's vigilant watch was sure to fight and abort any such moves.

It did not take Janet much time to go through the "Complaints Records" book which she had diligently kept since she assumed duties as Dental Practice Manager of BGMC. The records showed mostly complaints from patients against Dr. Glen. Most of the complainants had been pacified and/or transferred to other doctors even without involving Dr. Glen, in accordance with the patients' wishes. After further search through the records, Janet found a cursory request made two months earlier by a patient, 26 -year-old Ms. Laura Smith. Ms. Smith had been attended to by Dr. Doris and had expressed a desire to be seen thereafter by Dr Johnson. Ms. Smith had not in her request for a change of dentists, adduced any particular reasons to ask for a change. She was not obligated to adduce any reasons for requesting for a change of doctors. She had a perfectly successful dental filling done by Dr Doris. But in the *Optional Opinions and Reviews* box after the dental fillings which she had, Ms. Smith had stated thus: "Good job. But I will like during future treatments to be seen by the tall and lanky male dentist."

Of course, "the tall and lanky dentist" was no other than Dr. Johnson. No further reasons were stated by Ms. Laura Smith. She apparently only wanted "during future treatments to be seen by the tall and lanky dentist". Everybody knew the *tall and lanky male dentist* to be funny and amiable. He was therefore the natural choice of any young patient who was given a choice.

Janet immediately took note of Ms. Smith's next appointment date and headed back to Dr. Glen's office. The latter was still sitting with some printed papers in hand as if waiting for a feedback from Janet about the mission at hand. And, the mission at hand was the production of good enough reasons to discredit and implicate Dr. Doris and get her fired. By so doing, Dr Doris who was seen as an intruder and who was seen as not belonging to the Miami County demographic area would have been expunged from the system. By so doing, the impunity and sordid behavior between a Clinical Director and a subordinate staff of a public-grant-aided medical facility could go on impeded. By so doing too, space would be opened up for employment of the young dentist-wife of Dr. Glen's golfing pal who worked "too far away from home". The young wife of this pal would now be employed as replacement for Dr. Doris. That way too, there was the possibility of making an addition to the list of mistresses for a thrice-divorced Clinical Director who had roving eyes and who did not respect the marital status of his subordinate staff.

"Yes, Dr. Glen, you asked for complaints about Dr. Doris. I have found one, though it is not exactly in form of a complaint, but more of a request, and ....."

Dr. Glen did not allow Janet to complete her sentence. He sprang to his feet and literally snatched the paper which Janet was holding.

"Yes, I told you so! I knew there must be series of complaints against Dr. Doris. She is a meddlesome lady. And, according to your own words, she is *nasty and disdainful*. According to your own words too she reads and writes on activist websites at work. I knew there must be tons of wrongdoings which you probably had been hiding for her."

"No, Dr. Glen, this was not a complaint about Dr. Doris. This was merely a statement of preference by a patient for a particular doctor or dentist". Janet said trying to set the records straight.

"Yes, if a patient who was seen by a particular doctor suddenly states a preference for another doctor, there must be reasons for the preference. It is these reasons that I now want you to investigate and report back to me. You don't have to wait until every patient who is assigned to Dr. Doris opts out of her care or completely out of the Center". Dr. Glen said, staring straight at the diminutively-built Janet like a hawk about to pounce on a small chicken.

"Again, no, Dr. Glen. This is perhaps the one and only situation on record where a patient has opted out of Dr. Doris' care. Remember that this young patient has not alleged any mismanagement or wrong doings against her by Dr. Doris. She received her treatment successfully and did not complain. She indeed stated that the treatment was good. It was only in the optional opinions box that she expressed a desire to be attended to by Dr. Johnson."

Then, smiling mischievously, Janet, still looking at Dr Glen in the face said: "There may be other reasons why Ms. Smith wanted to be attended to in future by Dr. Johnson rather than by Dr. Doris. She has not called Dr. Doris a butcher or any such thing. Remember that this is a term which some patients had used in the past against you, and we did not fire anybody." Janet said. She was subtly alluding to a word which had once been used by a patient to describe Dr. Glen.

Dr Glen shrank back at the mention of the word *butcher*. His countenance soured. But he quickly recovered and dismissively asserted thus: "Both butchers and surgeons cut muscles and bones. And so, a loquacious patient who describes a surgeon as a butcher is not too far from the truth. There is no big deal in that allusion, Janet."

Having successfully reciprocated Janet's sarcasms, Dr. Glen remained unrelenting as he followed up: "I will like to talk to this patient who complained about Dr. Doris, when next she comes for her check-up. I will like to know why she suddenly prefers to drop Dr. Doris and switch over to another doctor. This case cannot be swept under the carpet any longer. Have a good day, Janet. But remember that a Clinic Manager is not expected to be colluding with a contriving doctor against the interest of patients, especially, e-e-r-r, especially when such a manager is still under a one-year probation."

Dr. Glen stormed out of the room while a thoroughly embarrassed Janet stood still for a while wondering where she had gone wrong. She however recollected herself and slowly walked out of the room back to her office, determined to keep her job by yielding to superior official fire power. The subtle blackmail was not lost on Janet.

Chapter 15

THE PLOT MATERIALIZES

Ms. Laura Smith was a simple fun-loving and out-going twenty-six-year-old single lady who would not mind funny stories even while she was in a medical facility. She had come for a dental filling and had been attended to by a lady dentist who had a little accent. While she was waiting, she had seen a tall and lanky young dentist who escorted his patient out of the surgery after a procedure. The tall young dentist had cracked some joke which made his patient laugh as the latter exited the room. Ms. Laura Smith had seen the conspicuous name tag with the boldly inscribed word "Dentist" on Dr. Johnson's scrub. She could not quite read the name of the dentist from a distance. But she wished she would switch to that laughter-inducing dentist during her subsequent appointments. She too would have liked to come out of the dental surgery with laughter on her face. She did not see the fun in being assigned to this very professional-looking middle-aged dentist who shared the same first name of Doris with her grandmother. The lady dentist also had a jaw-breaking surname which nobody would bother to pronounce. The absurdity of that surname could hurt a new dental filling if pronounced in a hurry.

During her initial visit Ms. Laura Smith did not mind being seen by Dr. Doris. Sitting on the dental chair, she had told Dr. Doris that even as a child that she had always been scared of dentists.

"I am usually scared of dentists and their instruments" Ms. Smith had told Dr. Doris.

"I have changed dentists ever so often, always hoping in vain to treat my many caries with medication rather than with instrumentation", Ms. Smith had continued as she lay back on the dental chair. She was a little agitated.

"It is no problem, my dear. You are not alone. I too as a child always felt so afraid of dentists and indeed anything that had to do with clinics and white-overall-wearing medical staff. But now that I am in the profession, I have gotten adapted. I assure you that even if initially it hurts a little, it is only for a very brief period of time and you will be completely fine after that. You will not even realize when the procedure is completed, I assure you."

Dr. Doris waited for a while for her assurances to sink in. She then continued: "And so, can I continue, Laura."

Ms. Smith nodded in the affirmative and opened her mouth for Dr Doris to proceed. The practiced professional in Dr. Doris came into play and in no time the carious tooth was taken care of effortlessly. The procedure was successfully completed.

Ms. Smith thanked both Dr. Doris and the young Dental Assistant. The latter did not appear to be paying any particular attention. She felt that Laura was a big girl and needed no special attention. She felt that the patient's expressed fear of the dentist's needle or a simple dental procedure was only natural. There were absolutely no unusual incidents.

There were no complaints whatsoever by Ms. Laura Smith about Dr. Doris or about the procedure carried out on her. In the optional opinion form she had simply graded her experience as "Great". She had however nursed a desire to see the *tall young dentist* during future visits. She had thanked Dr Doris and the Dental Assistant and went home with absolutely no complaints. It was only when she was called on phone by Ms. Kate the front desk patient-scheduling officer that she again expressed a desire, in future, to be attended to by "that tall and lanky dentist". Asked if she would volunteer a reason for requesting a change in dentists, Ms. Smith had replied: "I loved how that tall young dentist made his patients laugh."

During her scheduled follow-up appointment Ms. Laura Smith had been directed to see Dr. Glen the Clinical Director. At first Ms. Laura Smith had seen no connection between her preference to see Dr. Johnson and her instruction for an interview with Dr. Glen.

"Why exactly did you not wish to see Dr. Doris any longer." Dr Glen had insisted.

"No particular reason. I probably was persuaded by the laughter of the patient who the tall and lanky dentist was escorting to the door after the patient's procedure". Ms. Smith had replied, smiling. "Ha, Ha, Ha, who wouldn't want to leave a dentist's office laughing?" Miss Smith joked.

"You definitely told Dr. Doris that you were afraid of dentists and their instruments, right?" Dr. Glen had pointedly asked Ms. Laura Smith.

"I told her that I used to be scared of dentists and instrumentation, yes." Laura had responded.

"And in spite of your professed aversion to instrumentation she still proceeded to carry out instrumentation on you, right?"

"Yes, she did the procedure and you know what, I didn't even realize until the procedure was successfully over. It was amazing!" Laura said.

"Yes, but you pointedly told her that you did not want instrumentation, right?"

"Yes, at first!"

"OK, that's all we wanted to ascertain. You will now be assigned to another doctor of your choice. But first you will see Ms. Katelyn, the front desk officer who will give you further instructions about necessary documentation of what you have just told me. Rest assured that we are here to help you and we need your cooperation in righting the wrongs that have been done to you. Thank you, Laura and have a great day."

"There were actually no wrongs in particular. It was just an initial statement of aversion to dentists and a latter request to see another dentist", Ms. Laura protested, perhaps believing that she was misunderstood. She felt that the misunderstanding might count against her in her request for a change to see the tall lanky dentist of her choice. But Kate (Ms. Katelyn) was to reassure her that no harm was implied by Dr. Glen's interview with her. She was to be further instructed by the front desk staff.

Kate the front desk officer had a clear mandate:

"Get the patient. Ms. Laura Smith to write a formal and detailed complaint about Dr. Doris' administration of instrumentation on her against her expressed rejection of same, in her request for a change of doctors. Help her with the documentation where necessary even though she is well educated. She may not mean any harm to Dr. Doris and neither do we. But, according to the patient, instrumentation was used on her against her expressed wishes. This is a very serious offence we need to have good documentation and a cogent reason for any necessary actions."

Ms. Katelyn Sanders (Kate), was a very amiable junior staff of Beaming Grin Medical Center. She was not particularly academically-endowed. She alone in the Center, possessed no more than a high school qualification. She had joined the Center some nine years earlier as an Office Assistant and had risen without any further academic training to the post of a Front Desk Registration Assistant. Her only claim to superiority and power, in her rather warped view, was her skin color and the fact that her great, great grandfather was one of the earliest settlers in the community. Kate was overtly averse to "intruders" in her community. These, according to her were people who left their own communities to come *to invade* her community.

"These people know nothing about our deer-hunting and wild-turkey hunting past-times and our folklore". Kate was once overheard saying in reference to Dr. Johnson. She was further heard saying:

"I loathe the dominance of these foreign doctors and dentists in this our Community Health Center". But when confronted with the fact that none of the doctors and dentists in the Center was a native of her Community, her response was even more perplexing and warped:

"We can manage without them. They should all go, and leave us alone. My great grandfathers managed without them."

Katelyn's aversion for Dr. Doris was much earlier made more intense on the day that she, Katelyn repeated her parochial statements and was challenged by Dr. Doris who reminded her that there would be no functional Community Health Center to work at, if in fulfillment of her expressed desires all foreign doctors and dentists were to leave her community.

"Unless you and your friends go to school to become doctors and dentists, there will be no functional Community Health Center for you to work in, if in fulfilment of your expressed desires all foreign doctors and dentists left this Center. And remember that your definition of *foreign* includes Dr. Glen the Clinical Director who is not from this community, as well as Dr. Johnson who makes you laugh. It also includes many others." Dr. Doris had told Katelyn.

"No, Dr. Glen will stay. He is one of us. But the others should go home!" Katelyn had said. That was the extent of Ms. Katelyn's level of intelligence.

And so, when the patient Ms. Laura Smith went to see Ms. Kaylyn at the front desk, the latter was only too happy to help Ms. Laura in drafting a fabricated letter of complaint against Dr. Doris.

"You've got nothing to lose, I can assure you. A strong complaint will only facilitate your assignment to another Doctor", Katelyn had told Ms. Smith.

And so, a formal complaint in compliance with Dr. Glen's dictates, was soon drawn against Dr. Doris by Ms. Katlyn. The drafted false and incriminating accusations were handed over to Ms. Laura who, believing that the document was for her own good, immediately signed same even without reading the full contents and handed back to Katlyn Sanders the simple-minded but flippant front desk officer. The latter handed the signed petition over to Janet the Office Manager.

As Ms. Laura Smith left Katelyn at the Front Desk on that Wednesday morning, she did not feel that she had done anything particularly wrong. She did not feel that she had cost anybody his or her job. She did not feel that she had indelibly cast a shadow on the career or reputation of any individual or family. The lack of sense of guilt was enabled by the fact that there was no material inducement except perhaps the promise of a switch to "the tall lanky doctor".

"You had asked for a formal letter of complaint against Dr. Doris. Here you have a handful of it." Janet said as soon as she entered Dr. Glen's office the following morning with Ms. Laura Smith's signed letter of complaint in her hand. Dr. Glen's face glowed with expectation and excitement. He suddenly looked a perfect image of a child who was about to be handed a can of unexpected candies.

"Good job, Janet!" Dr. Glen exclaimed even before he read the contents of the letter. I have always known that you are a very efficient and pain-staking administrator. I hope you've made the original copy available to Little Cliff, I mean the CEO."

"Yes, I did. The CEO's advance copy went up to him this morning too."

Dr. Glen ran his eyes down the full-paged and well-chronicled barrage of false accusations against Dr. Doris:

"I had informed the doctor that I did not want the procedure."

"The doctor literally held me in captivity in the chair!"

"I was forced to open my mouth and forced not to shout out even when I felt pains from the needle prick."

"I was drugged into partial paralysis with intra-oral injections."

"I was thereafter forced to have a procedure which I neither signed for, nor consented to."

"I was talked down upon and was thereafter threatened into silence."

"I wanted to reach for the phone to call for help but was afraid that the needle would be used as a weapon against me."

"The dental assistant was sent away and the operating room door was locked against her".

"Thereafter, I was ordered to drive home from the Center without reporting to anybody or calling the police".

"I was threatened and forced to hold my peace for many weeks until the spell cast on me by the doctor was relieved by intervention of the front desk staff of the Center"

"I had to request for a change of doctors to escape repeated mismanagement from my former dentist who was very good and very professional but was no longer my choice."

Signed: Ms. Laura Smith

The concocted and largely ridiculous allegations were laboriously documented, but as was often the case in false concoctions, the subtle imperfections were very glaring, yet unnoticed by the conspirators.

Miss Laura Smith was given the document to sign and she did so without reading the document. Her attention was focused on having a change of doctors to the *tall lanky doctor who made his patients laugh*. Miss Smith might never get to know the full implications of her apparently-innocuous signature. If she ever got to know, it must have become too late to reverse her decision.

The last statement in the complaint ought to have rung a bell. "I had to request for a change of doctors to escape repeated mismanagement from my former dentist who was very good and very professional but was no longer my choice." The statement accused the doctor of mismanagement but at the same time said that the doctor was "very good and very professional". It contradicted the earlier cooked-up statements. One of the statements must be a fallacy: "repeated mismanagement" and at the same time "very good and very professional". Again, there was simply no way that the alleged events could have occurred on the day in question in a very closely-knit medical facility without anybody noticing. And the patient came out smiling, thanked everybody, went home and never reported until she came for a follow-up visit. The narrative was very amateurish and puerile at the very least. But it was not ignored. In the mad rush to indict, the conspirators had unwittingly inserted one true statement which ordinarily would have raised doubts about the authenticity of the other statements of indictment. In conformity with an African proverb: the deer that is destined to die does not hear the bell around the neck of a hunting dog. Ms. Laura Smith could not smell any rat in the bogus bundle of lies which she was given to sign. She happily signed, with a promise of having a change of doctors to the tall lanky doctor who would make her laugh. A self-implicating statement would equally be signed by her even if it was written on font size 24. An otherwise intelligent and amiable young lady, Ms. Smith meant no harm. She was assigned to the doctor of her choice, all right. But she did not collect any copy of the letter which she signed. She was not made to laugh after the check-up visit either. She simply went home.

The litany of purported abuses and forceful imprisonment on a dental chair in broad daylight was unbelievable, mind-boggling, and bordered on the absurd. It sounded unbelievable and ridiculous but it was documented on paper and signed. It was so very simplistic, a material which only the likes of poorly-educated Katlyn Sanders could write. But it was accepted. It easily challenged the credibility of any reasonable human being in 21st century America. But the litany which was chronicled with assistance from a designated staff member was accepted as gospel truth by a Clinical Director a well-trained professional and veteran of an otherwise highly-respected group.

The CEO was prodded by Dr Glen into accepting an otherwise incredible litany of obvious falsehoods. "Little Cliff" read the fabricated complaints levelled against an innocent and harmless staff member with shock. A mere phone call from the clinical Czar was all that made him do the equally unbelievable and unjust. He handed back the case to Dr. Glen to "investigate and make recommendation for punitive action to any extent seen commensurable". It was akin to a theatrical replay at the level of mere humanity, of an innocent biblical Christ being handed over by Pontius Pilate to his mob accusers and tormentors for trial, verdict and punishment. Inevitable verdict of guilt with crucifixion on a theatrical cross was of course to be expected.

Dr. Doris' the victim was to accept the injustices with equanimity and even prayers for his tormentors. But the irrepressible Dr Seene summarized her views to Dr Johnson in the following statements:

"Dr Doris is seen by Dr Glen as *a foreigner*. Dr Glen denies being a racist, but was once overhead in his frequent boasting fits disparaging colored peoples as *colored half-wits*. Doris is a citizen of the United States but this, in Dr Glen's opinion, is not her America. She is seen, especially by Dr Bob Glen as violating an expected norm by getting beyond the boundaries where people of her racial grouping were expected to remain.

"Doris is expected to be serving tea or doing cleaning jobs but has dared to break bounds by becoming a dentist.

"Even the most junior of the junior staff who are of a favored skin pigmentation in utter conceit, consider themselves her social superiors. They always have the conceited belief that they are doing her a favor by associating with her.

"These latter class often enjoy the privileges accruing from the conceit and will get away with actions and inactions for which the likes of Dr Doris will be severely punished.

"Dr Doris, and indeed all of us non-whites, especially the African Americans, South Americans and Asian Americans as well as even-handed whites, are supposed to be looking completely the other way, or cooperating sheepishly while our colleague at work, because he is white, bullies his way through the system, defrauds the polity or publicly rehearses immorality and indecency.

"Dr Doris, though taciturn, appeared not to turn a blind eye to a situation where a public-assisted medical facility was turned into a thriving enclave of dishonesty and falsehoods in medical billing and professional and moral unwholesomeness.

"In a nutshell Dr. Doris' sins, are our sins, no more, no less. They are the sins which each and every one of those of us, both black and white, who dare to oppose racism and racial discrimination in all its ramifications daily fight against. In the larger scheme of things, it daily becomes manifest that here in BGMC, we who are surviving, are bound sooner or later to also get punished." Dr Seene concluded.

Dr Johnson listened with rapt attention but said nothing. Even when he nodded his head in affirmation about what Dr Seene had stated, he was cautious not to appear too critical of the Clinical Director who had the first and last words about the renewal of his limited license to practice.

Events had moved on at neck-break speed after the submission of the made-up "letter of complaints".

"We have to move on fast before this Laura fella realizes that she has been used and comes complaining. We don't want to wait until she starts documentarily retracting what she had signed." Dr. Glen told Janet as soon as the latter reported to work the following morning.

"You know, Dr Glen, that I feel a bit guilty about Dr Doris. I find her harmless even when I do not wish to offend you. By the way, have you made the letter of complaint available to Dr. Doris yet?" Janet asked Dr. Glen.

"Not yet. I wanted first to ensure that Little Cliff, I mean, the CEO, was on board. You guys in administration have a way of successfully truncating things if you feel that you are not being carried along."

"Not when you as Clinical Director of the Center are involved, Dr. Glen. Even as the Manager of the Center, I am aware that my powers can only go so far. Again, in truth, I do not have much against this Dr. Doris. But where the boss says that his subordinate colleague is bad, who am I to say otherwise. I see Dr. Seene as a bigger problem but it looks like everybody is afraid of antagonizing her. Nobody wants her problem. This probably explains the descent on the scape-goat that is Dr. Doris." Janet said smiling. At this last statement Dr Glen's countenance changed. Janet had ostensibly overstepped bounds!

"Do you mean that I am unjustly pillorying Dr. Doris?" Dr. Glen asked, turning sharply to Janet. "I ask this question because it looks like no one can now move an inch within one's little space before appearing to unjustly step on the toes of one of these irritating black and other colored people who are increasingly all over the place. I am getting increasingly sick and tired of this virtual imprisonment! These people are suffocating us!" Dr Glen cut the image of a thoroughly distressed man in deep mental agony.

Even Janet was a little taken aback by the Clinical Director's unravelling. She had never imagined that the bigotry was so deeply-rooted. But she managed to assuage the visibly-agitated Dr Glen with gentler words.

"No Dr. G. I was only comparing two bad apples. I was only thinking aloud that the worse apple should have been discarded first."

"OK, then, Janet, you deal with Dr. Seene and leave me with Dr. Doris."

"Just joking, Dr. G. You are the boss. I only manage at your directive!"

The jockeying with the destinies of two innocent colleagues was soon interrupted by Debbie's entry into the room. Janet left hurriedly. She would not wish to play the obstructionist role which Dr. Seen and Dr. Doris were apparently being punished for, by Dr Glen.

Just before the monthly general staff meeting and two days after the submission of the letter of fabricated complaint to the CEO and the Clinical Director, Dr. Doris was handed a photocopy of the letter from Dr Glen. Janet walked into the Doctors' Room just as Dr. Doris was about to get into the surgery for the day and unceremoniously handed over the envelope to Dr. Doris. The latter at first thought it was a personal mail that was misdirected from her house to her work place. At first, she thought of dropping the mail into her purse to read it after work. On second thought she tore open the envelope just to glance over the content and source of the mail. She was shocked to read the litany of false and fabricated accusations. It was the kind of feeling that one could only imagine from a bad dream.

"Is it possible for human beings to do something like this? Is it possible for so much bad blood and gang-up to secretly exist in a place of work and we still exchange greetings and well wishes every morning with one another? Is it possible for any individual to lie back in bed and sleep soundly at night after so much fabrication of falsehood and ill-will against another fellow human being?"

But Dr. Doris was only seeing human beings in relation to herself. She was aware of the fact that she could only speak about the things that she dared not do to other human beings. There was no way that she could in reality speak for what others could do, or what they had indeed done. She had seen firsthand what others could do. She had seen the best of America. She now had evidence of the worst of America on her hands. She had a letter of fabricated lies right there in her hands.

"Could this be real or am in a bad dream? Could this be happening in a Christian America that I thought that I knew? Is this a true representation of my romance with America? Is this the promise, the great promise of America that I had made to Ron before we set out from our native land some seven years ago? Or, is this a mere aberration, an oddity from the worst representation of America, some devils incarnate?"

Dr. Doris was stunned. She involuntarily transferred the copy letter of allegations between her two hands two or three times before she read it again. She was a strong woman. She was equally religious. But the magnitude of the fabrications almost overcame her. She almost began to doubt the justice and fairness in the system. She said a short silent prayer and then quietly soliloquized:

"I will only write a letter of rebuttal of these false accusations and leave the rest to God and the conscience of my false accusers. This was a patient to whom I gave my best and with whom I exchanged banters. I remember her very distinctly because she was very fidgety at first before the procedure but later, after assurances, became very cooperative and thanked us profusely when we were done. And, I proceeded with her expressed permission to carry out completely successful procedures on her. I had gone beyond the call of duty to reassure her against her expressed fear of doctors and dentists. I could justifiably have referred her to a specialist who would let her go home momentarily on analgesics and anti-inflammatory medications and with the hurtful caries the moment that she expressed her dread of doctors. She arrived after the close of registration of patients for the day. But I had requested the front desk staff to still register her to be seen. I could simply have pulled off my gloves and said goodbye for the day as the front desk staff were all set to go home. But I had gently explained to her, reassured her and obtained a second consent from her after the general consent before I proceeded to attend to her. And after the successful treatment she had thanked us and left without any complaints, only for her to allow herself to be goaded into writing these falsehoods. Even if she changed her mind midway about receiving the treatment, as some patients do, she should have informed me. With three decades and longer of untainted service in the profession I stood nothing to gain or lose by letting her go if she so desired. But I chose to do the right thing and this is what has come of it. Yet I bear no malice. I know the source of this plot. I can fight back and vigorously too. But it's not of much use. I'll leave it to God and the conscience of the plotters."

Dr. Doris was still talking of conscience. She did not appear to realize that there was nothing like conscience in the terminology of her detractors. "Some of these people, a very tiny percentage of the population, live from day to day in godlessness, psychopathic depression and utter despair. It might not indeed fully be their faults. Some might have been acting under the influence of substances.

Some others might have come from very bad homes. In either of such situations it might not be entirely their faults. But one wishes that they would not take down some other innocent people to assuage their pitiable situations." Dr. Doris quietly said.

For the rest of the day after receiving the false accusations Dr Doris was not her usual self. She kept doubting whether it was all real life or her imagination that people could fabricate so much falsehood and heap upon an innocent colleague at work. Even though she was deep in thought, she tried to present a smiling face to the patients. But she was a little absent-minded and a little slower with the surgical instruments. Even Kim the Assistant who worked with her, noticed her doctor's clumsiness on that day. She had to call Dr. Doris' attention on more than one occasion. By midday break Dr Doris considered calling off sick for the rest of the day. But on second thought she summoned up courage and decided to weather the storm. She hummed her favorite song "Amazing Grace" as she worked for most of the rest of the day. She thought of calling her husband to inform him of the sudden developments at her work place. But she changed her mind and decided to let him know only after she got home. "These psychopaths are not worth glorifying by my spreading the grief which they want to spread.". She said.

On finally getting home and informing Dege, Doris was greatly heartened by Dege's reaction. Dege was not as religious as Doris. But after he read the litany of false accusations leveled against his wife, and listening to the latter's narration, he simply said to his hitherto greatly-saddened wife, "Bother not, Doris, we shall be fine. You must put up a cheerful face. Your detractors will only be very happy if they feel that their actions hurt you badly." Doris was further encouraged when Dege went on to quote Rudyard Kipling's "If you can keep your head when all about you Are losing theirs and blaming it on you. If you can trust yourself when all men doubt you But make allowance for their doubting too."

Doris paused for a while and further quoted. "If you can bear to hear the truth you've spoken twisted by knaves to make a trap for fools, … yours is the earth and all that is in it." Dege was so used to quoting Rudyard Kipling and Shakespeare that Doris no longer listened most of the time. But at that particular instance the Kipling quotation was so very appropriate and meant a lot to her. A hug of encouragement between husband and a hitherto embattled wife, greatly lightened the rest of the day for Doris.

Dr. Doris replied to the false allegations leveled against her in great details. She handed her response personally to Dr. Glen and copied the CEO. There was no formal query issued and there was no formal acknowledgment of the response from her. It was possible that the CEO who was initially goaded into believing Dr. Glen, was beginning to have doubts about the truth or otherwise of the whole episode. But he, like other members of staff of Beaming Grin Medical Center, always stood in awe of Dr. Glen who appeared with his boasts of medical and military superlatives, to mesmerize not just the Medical Center but also a lot of his peers in the small city's medical and dental community.

Dr. Doris just before the monthly meeting of the Center, had thought of informing Kim her young Assistant about the false accusations levelled against her. Kim was the only other person present during the procedure carried out on Ms. Laura Smith. If there was to be a witness to be summoned, Kim was the only one.

"I know they will contact Kim to also woo her against me. But I will rather not talk to Kim about this. Let them also woo her. Let me not, by talking to Kim about this, appear to be tampering with evidence or obstructing justice. They will talk to her and also woo her against me. She has quite some wants which she had sometimes expressed to me. If they promise her some favors in exchange for a lie against me and she consents, so be it. I will rather not talk to her about this until they do. That way they can make her promises which I on my part cannot make her."

True to Dr. Doris' predictions, Dr. Glen called Kim to his office and held discussions with her.

"Yes, Kim, you were assisting Dr. Doris on the day she forced a patient to have a carious tooth extracted" Dr Glen asked a trembling Kim. All very junior staff were usually scared being called to the office of the Clinical Director. Most of such calls were ominous.

"No, Sir, I don't remember any such case." Kim replied trembling out of fear that the Clinical Director might be having a case against her.

"A patient by the name Ms. Laura Smith had reported that you were assisting Dr. Doris when the latter forced a tooth extraction on her some time mid-September this year." Dr Glen said, looking the trembling young lady straight in the face as if positively demanding an affirmation from her.

"I do not remember, Sir, but I did not hurt any patient."

"This is not your problem, Kim. All I need is an affirmation from you that you were present and that you saw Ms. Laura Smith crying after the assault on her by Dr. Doris." Kim remained quiet for a while. She then looked up at Dr. Glen inquiringly as if to find out what he wanted her to answer. Dr. Glen on his part was standing over the frightened young Assistant like a hawk that was about to tear apart a little chicken.

"It's not your fault Kim. Just confirm to me that you were present and that's all." Dr. Glen said.

"Yes, I think I can remember the young man who cried profusely after his extraction." Kim said, relieved after the assurance that it was not about her.

"It is not a young man but a young woman." Dr. Glen corrected.

"OK, yes, I can remember the young woman who came with a baby that she was nursing."

"I don't know whether she was nursing a baby, Kim, but you can affirm that you witnessed Dr. Doris assaulting the patient."

"Yes Sir, yes, I remember precisely. I wanted to report but I changed my mind."

"Again, Kim, I don't know what you wanted to do but next time you should not change your mind. And I hope you do not change your mind about what you have just told me."

"No Sir, I am not changing my mind anymore about what you just told me. I will state it exactly as you said, Sir."

"OK then, you should state what you witnessed in writing just like you have narrated to me. You will then hand your statement over to Janet. After that you can go back to your work without any problems. By the way, what you told me is recorded and I hope you have no objections about that. Sorry I should have told you in advance."

"No problems Sir, I will do as instructed. But I wanted to know about the confirmation of my appointment which I had requested since four months ago, Sir."

"You will have that done soon after you have testified in this issue of Doris and her malpractices, right?"

"No problems, Sir. Thank you very much Sir."

In Janet's office, with Janet's help a three-sentence statement was made by Jim in her handwriting and handed over to Janet. Kim had stated thus: "I was present when Dr. Doris forced a patient, Miss Laura Smith, to have infiltration anesthesia and a dental extraction. The patient protested and cried, but Dr. Doris was very condescending. She kept the patient on the chair, carried out the procedure and told the weeping patient to cheer up and go home and continue with her pain medication."
Kim was the least difficult to convince among the chain of allies in conspiracy and falsehood. She had nothing to lose by lying against Dr Doris. On the other hand, by telling what she had seen as a simple lie, she was more likely to warm herself into the Clinical Director's good books and thus possibly get recommended for a raise. The deed had been done and the plot had been perfected. It was straight and easy, and everyone was happy except Dr Doris.

Dr. Doris had reported for work on the 4th day after the visit of the CEO to the Center. The incident concerning the patient who she had attended to many weeks earlier was no longer persistently on her mind. She had no reasons to fear or be apprehensive after a dental procedure for which the patient had thanked her and had gone home smiling.

As she drove into the staff parking lot of BGMC Doris saw the cars of many senior administrative staff of BGMC pulled in and neatly parked. She also identified the black GMC SUV that belonged to the CEO, Mr. Clifford. She also identified the ash-colored Chevy car that belonged to the lone female Member of Board of the center.

It was unusual for the CEO a Board Member and senior administrative staff of the Center to visit together in such large numbers so early in the morning. Dr. Doris immediately knew that something unusual was about to happen. She remembered that Janet in her loquacious and pedantic way had boasted during the previous day's staff meeting that there would be many far-reaching changes in the Center.

"Something big is about to happen to this Center." Janet had said. A volcano is about to erupt and much larva will be thrown sky high." Janet had said on entry into the Staff Common Room.

"What will set off the volcano, Janet; and what will the larva consist of?" Dr. Doris had asked Janet. Dr. Doris would not ordinarily have responded to an apparently silly comment from Janet. But somehow, she remembered that she was asked to write a report about an innocuous procedure which she had performed. Could the assemblage of the Board Members and senior Administrative Staff of the Center be in connection with her?

"I know that Dr. G does not appear to want any senior Doctor, worse still a senior doctor of color, to last long here since he came down. But

I have done nothing wrong to merit any fear of him. "Dr. Doris had muted to herself. Dr Seene who regularly made scathing remarks about Dr. Glen and Ms. Debbie ironically did not care a hoot about the goings on. And she was not asked to write any reports about any complaints from her patients. Dr Glen apparently would not wish to stoke a smoldering fire. The gentler and more taciturn underdog Dr Doris against whom there was already inherent bias, was an easier prey to attack.

When it appeared to her that enough attention was not paid to her glibly-talk about volcanoes, Janet had added: "We are not short of dentists and other doctors, and we can never be in want of such staff even if one or two doctors go. We have a long list of such personnel waiting in line to take up any vacant positions." Janet had talked so glibly in her usual boasts and so, not much interest was paid to her statement. And so, immediately Dr. Doris saw the array of administrative staff gathering in the clinic on that fateful morning, so soon after the plot against her came to the open, she figured that it must have to do with the malicious letter of complaint against her.

Dr. Doris had just emerged from the scrub-changing room when she saw Janet standing in front of the door.

"Dr. Doris, could we see you briefly in Dr. Glen's office".

Yes, events were coalescing and materializing so rapidly. The notice was very brief. Eight senior officers of Beaming-Grin Medical Center were already tightly-seated on a hurriedly arranged small oval table in Dr. Glen's office when Dr. Doris entered. These included the rarely-seen Chairman of the Board, the CEO, Mr. Cliff, the Clinical Director

Dr. Glen, three members of the Board of Management of BGMC who Dr. Doris had met on one or more occasions as well as two non-familiar faces, a man and a woman who were probably also members of the Board. They all looked so solemn. None appeared to want to have eye contacts with Dr. Doris. One of the familiar members of Board of Management seated there, the lone lady in the Board appeared a little nervous as she repeatedly removed and put back her eye glasses, finally loudly dropping the thick-framed object on the hurriedly-assembled meeting table.

As soon as Dr. Doris entered the room, Dr. Glen opened the discussions. He did not as much as allow Dr. Doris to sit down.

He cleared his throat and in a characteristic authoritative voice that did not acknowledge or defer to the presence of his employers or his direct boss who ought to be Secretary to the Board, Dr Glen stated:

"Ladies and gentlemen, you are all welcome to this emergency and extraordinary meeting which was necessitated by a very serious threat to the smooth running and integrity of BGMC. The Chairman has kindly allowed me to moderate this meeting since I am the man on the ground here."

Dr. Glen then paused for a while. He rolled his large eyeballs from one Board Member to another as if to gauge the mood of his listeners. He then turned to the direction of Dr. Doris. The latter was not as much as offered a seat, and was consequently standing surprised but defiantly, mid-way between the door and the oblong meeting table that seated the members of the Board.

"Yes, Dr. Doris, we, and by we, I mean all of us here including the CEO, have confirmed the complaint that you treated a patient without the patient's permission and against her will. You forced a patient to receive an injection and proceeded to extract her tooth without her permission or formal consent. This is a very serious offence which demands immediate and decisive action. It is tantamount to patient abuse. You humiliated and looked down on a patient who is a bona fide citizen of this community. And, the patient has threatened to stop using our facility for her medical and dental needs. She has even threatened further sensitization of members of the community against this body if nothing is done to appease her over this abusive malpractice. We do not wish to have any staff of this Center bring disrepute to the Center. We have investigated and consulted widely and have unanimously concluded that this body demands your immediate resignation. This same fate awaits your other collaborators and meddlesome staff whose cases will also be addressed sooner or later. If your conduct is permissible in some primitive far-away environment from where you came, it is certainly not tolerable here. The alternative to your immediate and unconditional resignation will be that we, and I mean the full weight of the Center, will take any and all measures at our disposal to have you do the right thing. These latter measures will of course include immediately firing you and levying further disciplinary and incriminating measures against you. And I can assure you we can always find more incriminating matters associated with your mistreatment of this patient."

As Dr. Glen spoke his hands were trembling. His lips were quivering. And even when he stuttered uncharacteristically, the lie was obvious in every word that he uttered. He could not as much as disguise the fallacy and devilry in his words. The full components of evil manifested in his facial features. In one piece he presented the full image of hate and repression.

As Dr Glen uttered the basketful of lies against her, Dr Doris looked the aggressor straight in the face. She had hoped that her genuinely innocent face and the helpless gaze of a mindlessly persecuted colleague would somehow mellow the cascading virulence of evil. They did not. Rather, the uttered lies that smacked of psychopathy and devilry, appeared to gather strength through the voice of Dr Glen. The latter's voice that appeared to stutter at the beginning became clearer and more distinct.

The faces of the other members of the Board were deep in gloominess. A few felt that the Clinical Director was overstepping bounds in his speech. But they all appeared to be mesmerized or under the spell of Dr. Glen's oft-repeated but unverified military gallantry as well as a constantly-manifested exaggerated professional excellence. But these factors however spurious, proved nonetheless effective for Dr. Glen as Dr Doris the victim, stood before them, humiliated without as much as a single sympathetic voice to speak up against injustice.

Dr Doris stood tall, dignified and defiant. Her piercing gaze which looked directly through the Clinical Director's bespectacled eyes appeared, even in silence, to successfully challenge the false might of the Clinical Director. The latter was savoring a brief moment of false triumph. He was probably thinking of how he would narrate his moment of triumph to his mistress, Debbie. "One bitch down, one more bitch in line to go. Dr Seene will be next in line to fall." He muttered to himself as he was done pummeling his helpless victim. Vulgarity was no stranger to the otherwise highly-placed Clinical Director.

When Dr. Glen finished his charges and verdict, silence fell in the room for a couple of minutes. It was akin to a one-minute silence observed for the demise of equity and justice. Justice that had departed from the system appeared to have dragged the voices of all that were in the room along with it. The attendees appeared to be hearing their own heart beats. One or two bent their heads down as if in mourning. The face of innocence that was being pilloried and utterly repressed appeared to be directing darts to their chests. But they remained silent nonetheless, mesmerized by their employee who they had conferred too much powers to.

When Dr. Glen the quintessential architect of the plot was done, he turned his gaze towards the ceiling and was again tapping the top of the table with his scrubbing-brush-withered fingers. He was neither smiling nor frowning. The face of evil would not be expected to be so blank.

Then, and most surprisingly too, a beaming, and maybe sarcastic smile exuded from the face of Dr. Doris. She was expected to be exploding with anger and disgust. And her face remained angelic to the dismay of the eight gloomy faces in the room. Many in the group were not privy to the plot. Only two were, the Manager Janet and the Clinical Director Dr. Glen. But all in the room had been briefed and fully-fed with falsehood. Most of them doubted the authenticity of the allegations and wondered at the speed with which the verdict and punishment were being meted out. They wondered whether they had at the same time conferred the powers of judge and jury to the Clinical Director. But they still were too mesmerized by the overbearing veteran and Clinical Director who appeared to bestride the Center's clinical activities *like a colossus*. The members all wore such gloomy faces as only falsehood could confer. But the face of the victim of it all remained bright, exuberant and pure.

Almost all in the room had expected loud protests, tears or wailing from the victim who was about to be suddenly and without justification thrown into the world of the unemployed. Even with the high demand for professionals in her field, an unplanned exit from a subsisting job was bound to have its deleterious effects on Dr Doris or indeed any professional. Sudden and unplanned exit from a job was not expected to be fun. It would indeed be expected to be more hurtful in situations such as Dr. Doris' in which the adduced reasons for exit were trumped-up utter falsehoods.

Dr. Doris had not in the wildest of her imaginations expected what she was witnessing. But she summed up courage. The middle-aged highly-experienced medical professional surprised everybody in the room. Almost all therein had expected her to react unfavorably to her ordeal. But, with a straight face and with head held high Dr. Doris looked Dr. Glen in the face for the entire length of time that the latter spoke. Even as she marveled at how human beings could so easily concoct lies and malicious falsehoods against other innocent human beings especially without justifiable cause, Doris mused: "What degree of hate or racial bias could propel humans to be so vindictive against other humans? Is this really the America that I had looked up to? Is this the America that I would wish for my children and my grandchildren? Is this indeed their America?"

Doris neither blinked nor bowed her head in defeat, melancholy or surprise. Paradoxically it became the role of the accuser and vilifying boss, Dr Glen, to bow his head. This occurred as soon as the victim stoutly and without mincing words gave a clear and distinct response

185

to the Clinical Director and the others gathered in the room. Even with the profound seriousness of the matter under discussion and despite the very obvious conflicting circumstances of the charges leveled against Dr. Doris there was resounding reticence from all the other members of the Board of Management of the facility. It looked as if the Clinical Director had cast a spell over all the others that were present in the room. In spite of the obvious profound injustice and exhibited malice, nobody in the room dared raise a voice. None dared to put in a word for justice or fair play. None even remembered the two words which even the worst kangaroo court was expected to allow: "Fair Hearing". All had relied solely on the list of trumped-up accusations which Dr Glen had distributed to the Members of Board and the written response which Dr Doris had submitted to Dr. Glen. There was nothing like cross examination of the accused or of any witnesses. Nothing was said about requesting the purported accuser Miss Laura Smith, to come and restate or confirm her case. None even muttered the probability or need for hearing directly from the lone witness of the purported assault, the Assistant to Dr Doris. Everything was done in keeping with the way that the Clinical Director had planned it all. The hearing and judgment were carried out in a hush-hush manner that was typical of kangaroo-courts. But even in kangaroo courts there were witnesses who might need to be cross-examined. In Dr Glen's court there were nothing like that. Luckily for both parties, the accused had decided not to contest whatever decisions that were arrived at by the assembled body as soon as she came into the room. She had made up her mind to go since the body that employed her could so readily abdicate its responsibilities to a conniving and morally-bankrupt fellow employee. She did not admit to any of the false allegations. But she did not feel it was worth the trouble to contest them, even if only for purposes of clearing her good name.

"It would serve no useful purposes. It would only amount to glorifying the body of evil. This body is obviously compromised by intimidation or by fear of Dr. Glen." Dr Doris said as soon as she saw the obvious ambush that was laid out for her. She thereupon mustered the courage to accept whatever was coming. Without previously ever contemplating it, she made up her mind that even with any and all allures of serving in a small-sized quiet rural community, that BGMC was not the right place for any professional of her temperament; one that was honest and dedication to duty. But even without that decision taken on the spur of the moment and even in the face of the unfolding conspiracies, Dr Doris did not allow her emotions to display on her face. Without any trepidation, she pulled herself towards the edge of the table as if to be more visible to her persecutors. She then cleared her throat and in her gentle melodious voice, she calmly said:

"I thank you Dr. G, for at least inviting me to make a statement before this bombshell." Dr Doris said, half smiling, half frowning. In the midst of the treachery and falsehoods she was surprised she could still call Dr Glen by his pet name, Dr. G.

At that perilous moment to compare the victim's countenance with the face of the famed Mona Lisa might sound spurious. It would have been seen as a major exaggeration worse than likening an African elephant in size to a new-born kangaroo. But perhaps it was only a minor exaggeration. Yes, the incongruity of comparison between Dr. Doris' and Mona Lisa's faces was only a minor one. Yet, both faces commanded deeper reflections for the true intent of either of them to be fully deciphered. Dr. Doris was no Mona Lisa. But even in the midst of the most provocative and the most challenging of human biases and near psychopathy, she had gently and with her characteristic soft and gentle mien and a plain countenance, continued thus:

"Mr. Chairman, Ladies and gentlemen, Dr Glen, the Clinical Director had issued me a query a few days ago. The issue was a patient who I had courteously and professionally treated and successfully discharged. The patient had expressed satisfaction and appreciation. Contrary to the false charges read out by the Clinical director, the procedure was fully read out to the patient and her expressed consent was obtained. That was in addition to the standard consent usually signed by all patients at the front desk before surgery. In my response to the surprising query from Dr. Glen, I had emphatically denied the false and obviously-trumped-up accusations. I hereby reiterate my complete and unequivocal denial of this evil plot. I have a good idea of why this plot is being hatched and executed against me. I would have loved to present my detailed defense individually and collectively to members of the Board here seated. But I believe that it will make little or no difference. This is because my Assistant who is the single witness that I would have produced has, to the best of my knowledge and belief, been thoroughly suborned and heavily intimidated by the Clinical Director. I have evidence for this belief. Racial hate, conspiracy, cronyism, advancement of immorality and unjustified malice run deep here. It is my belief that many members of the Board here gathered, are aware of the goings-on. Fear of, or reverence for, the Clinical Director may not allow for fairness and equity to prevail. Unfortunately, it is not my role or intention to begin to challenge or question the why and wherewithal of such fears. Even if I contest the falsehood and injustice and win, my triumph will not change the system. The courage to ensure the change by the responsible authority appears to be lacking. The powers of the Board and Management appear to have been abdicated to the Clinical Director as has manifested this morning. Forgive me if I erred in my latter view. But this is my humble opinion. I may have come from what the Clinical Director often and even to my face, referred to as 'some primitive far-away-environment'. But happily, even in that environment, educated people observed norms and decent behavior which were expected of all civilized human beings. I am a decent, truthful and fully professionally-trained citizen of the United States, justifiably proud of my heritage but devoid of irrepressible arrogance, falsehood and self-conceit. I therefore am happy to quit as you desire. My leaving without standing up to contest the falsehood and injustice may be viewed in some quarters as cowardice. In other quarters it may be viewed as subtle admission of guilt. In either situation I have no apologies, even when I know that neither situation applies here. The bottom line is that I leave with my full dignity and without malice. I leave with all innocence and a clear conscience. It is better that these burdens lie with the haters. I hope and pray that my departure brings peace of mind and a better sense of humanity to the few troubled minds who I have encountered here. I pray that these troubled minds will begin to have a change of heart and learn to sow seeds of love instead of hate, and humanity rather than devilry. I thank you all for giving me your ears. And I request that you please give me one or two minutes to step outside and confer further with my husband on phone before my final word."

As Dr Doris spoke, she could see a streak of tears running down the cheeks of one of the other two females in the room. It was not the victim crying. Rather, it was the Office Manager Janet, shedding tears. The lone female member of the Board held her head down but said nothing. Cliff, the CEO was gazing at the roof of the house. He too said nothing. All including the Chairman of the Board, appeared to have abdicated their positions to the Clinical Director. The latter remorselessly appeared to have sold his soul to the devil as he repeatedly and rhythmically tapped the top of the table with his fingers as would a drummer in a group music festival.

"Why was Janet crying? She was part of the plot. Could she be under torture by a sense of guilt? Or was she crying because I was not crying? Was she crying for fear that she might be the next victim. Whichever was the reason for the crocodile tears, it is already too late. It now makes no difference." Dr. Doris mused

"You can have ten minutes Dr. Doris", the Chairman of the Board said in response to Dr. Doris' request for one or two minutes. It was the Chairman's first statement in a meeting that he was expected to be chairman of. Dr. Glen then forced a wry smile in a vain effort to bring cheer to a room that was stricken with self-imposed burden of falsehoods.

Dr. Doris then briskly left the room. Her nimbleness and courage in the face of obvious persecution was surprising even to her two biggest tormentors: Dr. Glen and Ms. Janet. The victim's cheerfulness was surprising even to her. As Dr Doris opened the exit door, she could hear one of the men in the meeting say to the others in the room: "How come she is so cheerful in the face of all these?"

The question was not directed to Dr Doris. But the latter chose to respond albeit for the benefit of her ears only: "My cheerfulness is akin to the historical martyrs of old who smiled to their deaths at the hands of Emperor Nero." Nobody else might have heard Dr Doris. But the reply even when it was only to herself, strengthened the victim tremendously.

Within three minutes of leaving the room, Dr. Doris was back with a signed letter of "voluntary resignation". Yes, the letter was titled "voluntary resignation". Yes, it was voluntary resignation. But it was resignation that was forced on the individual out of malice.

Doris had spoken with her husband who though deeply troubled by the manifested injustice and bias, immediately concurred with his wife's opening statement as she narrated the events that led up to the call.

"These are not the kinds of human beings that I can continue to work with. It certainly is not part of the promise which I believe this country holds for those who work hard and who keep their hands clean. This is a different America, not the America that I know or envisaged. Therefore, it is better for me to immediately leave rather than to stand and contest the falsehoods. This is even when I know that if I double down on my innocence, the truth will eventually surface. But it is not worth the troubles. I believe that a better and nobler face of America stands out there waiting to be embraced."

 When Dr. Doris took up her pen to draft her letter of resignation, even in spite of her courage and resoluteness, she found that her fingers were trembling. Her fingers were shaking, not out of fear. They were shaking, more out of indignation and disappointment. It was disappointment at what she felt was failure of a well-trained professional and revered veteran who could not stand up to everyday temptations that average human beings should be able to withstand.

191

Her fingers were shaking out of great disappointment that a Board of what was expected to be distinguished men and a woman, had shamefully abdicated what was expected to be their constituted authority to a mindless or troubled bully who was not only destroying the reputation of an otherwise respected profession, but who, most unfortunately was also denigrating the honor of a greatly-revered veterans' organization, one that was perhaps the noblest on planet Earth.

For one moment Doris was tempted to ditch her initial resolution and her husband's advice. A voice in her momentarily persuaded her to withdraw the resignation and fight the injustice. For a moment she thought of standing up to Dr Glen and staying back to fight the injustice and racial bias.

"I will be doing injustice to many who are similarly discriminated against or who are tortured by mindless racists, bigots and bullies if I simply throw in the towel." But she again needed to reassured herself: "But there is no point in trying to contest this injustice and conspiracy even when you know you are perfectly in the right. You can never find peace of mind here even if you win in the end. Resign immediately and get quickly out of this devilish abode." She muttered to herself.

"I hereby resign with immediate effect, my appointment with Beaming Grin Medical Center." Dr Doris finally wrote.

It was all over; or was it merely seemingly so?

Psychopathy had triumphed.

Bigotry had won the day.

The pillar of moral rectitude and professional decency had been callously uprooted.

The forces of moral indiscipline and racial intolerance had assumed an upper hand.

It would be difficult for BGMC to be the same again.

"Dr. Glen can henceforth find peace in his multiple roles as Clinical Director, Distinguished and Unsurpassed-Surgeon, and Lover-Boy-in-Chief. At least he and the likes of him will daily see fewer faces of color from some *primitive far-away environments,* who appear to irritate them at work. Perhaps he and his likes will begin to enjoy monolithic skin and culture colors which are less irritating to their sense of equality. Perhaps his escapades at immorality will henceforth be better tolerated and more effectively feathered by the exit of my humble self, a *silently-nosy foreigner*, one who he feels is constantly opposed to what he should not be doing at work. Perhaps Beaming Grin Medical Center will, by my exit, be the better for it with unhindered, albeit unofficial padding of procedures or false billing of unperformed procedures for purposes of increased revenues. There will no longer be a Dr. Doris around, who, even with reticence and non-interference, would make one or two people look over their shoulders as they try to *pad* on performed procedures." Doris said as soon as she walked up to the corridor.

Dr Doris had mustered all the strength that she could to put up a bold face. She did not wish to appear to have been broken by the obvious conspiracies that saw her out. But though a strong woman, she was human. It took all the courage in her to walk upright to the Doctors'

Office and the locker room to gather her few belongings. Luckily all the other doctors and nurses were out either consulting or in the surgeries. There was none to say good-bye to, not even her bosom friend Dr Seene. She would have to contact them later by phone.

Streaks of tears had welled up in her eyes as she took the last few steps into her car. Doris was human, an ordinary woman like all else. "Naked came I into the world, and naked shall I return", the words of the biblical patient Job came readily to her lips as she painfully clambered into her car. And so, it was not long before her emotions fully weighed her down and she managed to take the driver's seat in her car before she broke down and wept bitterly.

Doris was a devout Catholic and as she sobbed, she quietly prayed:

"Good Lord, please give me the strength to overcome. Forgive me where I have gone wrong. And please forgive my detractors and help them to reform. But could human beings be so unjustifiably wicked to other human beings? Could so much evil parade under the cloak of men, and fabricate such imaginable lies to wreck so much unprovoked harm to other humans? Could so much evil exist in a Christian America, a country which I had always dreamt of, and truly loved? Is this truly my America? Good Lord give me the strength to overcome."

Doris was lamenting from a small medical facility in Miami Florida. She had uttered almost the exact same statement which was earlier uttered by her husband after the latter's momentary rejections in a New York library and during a book-signing exercise. Husband and wife had never discussed the sentence or used it simultaneously at the same venue. It emanated naturally and spontaneously from each person at different venues. Perhaps it was telepathy. Perhaps it was mere coincidence. In either situation, it was an expression borne out

194

of similar or near similar experiences of victims. These, like Dege and Doris and later, their son Ron, were victims of ethnic bias, bigotry and disdain for people who happened to look different. These latter consequently suffered as a result of a false belief by a few educated but ignorant vocal individuals who believed from their bubble that a certain class of people were not capable of doing any better.

Doris was lamenting a display of undisguised bias against her in Florida. She was in no position to know what was happening at the same time to her son Ron some three thousand and four hundred miles away in Portland Oregon. As she lamented her situation, Doris immediately remembered her son Ron. It was like telepathy as Ron in the midst of his own ordeals immediately remembered her loving mother in Miami Florida. Each silently had wished and prayed that the other would not suffer the same bias at their different places of work as the other at the opposite coast of the vast country. Each had also silently prayed that the silent majority of the population who were great neighbors and great colleagues at work and who were very exemplary in their relationships with other human beings would speak out more vigorously against the loquacious minority bigots in society. Each recognized that bigotry and chauvinism thrived where good men and women chose to remain silent in the face of overt display of the latter vices. As for Ron, he had learnt to say to himself at any turn of overt or covert bias:

"This is the country that I have known since my teenage years. This is the country whose citizenship that I now happily bear. This is the only country that I know. It is the country that has given me the best opportunities in life. And so, even amidst any and all biases, and no matter what any bigot or chauvinist says or does, this is my America."

Doris on her part, even when she shared similar views as her son Ron, would rather read *'The Word Among Us'* a book of daily prayers that appeared to have given her stability and peace of mind during her darkest days at BGMC.

After Dr. Doris handed in her hand-written single sentence resignation letter to Dr. Glen and left the room, silence and gloom descended on the room. Majority of the attendees at the meeting held their arms across their chests as if they were the people under persecution. They all looked into the emptiness unable to talk to themselves for a while. Majority of them inwardly felt that there was little merit to the allegations made against Dr Doris, especially since there was no credible collaboration and no cross examination of the alleged complainant. The hush-hush decisions appeared to have been all based on a simple letter from the Clinical Director to Dr Doris and the latter's response to the letter. But the Board Members all appeared to have been over-awed by the domineering presence and instigation of the Clinical Director who both the CEO and the other Board Members had deferred so much to.

Perhaps the Board members themselves were indeed all under persecution. But it must have been a different kind of persecution, one brought upon self by the individual, an iatrogenic persecution of conscience. Perhaps it was a self-imposed persecution of the mind brought about by complicity in attempting unsuccessfully to persecute an innocent soul.

Dr. Doris was very downcast on that her last day at BGMC as she walked towards the exit in the hallway. She was not downcast merely for loss of job. No, she was highly qualified and was certain that she would readily secure another job in a matter of days from one of the many health institutions that had been trying to recruit her. No, she was simply downcast at the injustice and harshness of the system in which she found herself. But she momentarily brightened up as she walked tall on her way out.

Mid way along the hallway Dr Doris had seen a young lady walking briskly towards the Board Members' Meeting Room. It was the young dentist, the spouse of Dr Glen's golfing partner.

In the previous couple of days, the young dentist had been frequenting BGMC. She had been conferring with Dr. Glen. She was smartly and formally dressed as one going for a job interview. Yes, it was Dr. Anne Williams the young dentist-wife of Mr. Phil Williams who was Dr. Glen's golf partner. Dr Anne Williams was at the Center for a scheduled interview. She was obviously pre-arranged to take over from Dr. Doris whose resignation was already fully stage-managed.

Dr Anne Williams did not as much as respond to Dr. Doris' friendly greetings as she walked briskly past the latter along the hallway. She might have been advised by Dr Glen not to talk too intimately with, or get too friendly with Dr Doris.

It was 10AM and Dr. Anne Williams was scheduled to be interviewed for employment by the Board of BGMC by 10AM that morning.

Some five minutes after Dr. Dori's exit from the improvised Board Meeting Room Janet the office Manager strode out to welcome Dr. Anne Williams into the room for her formal interview "for immediate appointment". Dr. Williams was already waiting at the entrance door to the meeting room by the time Janet got to the door. As Janet opened the door she smiled and jovially muttered to the hearing of Dr Anne Williams:

"One dentist, is on her way out and another dentist is on her way in. The difference is that one is a foreign American Citizen from some uncivilized primitive far-away environment and the other dentist is a real American Citizen. And you are coming at the time that we need this change the most. What a happy coincidence. Come right in, Doc."

The door of the interview room was half ajar, and so, Dr Glen could overhear Janet as she ran her mouth.

"How did you remember my exact words, Janet? I did not know you to have such retentive memory." Dr Glen who was sitting close to the exit door asked Janet.

"If you didn't know that I have a very retentive memory, then you probably did not know me well, Dr. G" Janet replied smiling.

"Well if I didn't believe you were smart, then I would not have hired you after your interview for the Manager's position."

"Looks like someone is informing our new Doctor that he graciously employed me in BGMC. Ha, ha, ha!"

Janet was making a joke. But she was also sending a message to inform the Clinical Director that she should not be used for the boosting of the Clinical Director's ego.

It was all smiles by all in the room throughout the duration of the ten minutes interview. The gloom had faded away. It was a happy welcome to a new dawn of brightness and cheer. Or, so it seemed at first.

There was no waiting time. Dr Anne Williams was handed her employment paper soon after the interview.

Chapter 16

RELIEF AT LAST FROM DEN OF REPRESSION

After Dr. Doris left the room the Chief *conspirator* and the *innocent Janet* that the Chief had recruited gazed repeatedly at one another for upwards of three minutes without a word. Each person was expecting the other to break the silence. Janet looked steadily at Dr. Glen as if to ask the latter: "What next?"

"What next?" The latter would have been a very appropriate question for Janet to ask, for it was more of Dr. Glen's war that he had gotten her to fight. The administrators from the General Office were more confused about the correct answer to the unasked question "What next?" Amidst the silence that prevailed for upwards of three minutes a heavy bulldozer that was doing some construction work at a nearby site had finally broken the silence with vibrating shock waves that reverberated and appeared to shake the entire building. The lone female member of Board of Directors of BGMC Ms. Nancy Rogers was not particularly happy with the obvious hush-hush way the issue of Dr. Doris was handled. She was even more perplexed by the accelerated interview and hiring of Dr Anne Williams. She had earlier learnt of Dr. Glen's scandalous escapades both in his earlier place of work and lately in BGMC. She was therefore suspicious that there might be more to Dr. Glen's enthusiasm about the entire incidence than met the eyes. She did not quite trust Dr. Glen. But she was powerless in the face of the CEO's deference to Dr. Glen in the matter. The CEO himself might have been suspicious of Dr. Glen's motives. But out of intimidation from the former, he chose to defer completely to the Clinical Director and maneuvered the Chairman to let Dr Glen run the day's show both for the termination of employment of Dr. Doris and for the hiring of the replacement.

Ms. Nancy Rogers was deeply religious. Even though she was one of the Board Members who took the collective unjust decision against Dr. Doris she felt some pang of conscience thereafter. But she did not readily express her remorse. On hearing the sound of the bulldozer and observing the shaking building, she had said: "The ground and the building are shaking! This is reminiscent of Golgotha."

Perhaps, it was reminiscent of Golgotha. But it was a mere human mimicking of the biblical quakes that befell Golgotha on the first Good Friday. But it was not Golgotha on that morning. It was a mere rehearsing of man's silly shenanigans, manifestation of rehearsals of earthly temporal power by mere mortals, puny humans who merely stirred up little storms in the teacup that was BGMC. The events of the real Golgotha probably occurred two centuries earlier. And it was for one who should be revered by all, and certainly who was revered by one third of all humanity to this day. Every comparison between the real Golgotha and the imaginary one was mere fantasy in the realm of mere humans.

Yes, there were no songs or dances of victory to sing or dance to. It was mere silence only briefly interrupted by the earth-shaking sound of a passing bulldozer, a handiwork of mere mortal man.

There was no music to listen to in the room which for that morning had a make-over with a small oval table. It was an oval table placed in a small room that was not The Oval Office known to all Americans. This mere mimicking of the real Oval Office was fake, for, it accommodated for that morning, *conspirators* both real and conscripted. The real conspirators came from the clinical wing of the Center. The conscripted arm came from the administrative wing in the Administrative Block a short distance away. The real Oval Office lay some three hundred miles away in 1600 Pennsylvania Avenue Washington DC. In the real Oval Office, real men and real women did not conspire. Even when they conspired it was called diplomacy or strategic planning, And They were not expected to conspire even when occasionally there could be atypical occupants. And if it was reported that there was atypical diplomacy, it might be fake news, and the reporting media would have to work extra hard to prove that they were genuine. No, in the real Oval Office real men and real women rallied together and did brain storming to solve the affairs of State. They rubbed minds (or were expected to rub minds) constructively in the interest of America and the world.

In the real Oval Office, there was true love for America; true love for core American values and not love for self and selfish interest. There was love for those values which were expected to fulfil the promise which America right from the time of her founders had bequeathed to the great people of America and to the world. In that real Oval Office there was no pettiness, (at least there was not expected to be one), no enduring conspiracy for evil, no meanness that would be institutionalized, no, not even in atypical times however badly one viewed any so-called Watergate or similar scandals, or any small-minded events that might come after those earlier scandals. Overall, even with any variations in style, one thing was invariable and certain in the real Oval Office, there was, or there should be love for America which transcended any pettiness or love of self. And when it concerned the good of America there was bound to be unity of purposes by even the greatest political, religious and other ideological opponents. Those were the peculiar qualities that made America and Americans unique. Those were the attributes that made America the envy of the world. The pettiness, meanness and hate that were manifested in the pseudo Oval Office in BGMC on that fateful morning were atypical of the real America. It was an atypical America in which psychopathy and meanness were displayed in their worst forms. It was a real counterfeit of the real Oval Office in which the worst of decent society was let loose to foul up an otherwise well-meaning health institution. And decent human behavior was left aghast; and evil thrived.

There was no formal music in the pseudo-Oval Office in the otherwise noble medical project called Beaming-Grin Medical Center or BGMC. On that fateful morning of her sudden resignation from the services of BGMC there was music. Yes, there was really good soothing stereo music. But the music was not inside the pseudo oval office in which Dr Glen and the bemused members of the Board of Directors of BGMC sat. No, there was music inside the sparklingly-clean BMW saloon car in which Dr. Doris was driving home.

Dr. Doris had initially wept on entering the car. But it was brief humanly emotion borne out of the sad thought of how low some human species could descend when they were in the firm grips of bigotry, passion and hate. But the good recorded music emanating from a CD in the car had all but erased the sad thoughts emanating from the encounter in the make-shift Board Room that was originally the Clinical Director's Office. And so, it was a relaxed Dr Doris who was driving to her happy home amidst some good music. And she drove home into the waiting arms of a loving husband and friend of more than three decades.

Perhaps there might not have been so much gloom; no, there would probably not have been so much psychopathy in the make-shift Board Room that morning if every aching soul in BGMC only had but one loved one and a loving smile at home. Perhaps a welcoming smile at home for every staff of BGMC, a dedicated spouse or a loving family member or friend to discuss with, would have helped to sooth away the many stresses and intrigues of everyday life in BGMC under Dr Glen. In a situation where all three, a dedicated spouse, a loving family member or a good and genuine friend were all absent, there was increased likelihood of constant anger and disgust being carried from home to work-place and perhaps again from work-place back again to the home. The aggregate of the unmitigated anger might trigger an unending vicious cycle which could only lead to a rising crescendo of anger, loss of empathy and complete disregard for the truth and for human decency.

Yes, the enduring "Hot Chocolates" hit song of the mid 1970's, "Love Coming on Strong" that played many decades earlier during her wedding again played as Dr. Doris drove down the beautiful road that led from her work place to her low-density residential area in her middle-class abode in Miami Florida. Dr Doris listened as she drove home. And the happy memories of her wedding day came back. And her mood was greatly lightened.

"This is but momentary disappointment. The meanness, shameless lies and intrigues that I witnessed this morning in the meeting with Dr Glen and his co-travelers, are not the hallmarks of the America that I know. They are rather aberrations of America of another age, an age that is certainly of a lower evolution. My America, the America of Lizzy my New York University friend, Dr Seene my BGMC colleague and friend and most especially the America of Dr Shelia my son Ron's erstwhile Chief Resident and great friend, the America that is my America, has certainly gone beyond that stage of utter meanness and wanton ethnic or racial hate. The latter is only good for the likes of Dr Glen. And I must always remember this." Doris soliloquized.

Dr. Doris took off two weeks of deserved rest before commencing search for a new practice. And, four days after her initial five applications there were favorable responses from four interviews. By the fifth week of her leaving Beaming-Grin Medical Center the highly experienced soft-spoken, mild-mannered dentist was snapped up by another Miami-based practice as a partner and at a considerably higher pay packet and much better working conditions and benefits. "BGMC's loss is our big gain. You are very welcome to our Miami Practice" was the welcoming statement made in front of many other staff by the Clinical Director of her new work place on Dr. Doris's first day at work.

"I assure you of my utmost devotion to this establishment, in services of God and country." Dr. Doris calmly replied. It was an emotional, albeit relieving first day at work for a seasoned and dedicated professional who had earlier found herself enmeshed in a well-built but managerially-corrupt work environment that was BGMC.

"If one door does not close, another may not open." Doris calmly said to herself as she was being shown around her new practice by the amiable new boss and obviously elated Clinical Director.

Chapter 17

WAS IT A COINCIDENCE OR WAS IT THE HAND OF KARMA?

As Dr Glen stepped into the Staff Common Room after the decisive and far-reaching Board Room meeting that ousted Dr Doris, he was accosted by his "dear Debbie".

"How did it all go, Dr. G?" Debbie asked quietly.

"You can hardly beat this, darling Debbie. This calls for popping of champagne. I had thought that some people had the guts to fight. Your friend Dr. Doris chickened out without as much as a protest. It is good riddance to bad rubbish. It is one down, two to go as the saying goes!" Dr Glen said gleefully, portraying such an image of high achievement that even Debbie was a little puzzled at the false sense of achievement in glorying oneself on triumph over a relatively helpless subordinate.

Debbie had asked her question quietly, almost in a whisper so that other staff members in the Common Room might not hear. But Dr. Glen had replied loudly and appeared to be purposely loud enough to attract the attention of the many other staff members who were loitering around the Staff Room. They had seen Dr. Doris walking briskly towards her car with her bag and all her personal working instruments. The nursing and clerical staff knew that some major developments had occurred in the administration and management of the Center. They saw one Doctor leaving without a chance to say goodbye. They also saw another Doctor walking in, smartly dressed, ostensibly for an interview for employment. A few of the staff had at one time or the other overheard Dr. Glen complaining about Dr Seene. They had thought that if anybody was to be forced to leave it would be Dr. Seene. They did not know how soon any anticipated changes would take place. The dried-up and flaking tree that many expected to fall was still standing. Instead, the apparently healthy blossoming live tree had suddenly fallen down. But even with the seeming irony, the vituperations and impunity that had emanated from both Dr. Glen and occasionally Debbie, made it obvious that it was only a matter of time before the offending dry tree would also fall.

"One down, two to go, you said. And I saw Dr. Doris driving off without greeting anybody. And Dr Seene is still in the Doctors' office making her usual gossip calls; what happened Bob?" Debbie asked Dr. Glen as soon as the two moved to one corner of the General Staff Room away from the rest of the staff members.

"Yes, one down, two to go. You may be one of the two, Debbie, who knows?"

"Well, since it is two to go, if I am going, you too will be going, who knows?"

"If I go, then everybody else will go. This is because there will be little or no revenue to sustain the place. Nobody will get paid. Yes! Then practically everyone else will go, that for sure!" The sense of importance and arrogance was infectious as Dr Glen spoke.

As the two love birds conferred, there was sudden silence in the room since everybody appeared interested to know what was going on. Debbie motioned Dr Glen about the increasing audience and the need to cease further discussions. So, the latter reluctantly left the Common Room and moved over to his office. He was immediately followed by Debbie.

"There needs to be a complete overhaul of the senior staff situation here. Sanity needs to be restored here." Dr Glen, emphatically said as he renewed the discussions and boasts alone with Debbie.

"I hope you guys will exercise caution and avoid massive staff overhauls. Such drastic changes could back-fire. Remember that this is a Community-owned health institution and not a private one where the owner could make relatively arbitrary changes. There could be a massive public out-cry if injustice is perceived by the general public. Such situations often have disastrous consequences if the necessary care is not taken." Debbie told Dr Glen. The latter was standing triumphantly in the manner of a conqueror who had suddenly accomplished an insurmountable feat. Then turning again towards Debbie in the manner of a vanquishing warrior to a crouching pet-admirer, Dr Glen said:

"As long as Dr. Glen is the major revenue source of this center no massive outcry will be of much effect. You need the revenue for staff salaries and the goose that lays the golden egg must be listened to."

Debbie smiled broadly and said:

"You are very right Dr. G. Yes, I have heard it said that he who pays the piper dictates the tune. And as you rightly said, it is Dr Bob Glen who pays the piper that is BGMC, from your surgical wizardly. Therefore, you have every right to dictate the tune. But a bigger threat to us is Dr Seene, not Dr. Doris. Indeed, I feel somewhat guilty about Dr. Doris. She was relatively harmless even though her silence sometimes spoke louder than words of meddlesomeness."

"Yes, but as a friend and an older colleague to Dr. Seene, Dr Doris should have advised the latter to exercise restraint with her meddlesomeness into other peoples' private matters. But she didn't. Instead she subtly relished the spectacle of condemnations and gossips. She needed to go first to serve as a lesson for others." Dr Glen said.

"Or, was it that Dr. Doris needed to go first to open a space for a charming young lady-doctor who allegedly got hired today." Debbie said, with a furtive look at Dr. Glen.

"How did you hear that so soon, Debbie?" Dr Glen asked.

"Wall have ears, according to Dr. Doris. We hear everything through some invisible cracks in the walls."

"Well, what else did you hear?"

"Ok, I further heard that the new young doctor's husband is a golf partner of a certain Clinical Director."

"Hmmm, so much already? Well maybe it was the meddlesome Dr Doris who might be feeding you with information. During lunch-break I often saw her reading one small book titled "The Word Among Us." I sometimes felt that that little book had some spiritual if not magical powers. You could always see Dr Doris' face lighten up each time she was reading that little book."

"Hmmm, I have never known you to be superstitious, Dr. G. Don't forget that I too am a Catholic like Dr Doris. I sometimes also read that book at home and I can assure you that contrary to your assertions, the book you are referring to is a great and perfectly harmless religious book of daily and weekly prayers. I can even recommend it to you even when I know you don't relate to any religious faith. By the way, the grapevine has it that a certain Clinical Director had received series of cards from the young lady-doctor who I further heard is very pretty and very ambitious."

"Wow, Debbie, don't tell me more, before those wide ears of yours begin to hear hallucinatory messages which bear no relationship with the truth."

"Ok but better be careful Dr G, before we start accusing Karma of some wrong-doings." The conversation ended suddenly with the entry of Janet into the room with a pack of files.

Chapter 18

THE SPEAR INCHES CLOSER

The days wore on very rapidly. Dr Anne Williams had started work as a replacement to Dr Doris. The new young doctor was smart and dutiful at work. What she lacked in the experience, dignity and religiosity of Dr Doris, she made up for, with her youthfulness, amiability and immense sense of humor. She easily won the admiration of the subordinate staff. She was always punctual at work like her predecessor Dr Doris. And being much younger and from the neighborhood, she interacted more freely with the junior and intermediate-level staff. Being from the neighborhood, she was personally known by a good number of the patients that utilized the clinic. She was however a little less restrained with her tongue. And, it was not long before words started filtering into many *expectant ears* about a certain randy Clinical Director's shift of unsolicited attention from a certain married Dental Assistant to a certain recently-married young doctor in BGMC. Credence was readily given to the gossips by the jealous Dental Assistant complaining to many people's hearing about the "misbehavior" of the Clinical Director.

"I cannot accept some bitch's intrusion into a genuine and sincere relationship just from the blues". Debbie was overheard saying along the corridor after she saw the Clinical Director talking for a protracted period of time with Dr. A, as Dr. Anne Williams was often called. It did not matter to Debbie that the discussions might have been work-related. And it did not appear to matter to the rather randy Clinical

Director that the young lady that he was paying unduly long attention to, was a married lady, indeed his friend's spouse. The very unethical aspect of both being colleagues who should have the highest respect for each other was of little consequence to the Clinical Director. It did not matter to the latter that the young lady was only being courteous and not in any way romantically attracted to her boss.

Debbie's suspicions about the goings-on did not appear to be an isolated situation. Or, she ensured that her suspicions were not restricted to herself alone. Three months into Dr Anne Williams' arrival at BGMC, the grapevine had it that the members of the Board of Directors of BGMC had scheduled another meeting in the mini-Board Room of the institution. It was the same improvised Board Room from where Dr. Doris was forced to resign some three months earlier. It was the same rectangular room that was fitted with an oval table to mimic an Oval Office. And the walls of that pseudo Oval Office had ears!

"I understand there is going to be a Board meeting here this Friday." Debbie had asked Dr. Glen.

"No, I am not aware of any such meeting. I am not a member of the Board but I am present at all the meetings as the Clinical Director."

"It is rumored that the Board is considering replacing some highly-placed staff of the center. The manager was overheard telling one of the front desk staff that there would be major administrative changes. She was said to have said that there would be *a Tsunami,* to use her very words."

"Who is Janet to be talking of staff changes here? If there is going to be a Tsunami, or a hurricane, maybe she would be the first victim."

The Clinical Director said arrogantly. He then sat down and casually crossed his legs atop the large writing table in his office.

"If there is going to be a senior staff replacement it will likely be Dr Seene. I remember that I had a number of times complained about her to Little Cliff. But I had really never insisted on Dr Seene's firing or demotion. Perhaps Little Cliff wants to keep the coast very clear for me by removing the two thorns that I often complained about. First it was that meddlesome Dr Doris. Next will be Dr Seene. Dr Johnson is a small fish and I can personally take care of his own case from my yearly report on him, if he starts being troublesome." Dr Glen rattled triumphantly.

Debbie felt reassured and left the room. But she was not out for long. She soon came back wearing an anxious look.

"Dr G, are you sure that you are aware of the details of today's proposed Board meeting? I just heard the nurses and other Assistants saying that the Clinical Director's position was under severe review by the Board. As a matter of fact, they are saying that the news all over town was that the Clinical Director of BGMC was leaving the institution. It was also rumored that the likely candidate for the high position was going to be a little-experienced young doctor. Two of the front desk staff who are from this town were there smiling from ear to ear. One of them had said jovially that it was high time for the sons and daughters of the soil to head the institutions in their native home. They also said ….". Debbie did not conclude her statement before Dr Glen cut in.

"Debbie, I am not in the mood for listening to any gossips from Attendants and Clerical Staff. I am trying to get across to Dr Williams about a case that I put her through with yesterday. Anne learns so fast. I love to teach such people." Dr Glen said with a slight tilt of his head to the left side of his neck, an idiosyncrasy for affection which Debbie recognized readily.

"Do you love such people or you simply love to teach such people?" Debbie asked.

"There is sometimes little difference between the two situations, Debbie".

"Well, Dr. G, there ought to be much difference between the two. From what people around are saying and from what I hear, even in spite of certain unusual behavior which I have recently observed in you, I advise you to be more careful."

"Nobody exercises more care than I do. Constant caution and persistent vigilance are traits that I learnt in the Navy. That was why I survived the many hazards in the military. Listen, Debbie, the Board of this Medical Center can hardly dispense with my services. I make so much money for them that if I should leave for a week, even in spite of the grants that flow into the Center's coffers, they will be hard put to pay salaries. That is why the Board invites me to all Board meetings. Whatever gossips that you have heard are mere gossips. There will always be something for idle minds to gossip about. As I had earlier said, now that I have seen to Dr Doris' departure, the next person that will find her way out is this Dr Seene. And after Dr Seene, I will sanitize the place further by dealing with the purveyors of these gossips." Dr Glen said angrily.

Debbie listened anxiously and then said: "Well, I hear the Board is meeting today. And I hear the meeting will be held here. And you do not appear to be aware of the proposed meeting."

Debbie had hardly finished talking when Janet walked in.

"Sorry Dr. G, I came to collect the July, August and September staff roster which I had given you last week for review at your request." Janet said looking like one in a big hurry.

"I have not yet finished scrutinizing it, Janet. You can come back for it tomorrow."

"I am sorry Sir, I need it now because the CEO had asked to take a look at it."

"What does Little Cliff know about the work schedules. I have not finished vetting those staff rosters, OK!"

"The CEO has asked for the 3rd quarter staff roster. They are having an Emergency Board Meeting here today."

"Emergency Board meeting? And nobody told me!"

"No Sir, it is a Board meeting and only members of the Board were notified."

"But, but, ... what, which Board Meeting exactly are you talking about, Janet?'

"I am actually talking about the draft duty roster which I gave you for vetting."

Dr. Glen stood still momentarily. He looked like one who was transfixed. But he soon recovered. He moved across the room to his writing table and slowly turned through a pile of files and extracted a file which he handed over to Janet. The latter zoomed away from the room as fast as she had entered. She appeared not to want to be around when the man who had interviewed her for her job would recover fully from a seeming trance.

On Janet's way out, she met the CEO Mr. Clifford. The latter had arrived a little early for the meeting.

"Hi Janet, I hope everything is set for the meeting. It is going to be a short meeting but I would want to look at a few documents well ahead of the meeting."

It was still 8.32 AM, and a little too early for the 9.00AM meeting. But from down the hallway walked up a lady and a gentleman.

"Ah, Mr. Thompson the chairman and Ms. Galloway are already here this early too!" Janet said.

Yes, indeed, the Board Chairman, Mr. Thompson as well as Ms. Galloway the only female member of the Board had also arrived well ahead of the scheduled time for the Board Meeting which was earlier scheduled to hold in Dr Glen's pseudo Oval Office. It was the first Board Meeting which was being held in the newly-renovated Conference Room of BGMC. A few other Board meetings had indeed been held in the Clinical Director's small office while the renovation of the Conference Room was going on.

"It must be something urgent." Janet said. "I wonder why the CEO directly instructed me to prepare the new Conference Room for this meeting. I wonder why he did not involve the Clinical Director as was usually the case."

By 9.40 AM Dr Glen who had uncharacteristically delayed his scheduled cases for the day was still in his office. He was still whining over the first Board meeting of BGMC to which he was not invited since he became Clinical Director.

The *real Board Members of BGMC* along with the CEO who was Secretary to the Board, soon met. Every member wore a long face. The usual pleasantries were missing from the day's meeting. The members deliberated on the single item agenda of the meeting: "The rapidly-deteriorating level of morality and professionalism among the top Clinical Staff of BGMC and the scandals which were raising eyebrows in the community."

The Chairman of the Board presided over the impromptu meeting.

"Lady and gentlemen" the Chairman started, "there are serious written complaints of salacious practices as well as complaints of overzealous professional practices written against the Clinical Director of this Center. Many similar complaints had in the past been ignored or swept under the carpet. All the renewed complainants had disclosed their identities with one of them threatening to take legal action if concrete steps are not taken to address the complaint. None of the complainants appeared to have been suborned. We can therefore not continue to sweep this dirt under the carpet or pretend that we have not been informed."

The Chairman adjusted his eye glasses and looked around the room for any comments. None came. He thereafter continued: "The confirmed sole culprit in all these allegations is Dr Robert Glen the Clinical Director of this Medical Institution. Dr Glen has betrayed the confidence we all reposed in him. He has shamelessly dragged the image of his high position in the mud. The most disturbing aspect is

217

that he has caused unjust disciplinary actions to be taken against innocent hardworking staff who disapprove of his shameful activities. He has caused a hardworking and very experienced staff of this clinic in the person of Dr Doris Jacobs to be asked to resign for absolutely no just cause. He had already concluded plans to have another innocent and hardworking senior doctor to be asked to resign. Worst of all, he is into the business of sexual harassment of his subordinate staff, something which this Center has zero tolerance for. His proven padding of cases for purposes of increasing revenue for the Center under his name is another serious matter which will be handled separately. Other confirmed allegations against Dr Glen are in the papers which have been distributed to you. Please take five minutes to read through those five pages of document before we continue with our deliberations." The Chairman removed his eye glasses and dropped same loudly on the table in undisguised anger.

The Board members had unanimously resolved that in the interest of, and for the survival of the Institution, immediate and drastic measures must be taken against the alleged culprits. And there was only one alleged culprit. And, the sole culprit happened to be the Clinical Director of the hospital.

"The Board has exhaustively investigated the allegations and has confirmed them to be true." The communique to be issued at the end of the meeting stated.

"The Clinical Director of the Medical Center was variously accused of sexual harassment and intimidation of some staff members of BGMC who were working under him. He was further accused of setting bad example to his subordinates in the institution, using the authority of his office. The Board of the Medical Center has therefore unanimously

218

resolved to summon the Clinical Director and directly put their findings before him. Thereafter in conformity with his conditions of employment, Dr Glen if found guilty, will immediately be fired. At best, depending upon whether he is remorseful or not, Dr Glen will be relieved of his Clinical Director position and still remain as a surgeon in the Clinic. The Board has also further resolved that to avoid any and all seniority squabbles among the senior serving doctors in the Clinic, the most recently-employed qualifying medical doctor or dentist in the clinic will be elevated to the position of Clinical Director since the position is purely administrative and advisory." The statement from the Board Chairman's Office further stated.

Paradoxically, Dr Anne Williams who was not too long earlier interviewed and brought into the dentistry unit, immediately came to mind.

"It is a smart thing to do, especially since Dr. Anne Williams is a native of the community." One Board member said. "Dr Williams' appointment will help mend fences with the aggrieved natives." Another Board member said.

"Elevation of the youngest among the Doctors will help avoid infighting for leadership among the older staff." The CEO concurred. The latter's concurrence sealed further debate about a successor to Dr Glen. The details of the resolution were not disclosed in advance to Dr. Glen and he was not in the least aware of the fate that awaited him as he waited ruminating over his non-participation at the Board meeting on that fateful morning.

Janet walked briskly into Dr Glen's office as the latter sat ruminating on why he was not invited in to the day's Board Meeting.

"Doctor G, the Chairman and members of the Board would like to see you in the Board Room." Janet announced to the sulking Dr. Glen.

"So, they now need me! I wanted to wait and see how they would navigate the rough clinical terrain here without my input." Dr Gen arrogantly told Janet as he hurriedly gathered some of his old Duty Roster files and followed Janet into the Board Room.

At first, Dr Glen appeared to be sulking over his being invited late to the meeting after the other panelists were seated. His sour countenance began to sour the more when he glanced at the unsmiling facial expressions of his once-assumed compatriots as they sat in judgment over other clinical staff members of BGMC.

Dr Glen looked around for an empty chair close to the CEO. That was the sitting position the equivalent of where he used to sit in the arc-shaped meeting room during previous meetings. But there was no empty seat. He therefore stood tight-faced clutching his pile of files close to the interviewee's chair located some distance away opposite the Board Members. He momentarily brightened up after a one-sentence welcome statement from the Board Chairman. The Chairman's brief welcome sentence was followed by Dr Glen's introduction to the other Board Members. These were members of the Board who Dr Glen had been holding meetings with in the recent past. The strange introduction of the Clinical Director was as if the Board Members did not earlier know Dr. Glen. And, the CEO who Dr Glen often disdainfully referred to as "Little Cliff", failed to thank Dr Glen for his services as was invariably the case, and of course as merited.

"Please sit down, Dr Glen." The CEO told Dr Glen. The soon-to-be ex-Clinical-Director again furtively searched visually around the Directors' table for an empty chair to sit on alongside the Members of Board as was always the case. But the CEO firmly pointed Dr Glen to the chair on which interviewees usually sat when they were being interviewed by Dr Glen and the Members of Board. The embattled Clinical Director hesitated and stood still.

There were a few seconds pause. Then once again Dr Glen the once all-powerful Clinical Director was ushered by Janet, not onto the table with the Board members, but onto the interviewee's chair which was set some distance away from the semicircular stand of the Members of the Board.

On being pointed towards the empty interviewee's chair Dr Glen's countenance immediately assumed an uncharacteristic frightened hue and his face suddenly turned pink. Impulsively, the subject followed Janet's outstretched hand-direction and walked up to the interview candidates' chair. But he did not sit down. He stood exchanging glances between the empty chair and the bespectacled Board Chairman who kept peering at the embattled Clinical Director through his heavy lenses. Dr Glen kept alternating glances between the Chairman and the empty interviewee's seat as if the chair was electrified, bewitched or dangerous. He looked every inch like a frightened overgrown school child. He immediately remembered the day that he and the technically *suborned* Board Members summoned an innocent Dr Doris and forced her to resign her appointment. It was in a different room. But the scenario was similar. At least he was being offered a seat albeit one far removed from the table. But that was a simple courtesy which he did not avail his colleague Dr. Doris.

"I will rather stand, Mr. Chairman. I would, e-m-m, I would rather stand" The embattled Clinical Director blurted, still exchanging glances between the empty chair and the once-familiar panelists now sitting in judgment over him.

The Chairman of Board loudly cleared his throat and without much ado, addressed Dr Glen. The humongous complaints were precise and were read out to Dr Glen in unambiguous sentences:

"Distinguished Board Members of BGMC, Dr Robert Glen, it is with much sadness and utter sense of disappointment that the Board has learnt of certain heinous practices which are alleged to have been going on in this institution. The Board has exhaustively investigated these allegations and confirmed them to be true. These reports and findings include, but are not limited to the following:

"1. That you, Dr Robert Glen, had on various occasions subjected your patients to unnecessary surgical procedures thereby exposing the Clinic to possible litigations and bad public image."

"2. That you Dr Glen had abused your office and set very poor moral examples to your subordinate staff by overtly-salacious activities, sometimes in the full glare of other members of staff."

"3. That you Dr. Glen had taken vindictive actions against members of staff who did not seem to approve of your indecent actions and that you had variously misled the Board of Management of the Clinic into taking unjustified punitive actions against such innocent staff. There are many other equally serious allegations against you as have been detailed in the document which I have here and have also distributed to the Members of Board of Management as gathered here this morning."

As the third charge was about to be read, Dr. Glens jaw dropped and his lips became agape. He repeatedly removed and replaced his eye-glasses several times. The once very powerful Clinical Director started trembling visibly. The Chairman of the Board decided to stop reading of further charges after the third.

"Can this be real, or is it a day-dream?" Dr. Glen quietly said to himself. He reached for his right ear and visibly pinched the lower lobe. He wanted to be sure that it was not a dream. He felt the pain. It was certainly not a dream. Dr. Robert Glen the once all-powerful Clinical Director of Beaming-Grin Medical Center was being questioned for demotion or removal by the Board of the Center!

"Do you confirm or refute the above-mentioned allegations, Dr Glen?" The Chairman's baritone voice thundered. The latter removed his eye glasses and placed same on the table. He then steadied his gaze at the fidgety Clinical Director who suddenly started sweating profusely. Nobody ever believed that the Board Chairman who was once considered weak when matters concerned Dr Glen, could be so firm.

There was prolonged silence from all sides.

Mr. Thompson after waiting fruitlessly for a response from Dr Glen, repeated his question to the latter.

"Do you admit or deny the above allegations, Dr Glen?"

There was again a short moment of silence as the Chairman started piecing together some loose sheets as if to assemble some documented evidence against the Clinical Director.

At that moment, a rattled Dr Glen who was not known to stammer blurted some incoherent words. He appeared to be choking in between words.

"I, … I, …". The words appeared to be choking Dr Glen so much that Janet had to rush up to him with a bottle of water. But Dr Glen recovered quickly and waved Janet and her bottle of water away.

"I, … I do not wish to contest any of your concoctions! I want to get out of this place!"

The once very powerful and dreaded Clinical Director immediately sauntered into the chair which he had earlier rejected. He sat for a few seconds and summed up courage and stood up and made to leave the room.

"Not so fast, Doctor." The Chairman interjected. "The Board will communicate its decisions to you by the end of today. Meanwhile we thank you for your service."

The due compliments tempered what appeared to be heading for a non-courteous conclusion.

As he wobbled out of the Board Room meeting, Dr Glen's legs missed occasional steps. But as the ex-military man that he was, he had summed up courage while still in shock. Dr Glen literally slumped into his office chair as soon as he got into his office.

"Please call me Debbie!" Dr Glen moaned across to Janet who followed him into his office fearing that he might collapse on the way.

"Please call me Debbie!" Dr Glen repeated.

"Debbie is not around but she made a signed document collaborating those charges against you by the Board."

"I can therefore not contest this! Et tu Brute, Debbie!" Dr Glen said almost in a whisper.

Dr Glen's decision not to contest the charges against him was vindicated by the revelation to him that Debbie had made a written statement to the CEO earlier that morning just before Dr Glen was called into the Board Room. The CEO had summoned Debbie just before the commencement of the meeting and ordered her to state the true account of what had been going on between Dr Glen and some members of staff including herself. She was given the ultimatum to state the truth or risk being fired.

Before Debbie was called in, the CEO who already had information about Dr Glen's flirtations with both Debbie and Andrea, had sent for Andrea the young blonde Dental Assistant who was Debbie's competitor for Dr Glen's attention. The CEO had tactfully offered a seat in the room to Andrea pending the entry of Debbie into the room. When Debbie entered the room and saw Andrea her competitor sitting in the room, she believed that Andrea must have narrated the details of her (Debbie's) relationship with Dr Glen. Debbie therefore felt that It would be dangerous for her to lie in defense of Dr Glen at that stage.

"This is a pretty bad situation. Damn it! I've got to be very truthful now!" Debbie muttered to herself. Debbie was a fairly decent lady even in spite of her detestable relations with Dr Glen. She was not used to gutter language but she had found herself in a very awful situation. Fearing for her job should she tell lies, Debbie felt that the best thing to do was to give a full and correct account of Dr Glen's flirtations with her and Andrea as well as his perceived unsolicited overtures towards the new young doctor, Dr Anne Williams.

"Dr G is not a bad man. He is indeed a very compassionate gentleman. I love him. But he finds it difficult to control himself when it comes to beautiful women." Debbie volunteered to the CEO. She made very damning and comprehensive revelations about her Clinical Director friend. And, those revelations included professionally-condemnable practices which Debbie witnessed while assisting Dr Glen in the surgical Operating Room.

"There can be no truer piece of information, than this one coming from someone who knows Dr Glen inside out." Mr. Cliff the CEO said.

As soon as Dr Glen found out that Debbie had spoken privately to the CEO, he felt that the game was up and that there was no need to contest the allegations levelled against him. Debbie had admitted all the accusations as they related to her, and offered to cooperate with the Disciplinary Committee of the Board at any time she was required to do so.

Debbie was not in Dr Glen's office when the latter sauntered in from the Board Room. Dr Glen's muttering of the words "Et tu Brute, Debbie,", on hearing of Debbie's promise to cooperate with the investigative committee of the Board, therefore did not get to her ears.

But, Janet was later to repeat the events in Dr Glen's room to Debbie shortly after the meeting.

"What did Dr Glen mean by that sentence Et tu Brute?" Debbie had inquired from Janet.

"Et tu Brute", stands for "*even you too, oh Brutus*".

"And how does that relate to me?" Debbie had further inquired.

"Those were the famous words allegedly uttered by Julius Caesar as he fell down at the final stab of betrayal from his bosom friend Brutus, in Shakespeare's *Julius Caesar*". Janet had explained.

Debbie brushed aside any comparison with Brutus.

"People can say whatever they want to say. I needed to save my job. And I told the truth. If there was any Brutus, it was Bob who was flirting around with Andrea and making irresponsible passes at the new young doctor even in spite of all I did for him." Debbie said in that rare moment of anger.

Yes, indeed, unlike Julius Caesar, Dr Robert Glen was an ordinary mortal and so could not utter his own immortal words. Yet he had earlier mustered courage and staggered into his soon-to-elapse office and slumped into the sofa. There was no Debbie to console him; none to gently if not romantically, rub his back. The latter was separately fighting for survival of her own job. As a Dental Assistant her own job was more readily dispensable than that of Dr Glen.

A provisional letter from Mr. Cliff the CEO to Dr Glen was handed over by Janet the Office Manager, to Mr. Glen about 1PM that day. The letter informed Dr Glen of the Board's decision to relieve him of his duties as the Clinical Director of BGMC. He was however allowed to remain in the services of BGMC, but merely as a surgeon. The alternative was that Dr Glen should immediately submit his resignation letter and quit his employment. The erstwhile Clinical Director was further warned that he should henceforth refrain from any and all the allegations levelled against him failing which he would be dismissed altogether from the services of BGMC. It was a one-two punch. It was as sudden as it was devastating.

All proposed surgical procedures lined up by Dr Glen for the day were cancelled. The reputed surgeon barely found the physical and emotional strength to hold himself up right for some hours. He remained back within his office for the rest of the day and waited for other staff of the Clinic to go home for the day before he hurriedly packed his personal effects out of his once-glorified office into the trunk of his car. But even in the midst of the turmoil the obviously brilliant surgeon and retired military man was able to mutter to himself as he drove out of the parking lot of the Clinic: "How are the mighty fallen, Bob!" It was self-chastisement that came a little too late. Unfortunately, he did not remember Dr Doris or the possibility of the thing called Karma, playing a role. It was a good thing he did not. He would have felt very saddened and his patients for the day might have been the unintended scapegoats.

Dr Bob Glen arrived promptly to work the following morning. He was unusually well dressed-up in black suit. He put up a cheerful face and walked straight to the Doctors' General Office. He carefully avoided the Clinical Director's Office even when the official letter relieving him of the office of Clinical Director had not been given to him.

But soon after Dr Glen changed his suit to surgical scrubs ready to start the day's work, Janet the Clinic Manager walked in and handed him a sealed letter. Dr Glen already imagined what was in the envelope. But somehow, he had hoped that by some slim chance that the Board Members might have had a re-think about their decision.

With trembling fingers Dr Glen opened the envelope. The first word that caught his eyes was the word "terminated". The courage in the renowned surgeon nearly evaporated. He staggered to a chair just in time before his worst adversary Dr Seene entered the room. He held his hands under the table to conceal the shaking fingers. Both adversaries carefully avoided eye contact. But the eagle-eyed Dr Seene had observed the nervousness in his erstwhile boss. She was gracious and immediately left the room to save Dr Glen any further embarrassment.

The word "terminated turned out to be part of a sentence warning the erstwhile Clinical Director that his contract would be terminated if there was a repeat of his misadventure. Dr Glen heaved a sigh of relief after reading the full text of his letter of demotion. As he opened the envelope, in his haste Dr Glen had accidentally torn through one third of the body of the letter. His eye balls rolled across the page as he read the full contents of the fairly-lengthy letter. He sat still for a while. The reality of the situation had only then begun to sink in. And, for the first time in many years he remembered his prayers!

"Oh my God, is this a dream?" Dr Glen muttered. He soon regained full composure. "I will rather resign immediately than face this humiliation!" He soliloquized.

But the once very powerful Clinical Director of BGMC could not summon the courage to immediately resign. There was nowhere that he immediately had in mind to move into. There was nowhere else to play the demi-god. He thought of his estranged family. He thought of sending for Debbie in spite of what the latter had revealed. Dr Glen had little or no friends outside his immediate work place. His eccentricity and arrogance hardly endeared him to any enduring friends. Debbie was still his best hope. But the latter was elsewhere fighting her own battles. He again remembered Dr Doris who he had been so unfair to in the recent past.

"Oh my God, could this be real?" He muttered again. "Could this be the often-quoted Law of Karma?" Dr Glen soliloquized. "What goes around has come around. And, painfully so!" He said.

Yes indeed, it was all real. Exactly six months to the day of Dr Doris' ouster and Dr. Anne Williams' initial appointment, the incredible happened. Dr Anne Williams was announced as the new Clinical Director of Beaming-Grin Medical Center! This was far above all her professional and academic seniors of the Institution. Even Dr. Johnson the tall jovial young dentist who livened up the clinic with his jokes and purposeful gyrating gait, was senior to Dr. Anne Williams. It was incredible. But it had happened. And, the ready question on every lip was: "What would become of Dr. Glen? Would he go or would he stay? Would he accept administrative directions from a professional junior? What would become of his boasts. Would he continue with his non-conventional practice behaviors? Could he afford to do without the mothering care of the Dental Assistant Debbie? Would the latter remain loyal to him without his exalted mantra of office and in spite of the massive waters that had flown under the bridge?"

On the second day after the Board meeting, Dr. Glen was still seen at work. Having earlier quietly evacuated his personal stuff from the Clinical Director's office, it was easy for him to come in, consult or operate quietly and go home without fanfare. To the greatest surprise of most of the staff members he had accepted to stay back with a demotion from his position of Clinical Director to simply being a surgeon in the Clinic. He was to serve under the administrative directives of Dr. Anne Williams who he had interviewed and employed barely six months earlier. He would retain his full salary as a specialist. But he would stop receiving the little allowance that he earned as a Clinical Director.

"Dr Glen was lucky he was not fired outright. Debbie his comforter-in-chief will no longer be available to rub his back and massage his ego. There will be no private office room for those silly romances. Her job is more dispensable than Dr Glen's and she had signed an undertaking to henceforth be of good behavior or risk immediate termination of appointment without further warning." Those were the words at every lip in BGMC.

"How are the mighty fallen!" was the exclamation repeated by Dr Seene as she walked into the General Office on the second working day following Dr Glen's fall.

"Dr Doris has thus, only been partially avenged. The poor innocent lady, a bona fide citizen of the United States is deeply religious and will not hurt a fly. She was unjustly persecuted because of her origin and the color of her skin. But she survived, albeit outside the stinking walls of Dr Glen's BGMC. She is indeed faring better elsewhere while her persecutors are beginning to pay heavy prices. Yes, if there is a just God, Doris and people like her will be more fully avenged in good

231

time. No evil done to man by man will go completely unpunished. This is a natural promise. This is the promise of my country. This is the promise of America." Dr Seene said, almost overwhelmed with emotions at the speed of development and change of guards in BGMC. There was already a silent air of jubilation among the staff of the Center.

"Who knew before now that Dr G was so loathed?" Dr. Johnson said in a low tone as he made his way out of the Staff Common Room.

"Like justice, the long arm of Karma grinds slowly but it sure grinds finely. Dr Doris has at last been fully avenged." Dr Johnson further said.

Chapter 19

"THAT TALL BLACK GUY"

Doris had been avenged and indeed exonerated at BGMC. Unfolding events following the demotion of Dr Glen from the office of Clinical Director laid bare the massive conspiracies and falsehoods that were concocted by the duo of Dr Glen and Debbie to push out people who they felt did not look like them to make way for their favorite staff members. This was without regard to the relative inexperience of a proposed new employee when compared with the victimized staff member. Often ethnicity or color of skin played a major role in who got away with poor performance in the opinion of Dr Glen and a few of the other management staff.

 The enormous bias and injustices meted out to Dr Doris by the duo of Dr Glen and Manager Ms. Janet, aided by the Dental Assistant Ms. Debbie had become public knowledge. The CEO of BGMC Mr. Clifford had felt the great need to make amends. He therefore wrote to Dr Doris and apologized. He further requesting the latter to withdraw her resignation and return to BGMC. But Dr Doris thanked Mr. Clifford for his apologies but declined the offer. She would not wish to be re-instated in the Center. She was already in a more rewarding place where she would no longer have to turn her face in the opposite direction at any renewed indecent behavior of cheating adults. She was not fully aware that the romance between the erstwhile Clinical Director and the Dental Assistant Ms. Debbie had been irrevocably broken. She was already part of a busy practice where her professionalism and her self-esteem were well respected and where she would not have to constantly look over her shoulders to be sure that a Dr Glen was not sniffing around to ensure that even very minor surgical procedures would have to be referred to him so he would boost his revenue figures. She would not have to keep worrying that a Dr. Glen who was not supposed to be supervising her work would be sniffing around her notes for any imperfections or errors, no matter how insignificant. She would not have to be worrying about whether her assistant was a paid agent of an all-controlling Clinical Director who was more interested in how much revenue was recorded against his name than about how satisfied his patients were with the services rendered to them so that they would recommend other patients to the Center and not ridicule an otherwise top professional as *the butcher of BGMC.* It was a most fulfilling change of job for Dr. Doris.

As Doris struggled with developing events at her work-place in Florida, Ron, Doris' *Baby of the House*, now a young college senior, had become an outstanding student in his college class in University of California Los Angeles. It was the same college which Mezie the son of Dr Seene of BGMC attended. Though in the same college about the same time, Ron and Mezie did not often get to meet each other in Los Angeles even when their two mothers were working in the same Beaming-Grin Medical Center in the East Coast. It was only as a result of Dr. Doris' travails in BGMC that both ladies who were already great friends in BGMC but who rarely discussed domestic issues got to know that their two sons Ron and Mezie attended the same college in Los Angeles California.

Ron had scored very highly in the nation-wide Medical Colleges Admission Tests (MCAT). He also had a very outstanding resume having done many volunteer services both in his High School and during his college years in University of California Los Angeles. He also had served for three consecutive years as his Class Representative in his college years in Los Angeles. His sterling and almost intimidating credentials made it possible for Ron to match in the medical school of his first choice, Columbia University New York. Ron, Doris and Dege could not be prouder at the turn of events. Mezie on his side, to the great joy of Dr Seene, had been accepted into Howard University Medical School in Washington DC.

As soon as they got to know about their sons' friendship, Doris and Seene, proud mothers of medical student sons often discussed and joked about how troublesome their once little boys were, before they matured into the delightful and promising medical students that they had become. "I remembered how apprehensive Ron used to be in high school any day that their monthly class tests would come up." Doris said to Seene. "He would get up from bed before anybody else and his dad and I would know that something unusual was in the making, because Ron would splash water all over the floor of his bathroom. He would inadvertently smear toothpaste all over his sink, in his haste to prepare early for school. And the lights would be left on till late at night and would again be on before we would wake up in the morning. On such days, Ron would need no alarm clock to wake him up." Doris would say. "By the time the alarm would ring, Ron would already have been studying." Doris said.
"It is almost a similar situation for Mezie" Seene said. "We were always aware of his test days by his haste and his taciturnity in the morning of his class tests. It would be as if talking to anybody would evaporate the stuff that he had memorized for the tests."

Both proud parents often compared notes and experiences on raising up their young sons even in the midst of pressure of work and work-place stresses by the mundane and indiscreet shenanigans of Dr. Glen, the Clinical Director, Janet the Office Manager and Ms. Debbie the Dental Assistant friend of Dr. Glen. The moral decadence and prevailing authoritarianism often brought revulsion and a sense of shame to both Dr. Doris and Dr. Seene. But between the two early middle-aged professional women, intimate discussions about their respective families, especially their respective sons, often brought great relief and joy even in the face of virtual persecution by their boss.

The years had passed on very quickly, and both Ron and Mezie had successfully completed their medical trainings; Ron from Columbia University New York and Mezie from Howard University Medical School in Washington DC. The friendship between both young doctors grew deeper after they realized that their respective mothers were friends and worked in the same medical facility. They came to realize that their respective mothers were victims of mutual discrimination at the hands of a "socially-demented Clinical Director", as Mezie had described Dr Glen after listening to tales from his mother.

"How come, a well-educated doctor who has also served in our well-disciplined military is behaving in such a despicable manner?" Mezie asked his mother. "It is most likely he had some very traumatic experience somewhere along the line. It is just not normal. "Mezie said.   No, it was not normal. And almost everyone else in BGMC knew that, except perhaps for Debbie and Dr Glen himself. And it had gone on without being checked for quite some time. It was the advent of Dr Anne Williams that constituted the last straw that was to break the camel's back. Dr Glen's cup got full the moment he started making overtures towards the married young wife of his friend. And it was that wrong move that stirred action from the Board of Directors of

BGMC. A thousand vindictive actions against Dr Doris or a million inflated procedures that boosted his revenue-generation ego, would not have changed anything. Mezie and Ron were overjoyed when they learnt that positive action had been taken to restore sanity in the center where their respective mothers had worked, and that the principal culprit had been sanctioned.

The matching process for Residency Programs for newly-graduated doctors were soon released nation-wide. Ron matched into his first choice for internal medicine in Oregon University Hospital in Portland Oregon, otherwise known as "Oregon Health Portland Oregon". Ron's friend Mezie, on his part matched into the surgery program in Presbyterian Hospital in Brooklyn New York.

The news had flashed that against the prevailing, albeit unwritten, tradition of the internal medicine unit of the University Hospital in Portland Oregon, by which non-white residents were practically unwelcome, Ron Jacobs a student of color, was offered a Residency spot. Unknown to Ron, he was the first colored Resident to be admitted to the Internal Medicine unit in Oregon Health in recent memory. Being a very affable individual, Ron quickly made friends among his colleagues in the Internal Medicine Residency Program. He was proudly black and never had a feeling of being different from any other Resident. If there were any reservations or bias against him from his Attending-physicians Ron did not observe these at first. Both in University of California Los Angeles and in Columbia University Medical School, he had no cause to see himself as different from any other medical resident. Inter-racial relations did not constitute an issue in either of those great institutions.

But, at the same time that Dr. Doris was being profiled and discriminated against at work by her Clinical Director Dr. Glen in Miami Florida, her son Ron who was in his first year of Residency training, was being harassed and profiled at his medical internship work place in far-away Portland Oregon.

Ron was not only the lone Resident of color in his class in the Medical Residency Program in the Portland Oregon Hospital, he was also the only colored doctor in the entire internal medicine team comprising of Interns, Residents, Medical-Attendings and other cadre of senior medical professional staff. Over the years, even when the leadership would not admit that there was a definite pattern of racial bias, it was an unwritten policy that doctors of color were not wanted among the internal medical team of the Portland Oregon Hospital. Everything possible was done to discourage intake of black residents into the Internal Medicine program in that institution. Ron's admission into the program was made possible by the directive of the Chairman of the Department that a nominal admission of one deserving colored resident for that admission cycle, to convey an impression that there was no racial bias. That directive was given after a newspaper article by a black candidate accused the Department of racial bias during previous years' admission cycles.

But it was a half-hearted decision and as soon as Ron joined the Department the already biased leaders of the Department wanted to prove that Black and Colored Residents were incapable of coping with the demands of the Internal Medicine Program in the Oregon Hospital. All eyes were centered on Ron at any time that he was on duty. The constant scrutiny on him made Ron jokingly once say to his friends that he was the only person who would not need police protection in the Department because according to him "I am followed around the Department by more than ten eyes at every particular moment."

In a mail to his parents in Florida Ron had written: "The constant scrutiny initially made me nervous. But that was only for a few days. Now I prepare my cases thoroughly and I study every case thoroughly knowing that the bar is set higher for me and that I will be very thoroughly drilled on every move, far and above what would be required of any of my classmates. Yet, I feel constantly strengthened by the ceaseless scrutiny and I find my skills getting more polished and more perfect by the day, knowing that I cannot afford to falter. I consider it a cross as well as a blessing that is consequent upon the color of my skin, a cross because of the angst of undeserved bias, and a blessing because of the excellence that comes from extra efforts to supersede."

Because of the desire to be very conversant with his assigned cases before the general ward-rounds with the Attending Consultant and the other interns and residents, Ron had made it a habit to arrive at the wards earlier than his other colleagues. That way he would thoroughly study his assigned cases many times over before the start of discussions. It was a perfectly-legitimate and indeed recommended habit which most interns and residents did not often adhere to because of the stress that was involved. But Ron, knew that he needed to excel before he would get a nod of approval from his all-white Attendings. And so, he needed to know every patient by name and the case presentations, discussions, diagnosis and treatment well in place if he must be accepted to be at par with his classmates. One morning when he was busy doing early rounds on one of his patients Ron saw one of the Attendings enter the ward at the far end of the ward. He saw the Attending look intermittently in his direction.

He then overheard the Attending discussing with one of the nurses who had joined him at a distance. The discussions were not going on in low tones or surreptitiously. The talk zeroed on a certain "tall black guy" who was most likely committing a horrible crime. The discussions were certainly not very complimentary. The language was indeed disparaging.

What Ron heard almost shattered his faith in the system. What he heard made him to start paying more attention to actions which otherwise he would in the past have completely ignored. And the statements were not the rantings of a poorly-educated-street urchin. No, they were carefully-chosen words from a highly-educated medical specialist, an internal medicine Attending who was in the business of guiding and counseling younger medical doctors. first year medical Residents who were often called "Interns", as well as the older medical Residents.

"Who is that tall Black Guy that I see bending over a patient down there?" The Attending -Physician Dr. Swanson asked the ward nurse Ms. Linda.
"Oh, that is Dr. Jacobs, Dr. Ron Jacobs, one of our new Interns", Ms. Linda replied.
"Doctor what? A black guy, a Medical Resident here in internal medicine? How did he get here?" Dr. Swanson asked.

"Do you mean when he joined our team?" the nurse replied, trying to quietly temper what was obviously an odious language.
"I mean what I said; how did he join this team." Dr Swanson insisted.

"I guess he joined just like every other Resident. He came in same day as Dr Williams this other new Intern checking on a patient closer to us." The nurse replied, smiling innocently, but obviously disapproving of Dr Swanson's statements and attitude.

But Dr. Swanson was not smiling. He was dead-serious. He appeared not to notice Dr Ron's friend and fellow intern Dr Roberts, who was equally checking on a patient closer to Dr Swanson. Dr. Roberts did not attract the attention of Dr Swanson. But Dr Ron Jacobs, *the tall Black Guy* readily did. *That tall Black Guy* must be up to something evil. And that evil must be consequent upon the color of his skin! Or, so did Dr Swanson imagine. And, the latter's squeezed facial contours revealed every bit of his amazement, hate and disgust. The mere idea of a black Resident in his Department was abominable and repulsive to Dr Swanson!

"I actually mean that tall black guy at the left end of the ward, the guy in white lab coat. Is he a laboratory Assistant or a doctor?" Dr. Swanson asked, his gaze still fixated in the direction of Dr Ron Jacobs. "Yes I know, Dr. Swanson. I have told you that Dr. Ron Jacobs is an MD and is a member of *Team B* of our latest batch of interns. He is not a laboratory Assistant. He is your junior colleague." The nurse a highly-experienced soft-spoken middle-aged white lady explained.

Ms. Linda had been in the Internal Medicine ward for quite a while and was not unaware of the apparent "for whites only" unwritten doctrine of the Internal Medicine Department of the Oregon Hospital Center. She was obviously embarrassed at the brazen display of racial intolerance which was made to the hearing of some of the patients. She had initially tried to parry and make light of Dr Swanson's question. But arrogance and bigotry rooted in deep-seated bias had spontaneously forced a repeat of the question by Dr. Swanson. "I ask you again, Ms. Linda, who do you say that *tall Black Guy is*? And why is he bending so close to that patient? Why is he so early to the ward when patients may still be sleeping? Why is he alone there without other members of his team? And why is it that I have never met him? I will like to see and scrutinize that patient's charts after that guy is done with him."

Dr. Swanson was fuming almost uncontrollably with rage and revulsion. And, his attention never quite left the direction in which Ron was examining the patient. He turned his gaze repeatedly in the direction of Ron and his patient, almost ignoring the patient who he was supposed to be attending to. In all these, he completely ignored another Intern, Dr Ron's batch of interns, who was equally checking on a patient closer to him. The color of the latter's skin, obviously made him less vulnerable, if not infallible, to Dr Swanson.

Ron heard every word of what Dr Swanson said. The latter did not speak in low tones. And he did not hide his disgust for a *tall Black Guy* checking on a white patient as an intern, in a Department which he, Dr Swanson, felt was an exclusive preserve for whites.

On his part, though his self-esteem and emotions were thoroughly bruised by the Attending Physician's comments, Ron tried his utmost to comport himself while he checked on the patient. The patient, a middle-aged white gentleman, had also overheard Dr. Swanson's comments. The former was obviously offended by the bigotry and overt display of racial bias against the young doctor who was simply doing his job.

"Never mind, Doctor," the patient calmly and slowly told Dr. Ron. "Ignorance and bigotry are not abolished even by a high position and a medical degree."

242

Then the patient, in further obvious attempt to change the topic and divert attention from the hateful gaze of Dr Swanson asked Ron: "Where did you originally come from."

"I am a citizen of the United States, and my parents and I immigrated from Ghana in West Africa." Of course, the patient meant well. But as Ron uttered those words, the import of the bias and hateful speech against him by his Attending Consultant stared him in the face. A situation that prompted his having to start explaining himself unlike his peers was most embarrassing to him. The humiliation in the presence of his patient, made him come close to tears. He was overcome by emotions. He briskly excused himself and went towards the nearby Staff Room. Midway he changed directions and headed for the bathroom instead. He did not wish to create a scene in the Staff Room. He desperately fought back the tears as he hurried into the bathroom.

"Do I really have to be an object of pity? Do I have to keep explaining my roots because of the color of my skin? Why can't I be accepted and treated equally as a man and an American that I am? Why must I be treated differently from my other classmates and colleagues just because of nature's protective pigments on my skin? Why do I have to be singled out for comments in a country in which I am a law-abiding citizen purely because of the chauvinism of a man who is supposed to be my Supervisor? I am a medical doctor here purely on merit. I have performed much better than most of my class mates academically. And so, why should I be the object of pillorying by my Attending?"

Ron then remembered what his dad had always taught him to do in moments such as he was in. He took five deep breaths and then quietly uttered the recommended sentences: *It's gonna be all right,*

Ron. You must never succumb to a bully. He wins and will taunt you again when he sees you cry. Stand tall, Ron, and stand up to the bully, and victory will be yours in the end." He recited to himself.

Ron soon returned to his patient with a cheerful face.

Strengthened by his father's prescribed ritual, Ron smiled and carried on with the patient examination. The patient noticed and said to Ron:

"Yes, Doctor, we all came from somewhere. If we did not directly, our fathers or forefathers did. Apart from the native Americans, our forefathers all came from different parts of the world. And it is this unity in diversity that makes our country America great. But some bigots like your Attending senior colleague down there, do not realize this." The patient said.

"Yes, but some people hardly realize this fact that the larger percentage of us are descendants of immigrants to this continent. Just a few people realize this. But the vocal few tend to overwhelm the silent majority" An appreciative Ron said, trying to sustain a smile.

"Yes, indeed," the patient said. "And it is more pathetic when bigotry emanates from educated people who should know. And it gets worse when a doctor appears not to know the reason behind nature conferring differing melanin loads to individuals from different climatic conditions. Is that man actually a Doctor? I have never seen him here since my one-week admission to this unit," the patient asked rhetorically, his gaze fixed in the direction of Dr Swanson's hate-ravished countenance.

Dr Swanson was not done. He walked straight to the bedside of Dr Ron's patient as soon as the latter left the patient to write his notes in the Residents' Common Room. He grabbed the bedside chart of the patient and before he could fully adjust his glasses the patient surprised him. "If bigotry was part of your medical school training, Sir, I would not like to be your patient. I certainly would not have you handle my chart."

It was a thoroughly stunned Dr. Swanson who found himself blurting incoherently: "I am sorry about that Sir. But we are not used to those guys in this Department."

But Dr Swanson was talking to a battle-ready patient, one of the often-silent majority, who immediately responded:

"Which guys, Doctor? If by those guys you mean people of other cultures or skin colors, then I am sorry, your Department must be living in the past. if that is your policy here, then you all need to be re-educated."

Ms. Linda the ward Nurse on Duty was standing not too far away from Dr Swanson when the patient, Mr. Patrick, went on the subtle offensive. She did not interfere in the brickbats. Indeed, she felt subtly happy that someone had stood up to Dr Swanson. An exchange that might have turned ugly was eventually happily aborted by Ms. Linda who soon stepped in and tried to reassure the patient:

"Mr. Patrick, Dr Swanson here, was only joking. I am sure he was indeed only joking." Mr. Patrick did not appear convinced as he quickly replied: "It will be good if the doctor was indeed joking. But I witnessed the events as they developed. And I do not believe that this senior doctor was indeed joking. If he was joking, it must be a most expensive joke, a very unfair joke to that young man who in my opinion deserves an apology from you, Mr. Joking Senior Doctor!"

Nurse Linda's intervention halted further verbal exchanges between Dr Swanson and Mr. Patrick only for a moment. Dr Swanson was to exacerbate the problem documentarily later. He quickly hung back the patient's chart and sluggishly walked away, disgraced to the hilt.

Dr. Ron was thoroughly embarrassed as Dr. Swanson's statements were quite audible even from a distance to the hearing of the other patients in the ward. It was not a case of mistaken identity. Dr. Ron like every other doctor in the medical team wore his white coat and had "Ron Jacob MD" inscription in bold letters, with the "MD" in red colors conspicuously inscribed on the name tag. And the name tag was stuck against the breast pocket of Ron's white coat as was the regulation in Oregon Hospital Center.

As he was still smarting from the humiliation in the ward from a senior colleague who was supposed to be one of his teachers, Dr. Ron got to the Doctors' Common Room to find that the new roster had him in Dr. Swanson's Renal Team with effect from the following Monday. It was a Tuesday and Ron was expected to make patient presentations along with one other Intern six days from that day.
It was the last of what the young Intern would have wanted: having to be assigned to the team of an Attending who had spoken so ill of him, even without having interacted with him. But true to his studious nature, Ron went ahead and prepared thoroughly for the patient presentation.

On the appointed Monday, Dr. Ron Jacobs was very apprehensive when he encountered the same Attending who had greatly embarrassed him without even knowing him barely six days earlier.

He had earlier resolved on seeing his name in Dr Swanson's team, not to appear shy or unduly offended about the duo's earlier encounter. Dr Swanson on his part had put up a wry smile when he made a brief eye contact with the young man who he had profiled in the ward six days earlier. But he did not make any allusions to the earlier meeting. It was obvious that there was no love lost between him and his Intern, the *tall Black Guy*.

Dr Ron picked up courage and delivered what the Chief Shelia, the most senior Resident, along with many other Residents greatly applauded. Dr. Ron Jacobs' presentation was followed by a presentation from Dr. Williams, the same Intern who was in the ward on the day that Dr. Swanson first encountered and berated Dr. Ron Jacobs. And Dr. Williams' presentation did not receive as much commendation as Dr. Ron Jacobs'. Dr. Williams presentation, according to the Chief Resident, was good but somehow, he could not quite arrive at the correct diagnosis of the case that he presented. That was unlike Dr. Ron Jacobs whose presentation, according to the Chief Resident and her other Senior Residents, was perfect and the diagnosis accurate. The Attending-physician, Dr. Swanson was thereafter required to appraise the presentations.
Turning to the intern with the wrong and unduly long diagnosis, and whose presentation was not well received by the generality of the team, Dr. Swanson said:
"Good presentation, Dr. Williams, even though you missed the diagnosis." Then, turning to Dr. Jacobs, and with a sudden countenance of disapproval, Dr. Swanson said:
"Yes, Doctor, e-m-m Doctor James, is that your name?"

"No Sir, it is Doctor Jacobs, Doctor Ron Jacobs!" Dr Ron Jacobs corrected.

"Ok, Doctor Jacobs, your diagnosis is right but your presentation is too long. Apart from the verbosity, I could not make out half of what you were saying. Where did you get your medical degree from?"

The transition from a voice of approval to a voice of contempt and hate was immediately glaring to all the assembled Interns and Residents. It was like a thunderbolt from the blues. But the victim Dr. Ron Jacobs apparently had prepared his mind adequately to receive the shock.

Again, he took a deep breath. He straightened himself up and courteously replied:
"From Columbia University, Sir."

But, even in spite of his courage and his bold countenance, Dr Ron's heart was pounding heavily with anguish. It was anguish borne out of the manifested unmitigated bias, double standards and discrimination, all for absolutely no reason other than his origin and the color of his skin. He felt sad that at every turn he was singled out for undue dressing down and needed to prove himself where his peers in the Department had a smooth sail through. Though saddened and naturally apprehensive about further bullying or biased statements from Dr Swanson, Dr. Ron managed to remain composed. But the ridicule and doubt were not yet over.
"Do you mean from Colombia in South America or from Columbia University Medical School New York?" Dr. Swanson blurted out.
"From Columbia University Medical School New York Sir." Ron answered hoping that a mention of his revered Alma Mater would earn him a favorable rating and perhaps some measure of deserved respect from Dr Swanson. But that was not to be.

"That's unbelievable! I am an alumnus of Columbia University Medical school too." Dr Swanson coldly stated.

"Great! What a great coincidence!!" Ron shouted in great excitement hoping that he was on the path of some kind of friendship and understanding with his prevailing tormentor.

But Ron's excitement was short-lived. Before his sparkling white teeth could again disappear behind his rich lips, Dr Swanson who displayed absolutely no emotions dryly said:

"Columbia University must truly have changed for the worse in recent years! In the Columbia University Medical School that I knew, they taught us to be precise and audible during clinical presentations. They also taught us to hold our heads high knowing who we were and where we came from. We were also made to understand that while we respected and appreciated whoever else came our way, that we would forever remain champions and leaders in academics and research. We were taught to hold high the torch of knowledge and retain our positions as the greatest intellectual people that God ever created."

As Dr Swanson spoke, he displayed a mien that smacked of snobbishness and lack of reality which was made more manifest by a fake smile that adorned his lips.

"The standards of the Columbia University which I once attended must really be falling from what I see. I am afraid Dr James that you may have to repeat this presentation." Dr Swanson said to the shock of all else in the room except himself. The degree of reprehension did not make for Dr Ron or any of the other listeners bothering to correct the mis-naming as Dr. James instead of Dr. Jacobs.

Dr Ron Jacobs and indeed all else in the room watched with perplexity as the boss displayed what was the worst manifestation of bigotry and racial bias that any human being could portray.

Ron in particular could not quite believe what he was witnessing. The meanness and brazenness were worse than what he and his beloved parents had always dreaded. Doris, Ron's mother, had during her ordeals in BGMC often prayed:

"Grant Lord that what I experienced at the hands of Dr Glen in BGMC will never be the lot of any of my children or indeed of any other American children."

Doris often also added "As an older folk and with sagacious tolerance and prayers I believe that I will be able to overcome the double standards and subtle but manifest bias of a few misguided bigots that I daily encounter at work in BGMC. But I know that Ron and my other children are not quite as prayerful and as close to God as they should be. Therefore, they may not be able to cope as well as I do."

Doris was absolutely right. In the Portland Oregon Hospital Center, it certainly was not the America that the zealous young Ron had looked up to. But he was happy that it was only a negligible few who exhibited such bigotry as he was witnessing.

The manifested psychopath in Dr Swanson was not done yet. After ordering a repeat of Dr Ron's clinical presentation he sharply turned to Shelia the Chief resident and ordered: "Chief Resident, you will supervise the repeat presentation and report back to me."

There was no acknowledgment of Dr Ron's order by Shelia, and that was unusual. The Chief resident's fair sense of judgment would not allow her to concur immediately with her boss. But as a subordinate who was indeed still in training too, she had no alternative than to silently accept and take note of the instruction.

Dr Ron was completely taken aback. The rebellious youthful tendency in him strongly urged him to immediately challenge the brazen injustice. But the good family upbringing and professional discipline acquired over the years, restrained any action which might be later regretted. He took a deep breath. He remained speechless for a while before he regained his composure. He turned in amazement from his equally-stunned Chief Resident Shelia. The latter did not shy away. No, even in the face of Dr Swanson's order, Shelia maintained continuous eye contact with the victim. Her unspoken message was clear: "Keep your cool, Ron." Dr Ron understood. He took a quick look at the sympathetic eyes of the other Residents and kept his cool. For a minute or two he looked around him in the manner of a wing-damaged bird seeking some form of support to fly off with its team. Dr Ron's fellow residents who had applauded after Ron's presentation were particularly stunned. But though doctors, they were all still in some form of professional training under the Attendings. And one of these Attendings was Dr Swanson. And he was right on the spot with the team. And so there was silence. It was deafening silence that spoke louder than words. Every member of the team in attendance was stunned at the obvious bias and bigotry being displayed against the only Black Resident in the Department. The discrimination was too brazen not to be noticed. But the boss had spoken!

Shelia the Chief Resident had submitted her scores for the different presenters including Ron's original presentation. Dr. Ron Jacobs' scores from the Chief Resident and the two other Senior Residents who were also allowed to score junior Residents were each much higher than those of the others who were Dr Swanson's favored interns. But this did not change the skewed view of Dr Swanson. His victim was purposely being held to a different standard, a higher standard, hence the original rejection of his excellent presentation and the order to him to repeat the presentation. Dr Williams who was in the ward on the day that Dr Swanson berated Dr Ron, though a mere intern like Dr Ron, had become Ron's friend and was following the ordeals of his friend. After Dr. Swanson's order for a repeat of Dr. Ron's presentation, Dr Williams had walked up to Ron and whispered into the latter's ears: "Don't worry, Dr Ron, it's gonna be all right." The spontaneous display of camaraderie was most encouraging to Ron.

During the repeat presentation, Ron though thoroughly saddened by the obvious bias that was being manifested against him, took the matter in good faith. He did not contest the boss' original score even when the latter was manifestly biased. He did not want to be labelled as "an angry Black Man". Although he was thoroughly devastated and saddened by the undisguised bias against him by Dr Swanson, starting with the odious ward encounter, he was happy to note that Dr Swanson's bigotry and hostility were not shared by any of the other members of the "Renal Team B" to which he belonged. His only worry was that his resilience in the face of overt bias was almost being stretched to a breaking point. He needed all the support that he could get. He very much wished that Mom or Dad was nearby. Physical family presence would have helped much more than mere telephone conversations. Mezie who was the closest friend that he had was two thousand and more miles away in Washington DC.

Midway through Ron's repeat presentation Dr Swanson, had pulled out his cell phone and started making a call. Making or receiving calls was most uncharacteristic and against established ward round rules in the Department. He later left the team momentarily as Ron was presenting. After some five minutes he came back and offered a brief and obviously insincere apology. "Sorry about that, Dr Jacobs." He said "But could you start the presentation afresh. I have missed the sequence." But Dr Swanson left the presentation on his own volition. And he rejoined when he pleased. By protocol he was not supposed to subject the presenter to a repeat. But he did, to the dismay of all. Each participant looked at the other in disbelief. Could this have been done to provoke the presenter into rebellion? Was the Attending Physician purposely tempting Dr Ron into disobeying orders so that a good reason would be found to suspend him from the unit?

Ron who was almost done with the presentation when Dr Swanson came back, remained silent for a while, not knowing how to respond to the new order. But luckily Shelia was around and had stepped in at the appropriate moment. She tapped Ron by the shoulder and whispered something into the latter's ears. "Don't get put off Ron. Remain calm. This is not the general policy here. But I want you to comply." It was most reassuring but Ron was still in shock. Shelia then tried other tactics.

'I was taking notes of the points that you might have missed while you were away, Dr Swanson. Can I summarize them to you so Dr Jacobs does not start the presentation all over again?" Shelia volunteered.

"No, Shelia. I want a complete re-do of the presentation from Dr Jacobs. You are not Dr Jacob's spokeswoman, are you?" Dr Swanson said angrily. The spontaneous and unprovoked bad blood was very glaring. "No, I am not, Dr Swanson. I was only trying to plead the cause of fairness." Shelia replied gently.

"We are doctors here and not solicitors. Could Dr Jacobs please restart the presentation, if you will?"

It had become obvious to everyone present that Dr Swanson had an axe to grind with the poor black Intern. It was obvious that he was rooting for a reason to discredit the innocent young man. At this juncture, almost all heads and eyes in the team turned towards the tear-filled Dr Jacobs. Whispers of "Get on Ron", "Just comply", "Get at it, buddy", "Do it Ron", from Dr Shelia and some other Residents filled the air. Those were whispers; but they were audible whispers. And, they transcended seniority and gender. Sympathy and support for Dr Ron Jacobs was unprecedented. Disapproval of Dr Swanson's unprecedented racism was undeniable. But Dr Swanson did not appear deterred.

Seeing that the traumatized intern was still in shock, Shelia who was standing at the back of Dr Ron Jacobs, again gently patted Ron on the shoulder. She inched a little closer and looked the obviously-downcast Ron straight in the face and in a compassionate consoling albeit, jovial voice, she quietly said: "Repeat the presentation, Ron. The boss' order is final law."

As Dr Ron Jacobs was turning the pages to restart the presentation, Dr Swanson, who all this while watched in amazement and anger at the support for Dr Jacobs, took a quick look at his wrist watch and said: "Dr Shelia, you and your two senior Residents should supervise and re-grade the repeat presentation and submit your reports to me in my office. He then turned and left the room.

Nobody in the room could recollect any precedent to what they saw Dr Swanson do. Re-doing and regrading the same presentation by the same Resident and the same Chief and Senior Residents who had earlier submitted their scores was unprecedented. It was absurd. It made no sense. But the boss had spoken!

And so, Dr Ron Jacobs re-did the presentation. And the Chief Resident and Senior Residents scored him again. Dr Shelia and one Senior resident each awarded the same "A" as they did earlier. The second Senior Resident changed her score from an "A" to an "A+". And the new improved scores were submitted to Dr Swanson in his office, but not before Dr. Shelia had made copies of each of the signed score sheets.

After she submitted the score sheet to Dr Swanson, Shelia walked up to Ron who was still recovering from the despair and said to him:

"Be of good cheer Ron. After the storm there will be calm. My grandparents were Irish. And I understand that Dr Swanson's grandparents were Irish too. There was a time when the Irish were marginalized, discriminated against and excluded from jobs and politics in this country. Like the Jews and the Blacks, the Irish were said to have suffered many forms of indignities. But they persevered, and kept fighting, trusting to the promise that a greater and more just America lay ahead and still held a promise for them. They believed that if the promise did not actualize for them, then certainly that it would actualize for their children or grandchildren. It is because of our grandparents' perseverance and strong belief in that promise that we are what we are today. It is not just a question of Black or White. It is more a question of the age-long desire of humans to dominate and decide the fate of other humans. As much as I know, bias is not institutionalized here; at least not any longer. But make no mistake about it, racial bias could erupt randomly. Like the doctors that we are, we know that melanin manifestation is only skin deep. But the promise and the concept of universal love for all humanity runs deeper and endures longer. This promise of equality and love of fellow humans is sure to triumph over all forms of bigotry and hate. This remains the promise that I know. And the majority of Americans know this too. It is the promise of America. It is your America as much as it is Dr Swanson's, as much as it is mine. And I want you to know this. Bigotry can triumph but only for a while. Love and inclusiveness are the only things that can endure the test of time. This is your country as much as it is mine, as much as it is Dr Swanson's. Let nobody intimidate you into believing otherwise. Again, this is your America as much as it is Dr Swanson's. and if anybody tells you that this is not your America, or displays such bias as to try to frighten you away from your dreams, tell such person that he or she lies. But you must continue to be smart. You must continue to hold your head high."

At twenty-nine, Shelia was only three or four years older than Ron. But she acted and advised Ron as only a mother would do. Her tenderness and assurance restored what would have been a damaging loss of faith in the polity for Ron. It was the Balm of Gilead that saved a nearly-drowning man and swung the latter back into the land of hope. When the saving angel that was Shelia removed her palm from Ron's shoulder the obviously grateful young Intern heaved a sigh of relief and said:

"Thank you, Shelia. I already know that the bar is often set higher for me and people who look like me. I already know that I am assumed to have failed any set tests or quizzes unless I can prove that I should pass. I saw the bias in full force a few days ago when I was examining a patient and Dr Swanson happened to be around. He made an audible disparaging reference to *a tall Black guy*. The reference was aimed at me and I heard it distinctly. There was no hiding the racial bias. That was ever before I joined Dr Swanson's team. I therefore knew that I had to work very hard, much harder than my fellow interns and Residents to distinguish myself in this Department if I must pass." Ron quietly told Shelia. He then continued:

"Like you know, I am the only Black doctor in this team of interns and Residents. There is therefore the rational tendency for my work and clinical presentations to stand out for greater scrutiny. I get that. But where I am singled out for unjustified persecution or where unfounded charges are cooked up against me simply because of the color of my skin, the hurt gets more unbearable. And so, I begin to ask myself whether there is indeed any hope for a fulfillment of this promise for me here in Portland Oregon. I begin to ask myself, "Is this truly my America?"

Tears had filled Ron's eyes as he uttered those words. But he was quick to pick up courage and dry his eyes.

Shelia watched with compassion the emotional torment which her Junior Resident was going through. She too was almost moved to tears. But as the Chief Resident she felt it was her role to manifest strength. Amidst gathering tears but with a strong voice that matched her tall but slender stature Shelia looked straight at Ron and said:

"This may appear not to be your America, Ron. Perhaps, not yet. It may appear self-delusional for you or any one of your skin color to believe that it is fully so even as of now. It is supposed to be. But in actual fact in most cases, it is not. Unfortunate as it is, this is still the prevailing situation in more ways than one. It is not yet an America that will give you a soft-landing pad. It may do so for me even without my asking because I am white. Certainly, in practical terms it is not yet for you because there are still many in the society who benefit from the privilege of being white. And they will not readily give away that privilege. And the awful situation is kept in place by a small handful of those vocal bigots amongst us. But you must not relent in insisting on your rights. America's freedom was not won on a platter of gold. And in spite of the Civil rights laws, you must realize that you must continue to fight for your rights since there are many Dr Swansons out there who have not yet fully come to terms with the dictates of that law." Shelia paused for a short while and continued:

"You have excellent human relations and intellectual qualities Ron. But these are not enough for Dr Swanson and the likes of him to simply accept you. But the biggest mistake that you will make is to be bogged down by their bigotry. You can, and must defy the odds and find your footing. You don't get into physical wrestling with a boar. Both of you will get dirty. And one party loves the dirt but the other gets badly damaged. And there are boars in almost every sphere of human endeavor and among all racial divides. You must sail above the fray. You must be smarter than the bigots. They are few in numbers but they drown the voices of the silent majority of good Americans. You and I, are Good Americans. The majority of us are.

"Therefore, we must not recompense to any man evil for evil. I don't know about your religious leanings Ron. I once heard you say that your loving mom reads a religious booklet every day. I remember you said that the title of the booklet is *The Word Among Us*. Or, is it *The World Among Us*? I took note of that statement and I believe it is a good thing for you. Her prayers must be part of what have been sustaining you. Yes, the scriptures are very clear about these. Repaying hate with hate will not advance you. It can only retard you. Hold your head high Ron, and continue to strive for excellence. At the end of the day, your hard work and perseverance will vindicate you. These qualities did so for my Irish grandparents. They are doing so for the Chinese and other Asian minorities. And they will do the same for you. And if you remain resolute and persevere, perhaps in a facility other than this, you will one day be able to come back here to tell every bigot that he lied. You will in good time certainly find that, contrary to every act of bias and for every different higher bar that is set for you, that you will come back to this very institution in this very city of Portland Oregon and announce it from atop those tram cars that hang so perilously across the street cars and a thousand bikes, and with an unambiguous voice say this to the Swansons of this world: *This is my America!* This is my hope and my prayer for you Ron. This is my prayer for us all." Shelia concluded. Ron listened attentively even as the tears again swelled up in his eyes.

As Shelia briskly made her way out of the building, Ron's phone rang. The call was from Ron's mother in Miami. It was at the point that she was exiting the corridor of Beaming Grin Medical Center, forced out by unmitigated bigotry, but strengthened in resolve by the mere words of little angels in human forms as exemplified by Dr Seene in BGMC and a Shelia in Portland Oregon. The exclamation had previously been uttered by Mother and son almost simultaneously from more than three thousand miles apart: "This is my America?"

Yes, the injustice was obvious. The Chief Resident was sympathetic. She had been very objective in her assessment of Dr Ron's work, but there was not much more that she could do in the circumstances since she too was still in training under Dr Swanson.

Was Dr. Ron Jacobs being paranoid or unduly sensitive? Certainly not. He was a mere victim of a despicable system that had run its course but had refused to give way to the realities of the times. Some staff members of the Department of Internal Medicine of the Portland Oregon Hospital were living in the past. They were only venting their frustrations that arose from their loosening grips on bigotry on an innocent Intern who was unfortunate to be under their momentary tutelage. Dr Swanson, though a relatively young man was reliving the tortured past of a system of oppression of his fellow human beings in the system in which he grew up. He saw the grips of his ancestors on power of life and death over their fellow human beings eroding and he had figured a quixotic retention of such powers. And when the latter failed, he loathed the sight of the likes of his former victims and saw everything about the latter as imperfect and unacceptable. The natural sequalae was hostility to anybody and anything that did not look like him. It was a pathetic situation in which both the victim and the oppressor each needed help.

Ron suddenly remembered his old classmate and friend Sui, who he met in California. "I now remember that I observed a similar increased scrutiny of Kui, the only North Korean American student in one of my classes in college in Los Angeles." Ron said to himself. "I remember that each time that Kui mentioned Korea, that people would seek to know whether it was North or South Korea. And being from North Korea, Kui was initially always lonely until one white student and I, made it a point to always discuss with him for company. Yes, I remember that It was only when two other Asian American transfer students from his part of the world joined the class that Kui, a very amiable student brightened up and was eventually elected the class representative. I remember that Kui's potentials became very evident with time and he became more vibrant and indeed started excelling academically." Ron reminisced.

Ron remained silent for a while and then said aloud: "But in the case of Kui, there was no intentional bias against him by the staff of the institution. In my case there was no problem from my fellow interns or residents. My problem emanated from the most unlikely of places, the academic staff of my clinical team. And, those were the very people who were expected to protect any marginalized team members against discrimination. The rest of the interns and Residents were very friendly and very cooperative. They portrayed the true face of America, the great premise on which America as a nation was founded, a free nation under God. It was Dr. Swanson who made all efforts to tarnish the commendable image of a great and wonderful people. But thank God for Dr Shelia and her likes. Thank God for the great majority of my class mates who, even at the risk of offending Dr Swanson, still kept close to me and provided me the much-needed emotional support." Ron soliloquized.

Dr Swanson was not done yet with *the tall Black Guy*. Two days after the tumultuous ward-round, Ron received a message from the Program Director of Internal Medicine Department inviting him "for discussions". "Perhaps the Program Director has learnt of the mistreatment by Dr Swanson and would want to apologize on behalf of the Department. Perhaps the Chief Resident or one of the Senior

261

Residents who felt offended by the overt prejudice had reported Dr Swanson's misbehavior to the Program Director. Perhaps the Program Director will be magnanimous enough to make amends on behalf of Dr Swanson." Ron thought.

On Dr Ron's entry into the Program Director's office, the latter went straight to the point.

"Yes, Dr Jacobs, I have received series of reports about your very poor performance especially in clinical presentation and diagnosis of cases in Dr. Swanson's unit Team B."

"It's no problem, Ma'am. I have successfully absorbed the shock." Ron replied mistaking the statement for an apology for the humiliating bias meted out to him by Dr Swanson.

"It is a problem, Dr Jacobs. Dr Swanson has reported that you come too early to the wards to examine patients, that you wake patients up from sleep at odd hours, that you bend unusually too close to patients while examining them thereby embarrassing them. He further reported that you are inaudible and incoherent in your case presentations and worst of all, that your clinical knowledge is too deficient as evidenced by the poor grades on your presentations by your Chief Resident. These reports have been compiled in writing and you will be required to respond to them in writing too within forty-eight hours. I must warn you that this report was also copied by Dr Swanson to the Chairman of the Department and the Chairman is very displeased with them."

To say that Dr Ron Jacobs was stunned by the reports communicated to him by the Program Director was like putting it mildly. Ron was completely flabbergasted. He opened his lips and shut them again, like a hungry pigeon, but could not utter a word. His legs wobbled slightly as he stared at the type-written document which the Program Director was reading from. He soon steadied himself on his feet. He immediately remembered the very encouraging and motivating words of Dr Shelia his Chief Resident. "But the biggest mistake that you will make is to be bogged down by their bigotry", Shelia had said. He also remembered a line in Rudyard Kipling's poem which his class teacher had made his class memorize as a high school junior.

The words of the poem ran through his memory almost emitting involuntarily from his lips:

"If you can keep your head when all about you Are losing theirs and blaming it on you / If you can trust yourself when all men doubt you; But make allowance for their doubting too ..."

"Rudyard Kipling could not have captured this situation better. But even the worst of Rudyard Kipling's imaginations would not have anticipated this magnitude of satanism." Ron mused. He had been too thoroughly emotionally mauled in the recent past by Dr Swanson to be derailed by the new false reports

After rattling the documented false accusations to Ron, the Program Director fixed her gaze on Ron for a few seconds. She appeared to be anxious for a response from Ron. The innocent but anxious face that was presented with a basketful of false and malicious accusations did not resonate in any way with the Program Director. She was not used to Black Residents in her Department since this category of Americans were unofficially, but very deliberately not welcome in her

Department for as long as the Program Director could remember. To the middle-aged lady behind the large office table which bore the prominent designation: "PROGRAM DIRECTOR", perhaps every black young man represented evil. Perhaps the young Dr. Ron Jacobs was a mere aberration who could readily revert to mischief or even serious crime. Perhaps the aberration before her that presented as an Intern was not expected to do an acceptable clinical presentation. Dr. Swanson's earlier question in the ward might in the opinion of the Program Director be quite appropriate: "How did *that Tall Black Guy* get here?" Perhaps, the opinion of being *presumed guilty until proved innocent* was one of the burdens of being black in America.

On the other hand, perhaps, the Program Director was non-racist but was only echoing the opinion of the Attending Physician, Dr Swanson. But certainly, her overt hostile attitude conferred an impression of presumed guilt against Dr Ron Jacobs by the Program Director.

Initial subdued anger readily gave way to good reasoning as Dr Ron Jacobs quickly forced himself to remain calm. Indeed, his thoughts ran as follows:

"Should I offer an immediate flat-out denial of these false accusations?

Or, should I admit culpability and apologize for offences that I did not commit so as to let these recurring issues rest?

Or should I offer to resign to let Dr Swanson have some peace?

Or, should I attempt some aggression? But, No! *The tall Black Guy* is an MD, and must toe the path of good reasoning" Ron soliloquized. "*The Tall Black Guy* is not expected to react like a so called "angry

Black Guy". My accusers are watching. Any discordant reaction or indiscretion would only go to vindicate my accusers' false allegations. Therefore, I must remain strong. I must not cave in. Bullies and bigots must not have their way. The world of a budding psychopath must not be allowed to expand." Ron said slowly to himself. The inaudible movement of his lips appeared to amaze if not rattle the petit middle-aged Program Director who must have been hearing a lot of unfavorable stories about the so-called *Angry Black Men.* Perhaps Dr Swanson's false tales had also negatively influenced other Departmental Officers including the Program Director. Otherwise how come she appeared to have made up her mind that Dr Jacobs a very amiable and jovial young medical doctor, her Intern, could be readily guilty of the allegations or could be suspected of possible violence?

All sorts of ideas and fears went through the Program Director's mind as she steadied her gaze on young Dr Ron Jacobs, *the tall Black Guy* who had been declared as incompetent, albeit unfairly, by his unit's Attending Physician.

If the Program Director was expecting some incivility or unprofessional behavior she must have been disappointed. For, when he recovered from the shock, Ron again politely denied all the charges and requested for a copy of the allegations.

"I will be glad to respond to all those allegations to prove that they are all false, Ma'am. There are witnesses who can collaborate the mendacity of the allegations." Ron said as the unimpressed Program Director quickly made a copy of the allegations and handed it over to Ron.

Chapter 20

THE UNMASKING OF A BIGOT

Back in his apartment and clutching the letter of fabricated accusations in his hands, Ron immediately contacted his parents Dege and Doris. He did not want to alarm them, especially when he knew that his mom might not sleep for the night if he painted the picture of one who was in great trouble. He started by cracking a joke about how he parked his car in the Walmart Mall and could not locate it for nearly forty-five minutes because he was looking for a blue-colored car which was his mom's car color instead of his brilliant-red colored new car. After making light of the conversation, he mildly informed mom and dad of "a small problem" at his work place. "It is like a fender-bender problem, mom, and so, you must not get alarmed." He said.

Ron knew that his mom Doris could be very disturbed by such acts of unprovoked hostility towards his "baby" if he told the full story. Having experienced similar bigotry in her former working place BGMC, Doris knew what it meant to work in a very hostile work environment.

"I can tolerate color-based double standards against me. But I certainly would not want my baby to experience same under any circumstances" Doris muted.

Dege was more diplomatic about it. "Man is by nature a predatory animal. And since predators readily pounce on the weak, you must endeavor to be strong, Ron." Dege told Ron.

"But how does one display strength in a system where the odds are skewed against the individual from the very top. The Department Chairman and the Program Director are expected to protect me when racial predators like Dr Swanson descend on me. But alas, there appears to be collusion between all my bosses from the very top. Only Shelia my Chief Resident can speak for me. But unfortunately, Shelia is also a Resident and not yet a faculty member." Ron said.

"The lone tree in a desert gets twisted and toughened by being blown hard and mercilessly by the strong winds. Such a tree learns to survive tough times, so must you. State the facts as they are, Ron son, and you will be vindicated in the end" Dege concluded in a return phone call to his son.

Ron's response to the Departmental query was prompt and precise:

1. "I have never been to the wards earlier than the stipulated time and the clock-in time as well as the cameras in the corridors and the wards can bear witness to this.
2. "I do not wake up any patients from sleep and I do not bend too close to patients as can also be confirmed by the nurses and the ward cameras.
3. "My clinical knowledge as well as my case presentations have never gone below an "A" as can be confirmed by my Attendings in other Units that I have rotated through. The same applies to my scores by my Chief Residents.
4. "I am very audible and precise and have maintained the highest standards of clinical judgment as my patients, the nurses and my Chief Residents can attest.
5. "I am ready, even at the shortest notice, to face any panel to further prove my innocence and demonstrate that these

allegations are malicious and completely based on bias, forgeries and lies at the highest levels of the management in the Department. Such a panel will also prove that "that *tall Black Guy*", a derogatory term by which I am addressed by a senior colleague and Attending, is only being unfairly targeted and maligned.

6.   Again, I request that you kindly study the related cameras and obtain the opinions of the related patients if necessary, to prove me right or wrong."

Dr Ron's documented response must have rattled the leadership of the Internal Medicine Department, more so, the arrowhead of the bigotry, Dr Swanson. They probably had expected to intimidate *the tall Black Guy* to scamper like a frightened dog with his tail between his legs. But with the response from Dr Ron, it was obvious that photographic evidence of the concocted lies would be made public. "Who knows how many people that intruding guy has discussed these matters with? We certainly do not wish to wash our dirty linens in public." Dr Swanson told the Chairman.

True to Dr Swanson's fears, Dr Ron Jacobs had also copied his response to the query to the Chairman of the Diversity and Anti-Discrimination Sub Committee of the Oregon Hospital Board. The latter Sub Committee had been set up a few years previously following reports of discrimination and marginalization against a section of the Hospital Staff by the Management. Dr Swanson had expressed his fears to the Program Director as soon as a copy of Dr Ron's response was presented to him. Ron had learnt from one of the clerks in the Chairman's office that there was an overnight order by the Chairman of the Department that all the corridor and ward cameras should be studied for Dr Ron's movements. The results of those studies must have demonstrated certain lies by a certain highly-placed Attending called Dr Swanson. Hence the sudden volte face by the once arrogant Dr Swanson. The latter thus discarded all arrogance and decided to descend from his high stool. He immediately dropped a voice message to his former victim, *the tall Black Guy* who, according to his assessment, must have studied in Colombia and not Columbia University and whose name he had never bothered to know.

"Hi Ron, I meant no harm in my address to you in the ward and during the Case Presentations. As a fellow Alumnus of a great Alma Mater Columbia University Medical School, I was only trying to make you a better Doctor. I was only trying to ensure that the C's which you have been scoring in your Chief Resident's assessments could transform to A's. Let's make out time to talk this evening. Best. Dr Swanson."

Ron had again immediately contacted his parents about the unfolding drama in his place of work. In the midst of the persecution in his work-place, Ron found his parents as his best counsels. The Chief Resident Shelia had helped him immensely to maintain his on-the-spot sanity in the hospital while his parents Dege and Doris provided the necessary pillar of long-term emotional and strategic support.

Doris on learning of Dr Swanson's volte-face had felt excited about the prospects of reconciliation and had said: "Good, if Dr Swanson meant no harm. He may even become your friend after this since I understand that he is also a Catholic.

But Dege was not so readily taken in by the voice mail. "I believe in forgiving but not forgetting." He said. "A great American President had once advised that even as you trust, you must also verify." Dege advised.

On his own part, Ron for the first time in the unfolding drama spoke out forcefully.

"Some people persistently take other people for fools." He said. "Someone sees you as something less than human. Then as it pleases him, and in furtherance of his own purposes he suddenly does an involuntary U-turn. Under pressure he suddenly warms up to you, all at his own time and at his whims and caprices. Dr Swanson said that he meant no harm. Nothing could be further from the truth about his statement. The cameras must have been reviewed and the nurses have been interviewed and the big falsehoods have been exposed. And the mysterious alterations of a Chief Resident's scores from A's to C's have been discovered. And the lies and forgeries by a supposedly respectable and highly-rated physician who was silently being consumed by bigotry and racial hate have been exposed. Someone's 'reputation' or lack of it must be about to be on the line. Some big guy's treasured job may be hanging in the balance because of unbridled arrogance, chauvinism and falsehood, hence this hasty apology which is laden with more falsehoods in converting my scores of A's and A+ to C's all in an effort to prove his point of incompetence on my part. No, Dr Swanson meant harm. Even when we must make peace, we must not deceive ourselves. And peace must not be entirely at Dr Swanson's terms" Ron emphatically said.

As Dr Ron Jacobs had copied his response to the issued query to the Chairman Internal Medicine Department as well as the Chairman of the Hospital Board of Management there was little or no chance of the serious complaints being *killed* in transit. Racial discrimination was a malady which the Board of Management of the Oregon Hospital had three years earlier declared zero tolerance for. That declaration followed a scandal which had earlier rocked the facility and which adversely affected the grants being awarded the medical facility. It happened that some Departments as well as some individuals among who was Dr Swanson, had remained impervious to the changing times.

Ron had routed both copies of his letter of response to the issued query as well as complaint, through his Program Director with advance copies to the concerned officers. The copied officers even when they might secretly share some of Dr Swanson's opinion on racial superiority or racial bias, needed mandatorily to act on the complaints. There was not much hiding space any more for Dr Swanson. Investigations were variously commenced. Some disturbing truths soon came to the open about institutionalized bias and marginalization of a section of the American community in the Internal Medicine Program of the Medical Center. This same Medical Center had hitherto prided itself in the immediate past three years, as "an equal opportunity institution". Yes, Oregon Medical Center especially its Internal Medicine Department, might have been *equal opportunity* in the racial composition of its patients. It might indeed be collecting higher monthly payments from the federal and state coffers for medical treatment of its majority colored patients who were often poorer and sicker. But the Center was not equal opportunity in staff hiring. It certainly was not equal opportunity in its treatment of its Resident Physician staff who in the unlikely event of their being hired, were harassed out as quickly as they came in.

"The truths are ugly." The Departmental Chairman of Internal Medicine stated in a circular letter to Staff of the Department. "And, the uncovered truths especially as they relate to Dr Swanson must not get to the press. Irreparable damage to the reputation of the Center and this Department may result if the truth gets out to the Press." The Chairman further stressed at a meeting between him and the Program Director and other Attendings in the Department.

Evidence of attempts at redressing the situation soon got underway. There must at least be a semblance of honest attempts. And so, Dr Swanson was secretly compelled to retrace his steps. He was advised to make amends. That was why he had to swallow his pride. That was reason for the hasty reconciliatory moves. And he suddenly remembered the real name of *the tall Black Guy*. And he addressed him by his first name. Unfortunately, an arrogant bigot could not find himself climbing down fully from his high horse. His quest for reconciliation was still characteristically laden with further falsehoods. He had earlier tampered with the scores that were awarded by the Chief Resident Shelia, as well as the scores of an "A" and an "A+" awarded by two Senior Residents to Dr Ron Jacobs. The earlier altered scores were an attempt to prove the intellectual inadequacy of his victim. But, consumed by his hate, Dr Swanson had forgotten that the Chief Resident and Senior residents who awarded the scores were still available. And the latter had readily testified to the forgery when summoned to testify after Dr Ron's rebuttal letter to the query issued to him. The Chief Resident and two Senior Residents had produced copies of their scores to the panel. Dr Swanson was at first reluctant to provide the original scores which he had altered. Upon insistence of the Departmental Chairman, he had to comply. And the cat was let out of the bag! The review of the forgeries along with the video of the corridor and the wards readily vindicated the victim. And the disclosures as well as interview of the patient who Dr Ron was examining in the ward on the day he was verbally assaulted in the ward readily implicated the forger, racist and bigot, Dr Swanson. To double down on the falsehoods would be suicidal for Dr Swanson. And so, attempts at fence-mending had to be made.

Yes, attempts to mend fences were being made. But the horses had left the stable. The bond of professional friendship and trust had been seriously broken.

How would a young intern again have faith in the impartiality of the faculty and staff of a Department with the continued presence of a Dr Swanson. Even if the latter appeared to apologize, such contrition was only being feigned. If he had another opportunity he would strike his victim in a manner such that the latter might never recover from. The fact of forgery of scores awarded by the Chief Resident were incontrovertible evidence of abysmal insincerity and lack of honor. And the culprit did not resign. He was not forced to resign. His mere words of contrition were accepted by the Department. What was the guarantee that after the storm died down that it would not be business as usual?

Dr Shelia the kind Chief Resident had again come to the rescue. She was on her way out after completion of her Residency Program and an extra year thereafter. She and a few other Residents had been following up on the injustices being meted out to Dr Ron Jacobs. Upon request from a committee which was reluctantly set up by the Internal Medicine Departmental leadership to study and report on the "bias allegation", Dr Shelia had submitted a copy of her original assessment of Dr Ron Jacobs. In the original score sheet, Dr Shelia had scored Dr Ron Jacobs A's in all the areas being assessed. But in the copies which Dr Swanson had submitted the scores were visibly altered to C's. The forgery would have been grounds enough for immediate resignation or firing of Dr Swanson from the services of the institution. But three weeks after the discovery of the forgery and racial bigotry against a defenseless intern, Dr Swanson was still in service as an Attending Physician. He was only reprimanded and told to invite Dr Ron for "a friendly chat." That was the origin of the crocodile-tears-like note from Dr Swanson to Dr Ron.

"Have you been invited by the Department or the Board about your complaint?" Dr Shelia asked Ron.

"Not really. I was only asked to respond to the false accusations against me by the Attending." Dr Ron replied.

"And how comfortable or safe would you be to remain in the Department after this incident?"

"I know it is going to be rough. But I have little or no choice. I now regret having this place as my first choice after the matching interviews. I saw this as a great program and I ranked them highest in order of my preferences. The fact that there was no Resident or Attending physician that looked like me when I came for the matching interview should have been a warning sign to me that there might be racial bias somewhere. I wanted a relocation from the East Coast to the West Coast. I had many options including one other great program which, even against the matching interview rules, literally told me after the interviews to consider myself accepted if I ranked them high. But still I chose Portland Oregon. Now I know better, alas, too late." Ron said. He looked sad and dejected.

Ron then continued:

"My worry is that they will allow me to waste time here and later force me out at the slightest excuse."

"You are perfectly right, Ron. I must say that I thoroughly enjoyed working in this unit. But as regards your situation, it is certainly very different. Like the Irish of old experienced discrimination, your skin color or ethnicity may still not be welcome to some people here. Throughout recorded human history humans have in times of uncertainty and immense challenge descended into, and taken refuge or solace in racial or tribal formations. They make efforts to emasculate or diminish those other groupings who they see as different or as threats to their existence. I get that. But in this particular situation, I don't see how you pose any challenges to Dr Swanson or the likes of him. It pains me that some well-educated people who should know better are active participants in this bigotry. I wish I could be of further help. But I am not a member of faculty. Besides that, I am on my way out having completed my Residency requirements. Indeed, if I were to stay longer, I may suffer recriminations for awarding the merited grades which Dr Swanson did some doctoring on. I sincerely recommend that you seek a transfer to another Residency Training Program. That way, you will ensure that your potentials which I see as very immense, are fully attained. You can always count on me to assist in any way possible including recommendations, in seeing the latter actualized. Good luck Ron."

As soon as he got back to his apartment after his discussions with Dr Shelia, Ron discussed with his parents who, without hesitation.

supported Dr Shelia's advice for a transfer to another Residency Training program.

"I sincerely recommend that you seek a transfer to another Residency Training Program." Shelia had recommended. The latter's words reverberated persistently in Ron's ears.

"But how will I restart an application process for Residency transfer midway into a Residency Program? How will I fit in anywhere else long after the matching processes have ended? And in the event of my deciding to try, who in this Unit will recommend me for this kind of a transfer? Is it Dr Swanson, or is it the already biased Departmental authorities?" Ron asked himself. The resourceful and ebullient twenty-four-year-old was almost beginning to lose faith in the ability of the system to protect people like him.

"And if I choose to stay back in the face of the discrimination and the higher bar being set for me, the outcome is as good as obvious: they will inevitably find cause to boot me out unceremoniously. And with the kind of bias that I see in Dr Swanson's eyes, with his manifested penchant for falsehood and alteration of scores, they will make sure that I do not get accepted anywhere else." Ron bemoaned.

And so, mid-way into the first of his projected four-year Residency, Dr Ron Jacobs faced a near similar fate at his place of work as his own mother had faced three thousand and four hundred miles away at the East coast of the country. The situations were dissimilar in the sense that a reason was fully hatched that forced the mother to resign while the son was about to resign before a reason would be fully hatched to compel his resignation. But the situations were similar in the sense that the ultimate reason for leaving in each case was unbridled racial hate, double standards and bigotry, all hatched and executed by a supervising member or members of staff, co-workers who were expected to cooperate with one another and see one another as loving members of the human race. Yet, in each of the two cases for mother and son, even with the great distances apart, there was invariably *an angel* who manifested the true spirit and true promise of America and the best in humanity. In one case there was Dr Seene. In the other case there was Dr Shelia. In each of the two cases, there was resounding hope for future actualization of that great promise which the Founding Fathers of the country had envisaged and sacrificed so much for. Above all, in each case the purveyors of discrimination and double standards were only a small minority of the general population of staff members. And, as it was in each of the two medical institutions, so it was in the general society. The vast majority members of the society were friendly, great fellow Americans, open-minded, cooperative and loving. But one thing that the greater majority of good people lacked was the strong voice to drown the evil voices of the few haters and bigots. Yet, as succinctly sung in the 1970 Osmond Brothers song: "One Bad Apple Don't Spoil the Whole Bunch." Certainly not!

Ron's excellent credentials readily got him another good program within six weeks of his application for a transfer. A Resident had dropped out for medical reasons in a similar program in his Alma Mater early in the first year. And Ron had applied for a transfer to several places including his Alma Mater. It was a most unusual time to apply or get accepted for a position in the program. Ron's records were very good in his medical school classes. He did not need recommendations from the Portland Oregon job. The Oregon Program Director's signature was only required as evidence that Ron had started his Residency Program somewhere and was eligible, if released, for transfer upon acceptance elsewhere. She was only required to confirm that her Program was prepared to release the applicant to another Residency Program.

The Program Director in the Oregon Program, as well as the Departmental Chairman, were only too happy to let Dr Ron Jacobs go. They were indeed anxious to avoid undesired scrutiny into their utterly lopsided and discriminatory admission records. Dr Swanson on his part when he heard that "The Tall Black Guy" whose presence had bothered him so much had applied to transfer out, felt greatly relieved.

"I will issue him with an excellent recommendation letter if this will facilitate his exit." Dr Swanson had happily told the Internal Medicine Program Director. He was smiling and appeared to be joking while he made the latter statement. But he was dead serious about the statement. He was also dead afraid lest his bias and bigotry should become public knowledge.

Ron was very pleased to leave Oregon. And Dr Swanson and his group too were very pleased to revert to their unofficial but de facto *for-whites-only* practice policy in the Department.

On the final day of work in the Internal Medicine Department in the Oregon hospital, Dr Ron Jacobs remembered the last statement of Dr Shelia his erstwhile Chief Resident:

"My grandparents were Irish. There was a time when the Irish were marginalized and excluded from jobs and politics ..."

Dr Ron Jacobs sighed audibly. He momentarily halted the gathering of his personal effects from the locker that was assigned to him in the Residents' Common Room.

"Will there ever be a day when one who looks like me be able to stand in his or her work-place here in Portland Oregon and like Dr Shelia, say:
"There was a time when Blacks, Browns and other Colored People like me were marginalized and excluded from fair treatment and respect by the authorities in this Department? Will there be a day when a Resident in this Department will work in the wards and hope not to be stalked or held to a different standard than his or her other colleagues? Will there be a day when the Dr Swansons of this world will retrace their paths and come to realize that their time is up and that their era of chauvinism and bigotry belongs to the past? Yes, I believe there will be. I believe that the time is near if not here already. Dr Shelia and Dr Steve make me to so believe. And I believe them. But I must go!"

Ron paused for a while and continued with his packing. He suddenly realized that there was indeed very little stuff for him to pack; only a spare white lab coat, a stethoscope, a patellar hammer and a diagnosis-equipment box.

"Could I have anticipated a short stay in this Department from the start? I seem to have even fewer equipment in my locker than I had as a medical student." Ron said.

Yes, Ron indeed had fewer equipment in his locker in Portland Oregon than he had as a medical student. But the truth was that as a medical student Ron and his classmates had equipment that spanned several Departments. But as an intern in Internal Medicine, the equipment in his locker were narrowed down to the relevant ones with all others provided only on demand by the hospital wing. Perhaps some degree of paranoia had momentarily crept over the young Medical Intern because of the circumstances in which he found himself.

Ron repeated Shelia's statement to himself and involuntarily sighed again as he calmly muttered:

"I can take solace in Shelia's statement and I hope and pray that such a time comes soon for equity and banishment of bias from people's minds. I can take solace in the belief that such a time will come soon when there will be fairness in work places and there will be redressing of the wrongs of the past. I look forward to such a time when people of my skin color will not have to worry about being held to a different standard in work places, a time when privileges be they *white privileges*, *black privileges* or *brown privileges* would not be granted, based on the color of the skin. I look forward to such a time when people like me, be they in Portland Oregon or in Miami Florida, would not have to worry about rampant profiling that is subtle but still persistent; one that stares us in the face and yet is brazenly denied. Yes, I take even greater solace in the realization of Dr Shelia's practical and commendable examples, examples which portray *Profiles in Courage* and which fully demonstrate that even in the midst of a predator-world, that the tenets of humanity can still be upheld. And I take the most solace in the same Dr Shelia's statement about the promise of a more inclusive America, an America where any existing wrongs and many of the previous wrongs that still hold a section of the American society down, will begin to be righted."

When he finally swung his spare lab coat over his shoulder on that last working day in Portland Oregon, Ron pulled out the handle of his wheel-fitted medium-sized travel bag and sharply headed for the exit door. He did not look back.

"Like the exit from the biblical evil city of Sodom I shall not look back. I do not wish to turn to a pillar of salt like Lot's wife who was said to have disobeyed orders and looked back", Ron said. He vividly remembered the biblical stories which his highly religious mother told him from the Bible as a child.

Yes, indeed Ron did not look back as he made his way from the locker room to his car in the Doctors' car park. There were no parting niceties, no eulogies. No, there was not very much to miss on either side. On his way, Ron had met **Dr Steve**, the new Chief Resident of the Department. The latter apparently had been briefed by Shelia the erstwhile Internal Medicine Chief Resident.

"I hope you do not take it personal Dr Jacobs" Dr Steve told Ron. "Whatever that transpired between you and Dr Swanson must not be taken as the overall view of the entire Department. Shelia has narrated everything to me. You have this one promise from us, and that is, that you will eventually see that other good face of America. I too am a son of Jewish immigrants from eastern Europe. My parents' spoken-English was reportedly not very good initially. And they suffered lots of ridicule and subtle discrimination. But they eventually fitted in very well and I can proudly say today that we as a family have finally achieved the long-sought American Dream. I am confident that in good time that, that same promise will be fulfilled for you no matter where you ultimately find yourself. It will surely one day be your America too." Dr Steve paused for a while as if to assess the soothing effect of his statement. He then asked: "Where exactly are you going to continue your Residency?"

"Columbia!"

"Where, Colombia? In South America?"

"No, Columbia University, New York!" Ron replied, immediately remembering Dr Swanson's earlier surprise and statement when he mentioned to Dr Swanson that he did medicine in Columbia University Medical School.

"Wow! How did you make it to Columbia, especially as a transfer Resident?" Steve, the new Chief Resident said. The expression on Steve's face, unlike that of Dr Swanson, displayed honesty, admiration and well-intentioned surprise and good will. The confusion between Columbia and Colombia in both Dr Swanson and the new Chief Resident was not unnoticed by Ron. It probably was a result of Ron's pronunciation of the words. He knew that Dr Swanson's confusion was spiteful while Dr Steve's was genuine.

"It is perhaps part of *The Promise of America,* the new America which your generation and mine sincerely look forward to", Ron said with a gentle smile on his face.

"I sincerely wish you well, Ron. Do, let's stay in e-mail contact. And let nobody or the fact of any failures on our part here in Portland Oregon lead you to believe that this is not your America, your experience here notwithstanding. Even if earlier generations did not achieve the desired equity, our generation, yours and mine, must work extra hard to ensure inclusiveness and to make things work." Steve spoke softly and with obvious pain that manifested real empathy. He then pulled out his business card from his wallet and handed one over to Ron.

"Thank you, Steve." Ron said. "Sorry I don't have a business card to give you. The Department uncharacteristically did not make any for me even after my many months of stay here. All my other fellow interns were issued business cards but I was informed that my own was still in print each time I requested for it. They appeared to have foreknowledge that I would not last long here. But you already have my email address in the notice board. I will endeavor to contact you first as soon as I am settled down back in New York City."

Yes, it was just after the exchange of farewells that Ron remembered that the business card which he applied for through the Departmental office many months earlier had not been issued to him. That was even when his other Intern colleagues who started the program with him and who in some cases had applied for the business cards later than he did, had all received theirs. Ron had not at that time complained about the discrepancy. But with the turn of events on that his final day at the Oregon Hospital Center, it occurred to him that the non-issuance of the business cards by the Department might not be merely a coincidence.

"It no longer matters, whichever way. The business cards, if they were issued by the Department on schedule, might today have constituted a nuisance to me. Perhaps it is now good bye to bad rubbish." Ron who was not used to foul language uncharacteristically sneered.

With a warm handshake, Dr Steve the new Chief Resident, and Dr Ron the intern who was literally forced to flee, said goodbye to each other. There were no celebrated farewells as was the practice for other outgoing members in the Department. There was not as much as a brief get-together to honor a relocating Departmental member. Perhaps it was feared that speeches made at any such gathering might reopen an already irritating wound of acrimony. Perhaps the subject of such an arrangement was considered too insignificant or too undeserving. But for Dr Ron Jacobs, the thought of a new America as aptly and eloquently enunciated by Dr Shelia the immediate past Chief Resident, was good enough and surpassed what any send forth party might have provided.

Chapter 21

FULFILLMENT OF THE PROMISE

Ron saw a missed phone call when he reversed his phone from airplane mode as he landed in John F. Kennedy Airport New York. The call was from his mother Doris in Miami Florida. Ron listened to the voice mail.

"Just calling to know whether you have boarded the flight. Let us know when you arrive New York. Love, Mom."

Dege and Doris had been following their son's travails in Portland Oregon. Again, they marveled at the big irony that mother and son were facing similar discrimination ordeals from both the East and the West coasts of the country that they had come to know as their home, one they were both citizens of. And it was happening about the same time. The difference was that whereas in the institution in Miami Florida there was no official policy of discriminating against people of color, there was a definite unwritten policy in the Internal Medicine Department in the relevant Institution in Portland Oregon. While Dr Glen's misplaced wrath and bias were concocting charges against Dr Doris purely on account of the notion that she did not belong to the system in BGMC even with the latter' American citizenship, a bigoted Dr Swanson was pummeling the young Ron on the basis of the latter's skin color in Portland Oregon. There were marked similarities in the response of the top management at both Portland Oregon and Miami Florida in response to the fear that the

285

prevailing overt discrimination in the institutions were about to become public knowledge. The top management of each institution was worried about the possible dent on the reputation of the establishment as soon as the allegations of racial intolerance and bias were brought to their notice. They commenced investigation and necessary action about the report, hence Dr Swanson's panic and quest for amends. However, the top management of BGMC which was equally a publicly supported Non-Profit did not appear to be bold enough to take immediate action against the machinations of an appointed Clinical Director who was assuming more powers than he was entitled to and was steadily dragging the reputation of the institution to the mud until there was a massive outcry in the small city. In each of the two institutions there was an official open-door policy for all Americans. The Mission Statements posted on the walls in each of the two institutions included in bold capitals: "This is an equal opportunity institution" But in practice the Oregon institution did not appear to acknowledge the existence of this policy in her Internal Medicine Department. And if by mistake a *wrong skin color* or a "tall Black Guy" got admitted for Residency, a higher bar must be set for him to discredit him or force him out of the establishment. There was sure to be a Dr Swanson who would ensure that the admission *error* was corrected by harassing out the unwanted individual.

In the case of BGMC there was no official policy, written or unwritten, against the interest of staff who were citizens but who were non-indigenes of the locality. But it was in the era of a morally-decadent Clinical Director who saw himself as a super-hero for reading medicine or dentistry and serving as a dental surgeon in the military. Therefore, in his warped view, discrimination and recrimination were as good as official policies.

Ron had a simple explanation for the events and had summed them up in a mail to his parents thus:

"Mother Nature has a way of sorting things out. And every cloud has always had a silver lining. Thus, the simultaneous, albeit isolated, racial persecution experienced by Mom and me provides a bigger and more enduring bond between us as a victimized family. Happily, the isolated incidents even when they hurt mother and son momentarily, none overshadows or imperils the strong and more enduring show of solidarity and camaraderie that exist between Mom and the ranks of the good staff of BGMC in Miami. And, the likes of Shelia and Steve in Portland Oregon Hospital Center, represented the best of America and in a few unspoken words stoutly convinced me that that notwithstanding the racial bigotry of the Swansons and the Glens, and even amidst the bias and double standards manifested by a few, there is no greater or more benevolent country on the surface of planet Earth than our America. We belong here. We are citizens of this great country. We love this country. We came here legitimately. We live here. We pay our taxes here. We obey the laws. We have sworn *allegiance to the flag of the United States of America and to the Republic for which she stands.* This is now our America." Ron said.

He then continued: "The echoes of the derogatory language used by Dr Swanson against me will gradually fade away. Those hateful words torture more the hater rather than the hated. Yes, but the compassionate counsel of Dr Shelia will remain ever green in my memory. Like mercy as advocated by Portia in Shakespeare's Merchant of Venice, *it blesseth him that gives and him that takes.*" Ron was speaking to his mother in a telephone conversation after he had settled down in his scantily-furnished studio apartment residence in Manhattan New York.

"Yes, Ron, it hurts the most when one's professional colleagues like my Dr Glen and your Dr Swanson who should be one's brothers turn around to be the predators and tormentors. But I am happy that you still remember the Shakespearean quotations that your dad taught you as a high school student."

"Yes, Mom, literature and the prayers that you taught me are mostly the things that sustain me. There is hardly any situation that I cannot find a soothing literature or biblical equivalent to explain with. Literature quotes from Shakespeare and many great writers like Henry Longfellow, Rudyard Kipling, Chinua Achebe, and many others are soothing balms to me in times of uncertainty and near despair. These verses engage and sanitize me just like your little book "The Word Among Us" which you seem to find solace with, Mom, ha! ha! Indeed, it comforts the most when one realizes that there are other colleagues, like your colleague Dr Seene and my Dr Shelia and indeed many more like them, who represent the face of the best of America, and who do not share in the bias and bigotry of the few." Ron said.

"I am surprised you appreciate my little prayer book Ron. I have tried unsuccessfully to introduce *The Word Among Us* to your dad. But he appears more interested in literary discourse like you. Yes, indeed the greater proportion of our society is generally amiable and great, but non-vocal. It is only unfortunate that the noisy few who cause the most havoc appear to define the system. The latter are the more visible and more vocal while the more reasonable majority sit by the sidelines and allow their voices to be drowned by the minority mob." Doris said.

"Yes, indeed Mom, it is simply disgusting when one sees seemingly respectable professionals who one should look up to, telling bare-faced lies against their junior colleagues and doing so in a shameless display of bigotry and hate. Dr Swanson who I told you about was a perfect case in point."

"Yes, Ron, but you see, most bigots invariably end up as utter losers. They may make the waves, but most times only momentarily. Those that somehow succeed still pay the price someday. And when realism and good reasoning stare them in the face, they melt and limp back to their primordial bases like chickens that were accidentally soaked in bowls of crude oil. And they make pathetic sights."

"Very true, Mom. I know because I witnessed it firsthand. Shelia and Steve made me proud of my generation. They made me proud of my Americanness. They reaffirmed my faith in the system. And, the promise of a greater and better America which they variously espoused, today appears to be getting fulfilled before my very eyes." Ron said.

"Your generation holds the promise Ron. As for me, I feel sad when I see my generation of Americans behaving as if we are still in the fifteenth and sixteenth centuries when it comes to race relations. I feel sad when we appear not to have evolved as fully as your generation, Ron. Sadly, we still have the Dr Glen's of this world, and your Dr Swanson, too. But we also happily have Dr Seene and your former Chief Resident Dr Shelia and the likes of the latter, who are prepared to maintain the moral conscience of their professions and indeed of the nation even in the face of subtle repression and threats." Doris said.

As mother and son chatted and respectively recounted their experiences from New York and Miami, there was an incoming call in Ron's cell phone. It was a call from the least expected of persons. It was a number that Ron had earlier wanted to delete from his contacts.

"One moment, Mom, I'll put you on hold for a second or two."

"Hello, am I speaking to Dr Ron Jacobs?" The caller asked in a rather vibrant voice.

"Ron's here, who am I speaking with?" Ron replied in a drawn voice and slightly squeezed facial expression. He feigned ignorance of who the caller was even when the caller ID flashed on his cell phone. Even if the caller ID was absent Ron could not so readily miss the deep melodious but often cruel voice that he first heard in his second month in the Male Medical Ward on a certain day in Oregon Hospital Center in Portland Oregon. It was a voice which was very repugnant to the *Tall Black Guy* whenever the latter remembered the person who he first heard that otherwise innocuous phrase used so antagonistically from.

"Yes, Ron, this is Pete, Dr Peter Swanson calling from Portland Oregon, how are you today?"

Ron almost froze with anger and anticipation. He felt like either smashing the phone on the floor or at best switching off the call so as not to continue to hear the sallow Satanic voice that appeared to be feigning an Angel's. Better reasoning however prevailed as Ron immediately remembered a religious quote which his devout Catholic mom always quoted to him whenever he complained about wrongs done to him and his plans to retaliate: "Vengeance is mine; I will repay, says the Lord." Doris had always quoted to her son. Remembering the latter quote, Ron calmed himself down and told Dr Swanson:

"Could I put you on hold for a minute, Sir."

"Yes, take your time Ron."

Ron with trembling fingers put the caller on hold and switched back to his mother.

"Guess what Mom, talk of the devil! Guess who is on the line just now, it's Dr Swanson! Dr Swanson of all people! What do I tell him? I wish he stayed his distance from me. Should I simply cut him off or quietly make him know how I feel about his hostility?"

"No, Ron, let me hang up while you hear him out. I would rather we suspend our own conversation so that you can discuss with him. Give him all the time that he needs unless he reopens hostility. Remember the Shakespearean piece titled, *A Father's Advice to His Son,* which your dad taught you as a primary school student: *Give thy thoughts no tongue*, it stated. And it further stated: *Give every man thine ear but few thy voice*. Therefore, be nice. It costs nothing. Listen to Dr Swanson and hear what he says even if you don't approve of what he says."

"Ok Mom I 'll get back to you." Ron said as he switched back to Dr Swanson.

"Yes, Dr Swanson, sorry about keeping you waiting." Ron told Dr Swanson.

"Yes, Ron," Dr Swanson started. "I just want to once again apologize to you for all that transpired between you and me while you were here with us in Oregon Hospital Center. It was all wrong judgment on my part. I over-reacted to some bad experience which I had with some black neighbors in Alabama where I was raised as a child. I sincerely apologize and if there is any recompense that you think I should make to lighten the pains which you obviously feel, kindly let me know. I know that I cannot wipe out the memory, but at least I can make some amends."

Dr Swanson sounded compellingly penitent. He then paused for a while, apparently to hear Dr Ron Jacobs.

There was momentary silence. Ron was taken completely unawares. He was lost for words. He had been raised in the Catholic faith by his very religious mother and not-so-religious but obviously God-fearing father. He never missed Sunday Mass in company of his mother even in his relatively rebellious teen years in Los Angeles California.

When Ron did not speak, Dr Swanson continued:

"Again Ron, it was all my fault and I promise to apologize in writing to you if you provide me with your mailing address."

The mention of a promise rang a bell in Ron's ears. He immediately remembered the first promise, the original and more genuine promise first mentioned by Dr Shelia and later repeated by Dr Steve, who took over from Dr Shelia. Ron soon regained his composure.

As Ron made to reply with kind words to Dr Swanson, a completely contrary regular statement by his good friend Mezie appeared to overshadow all reconciliatory thoughts. *Two Eyes for an Eye,* was the title of the novel which Mezie had once given to Ron when the duo faced subtle discrimination from a few neighbors as the duo grew up in their Los Angeles neighborhood. The latter dogma appeared to be Mezie's defensive opinion for a while. But then the nobler quote from his mother also gently reverberated in Ron's ears: "Recompense to no man, evil for evil." Ron had once checked out that quote and found that it was derived from the Bible. He did not read the Bible much but he always admired his mom's biblical quotes.

As the suggestion of love and forgiveness appeared to overshadow other suggestions of hate and revenge in his thinking, Ron picked up courage.

"What should I say?" He murmured to himself.

"How best should I frame my words in order not to appear to still nurse the hurt?" He again said quietly to himself.

"Or should I simply bare my thoughts to Dr Swanson and thereafter put it all behind me?"

The built-up anger in Ron had gradually melted away especially with Dr Swanson's manifest penitence. All that remained was the desire to extinguish the last bits of revulsion and thereafter to enjoy the clear conscience and magnanimity in reconciliation with one who had hurt one so tremendously.

"Love trumps hate." Ron said. "I will toe Mom's path this time around and try to love my enemies. This is more so when the erstwhile enemy has brandished an olive tree." Ron again soliloquized. Dr Swanson waited patiently while Ron struggled with himself about the appropriate response to give to a repentant adversary who obviously had hurt him so badly in the recent past.

Then, Ron took a deep breath and slowly and quietly replied:

"Thank you, Dr Swanson. My sojourn in Oregon Hospital Center was one of the most difficult times of my life. I thought I came to a great program. But I was utterly disappointed. But be that as it may, I greatly appreciate and accept your apology. I come from a practicing Christian family and my parents always taught me and my siblings who also happen to belong to this noble profession, that forgiveness and love were the best tenets that any human being could have. And so, much as we cannot easily forget, let us here and now forgive each other for whatever wrongs we might have done or caused to be done to each other."

There was mutual silence again for a while as if each person was weighing the feasibility or genuineness of the uttered words. When he did not hear for a while from the other end, Ron tried to confirm Dr Swanson's presence: "Are you still there, Dr Swanson? Ron asked.

"Yes, indeed Ron. It's just that I feel so guilty. But I thank you sincerely for your graciousness." It was all so unreal to Ron, hearing the man who just a few months earlier was a terror to him. "Was the repentance genuine, or could it be that the authorities in the Oregon Hospital Center had prevailed on Dr Swanson to ensure he made up with his victim? Could it be because Dr Swanson had found out that Ron had flown higher out of his reach and in spite of his impediments? "In either situation I am happy and grateful that my conscience will now be clear. I am relieved that I bear no malice any more towards anyone." Ron said.

There was another pause of ten to twenty seconds. And finally, Dr Swanson took his own deep breath and in an uncharacteristically light voice said:

"Is it a deal, Ron?"

And without any hesitation, Ron replied:

"Deal! Dr Swanson."

Thus, was the deal of mutual forgiveness, incredible as it seemed, signed, verbally over the phone between Ron and his one-time-tormentor, Dr Swanson. Even the dramatis personae found it incredible that it was happening. It happened so quickly and was completely unexpected. But it was true. A few more pleasantries followed and lasted for another five or six minutes. Ron was very surprised to find out that Dr Swanson had done quite some research into his family background. He even mentioned Ron's Mom's name and complimented her! "There must have been quite some discussions about me in the Department after I left." Ron said.

"We are all trying to make amends for all that had transpired." Dr Swanson replied with a sigh. It appeared so very much out of the blues.

Again, it sounded so very unreal, but it was true. Dr Ron Jacobs, the erstwhile *outsider Medical Intern* in Oregon Hospital Center in Portland Oregon and his erstwhile Attending Consultant Dr Peter Swanson who was his worst enemy, had reconciled! And only one phone-call did it! The *tall Black Guy* who was believed to merit coming from Colombia instead of from Columbia University New York, the guy whose case presentations always scored an "A" from other assessors but always a "C" from Dr Swanson the Attending Consultant in the hospital, had mutually buried the hatchets with Dr Swanson. They were never again to call each other derogatory names; never to remember each other with revulsion and ill-will, but as mutual citizens of the same great country, never again to see America as "My America, and Not your America".

And there at the Miami end, Doris sat literally glued to her seat waiting for a call back from her son.

At last the call from Ron came in.

"It is unbelievable, Mom, but it's true. Guess what? Dr Swanson and I have reconciled. We have forgiven each other. We have exchanged contact information. I feel like a heavy load has been lifted off me." Ron said excitedly to the mother.

Doris was silent for a few seconds. She appeared to want to be sure that she heard Ron correctly. She then heaved a deep sigh of relief and said: "Thank God for the reconciliation, Ron. Did you say that you and Dr Swanson have forgiven each other? But you never wronged Dr Swanson! Perhaps it was the color of your skin that wronged him? I wish to God that we could each look beyond the color of the skin and search for those things that bind us together. It would be great if we assessed all fellow humans based on their good works; on how sincere and how honest such individuals are, how hardworking, how benevolent, how God-fearing and generally how humane. I wish we could, as Martin Luther King had espoused, judge our friends, neighbors and all we interact with, based, *not on the color of their skin but on the content of their character*. I wish indeed that we would never judge at all, but process objectively, and at all times be ready, willing and able to help provide a level playing field for all. I wish we could at all times strive as much as is humanly possible, to help make the world a more pleasant place for all humanity. I nevertheless am happy for each of you, you and Dr Swanson who I have never met. And, I am grateful to God that each of you can now harbor love rather than indignation and hate, goodwill instead of spite." Doris solemnly said.

"That's very true Mom." Ron interjected, feeling some sense of guilt that he too might have been too hasty in judging Dr. Swanson.

"I too might to some extent have been in too much haste to judge Dr. Swanson. He might indeed have been reacting to some very bad experiences he might have had in Alabama as he said. This thing they call post-traumatic stress disorder or PTSD could manifest in various ways. Or could it be that I on my part had been too unforgiving? Could it be that I had been too judgmental? Could I too have been biased in my view about Dr Swanson?". Ron said, trying to be fair.

Just as he and his mom discussed, Ron's mind raced back to his first day in America. He remembered his little cousin Nathan innocently playing with his toys. He remembered the four-year-old Nathan painstakingly coupling his toys and agitating them to entertain the visitors to their Rancho Cucamonga home. He pictured in his mind's eye, the innocence and simplicity that pervaded the young boy's world and wondered why such innocence could not be practiced by him and other adults.

"Perhaps, if I were to try to be as simple-minded as little Nathan, I might be more forgiving and indeed happier." Ron said.

As if to consolidate the forgiving spirit needed at that moment as well as the simplicity of little Nathan in Rancho Cucamonga California, Doris said to his son:

"I wish Dr Glen of BGMC could also call to apologize for the conspiracy and injustice against me. He was in the military in the service of our country. Who knows what could have happened to him while he was serving overseas? Who know what traumatic experiences he might have experienced while in the air or over the Sea of Japan? One may never know what contributed to other people's peculiar behavior unless one deeply researched. I truly wish Dr Glen could initiate mutual reconciliation. But that's not likely to happen since he has been stripped of his leadership role in BGMC. But as a Christian, why can't I initiate action on this? Why can't I take the first step? Since I know that self-pride, remorse and shame for what he did to me and what became of him will not allow Dr Glen to call or apologize to me, I can write and inform him that I have forgiven him. Now that he is no longer in charge, he may be better disposed to read my mail without feeling that I am seeking some kind of favor. He may therefore respond appropriately. Even if he does not reply my mail, I will still be happy in the realization that I have initiated action and played my part. That way I might be able to attain the desired biblical child-like life. That way we may again be as happy as we were on that our first day in America when your little cousin displayed his many toys and was selflessly entertaining us with the sleeping passengers in his toy-trains." Doris said.

Later that evening Doris called Dr Seene to ask for Dr Glen's phone number.

"Do you happen to have the contact number for Dr Glen?" Doris asked Dr Seene.

"Which Dr. Glen? Do you mean the braggard lover-boy of BGMC?"

"No, I mean the erstwhile Commanding Officer of my former work-place. Ha! Ha! Ha!" Doris said.

"I understand Doris, but you know I have little or nothing further to do with Dr. Glen and his antics since I left BGMC. I had since deleted Dr Glen's contacts from my phone. I did not wish to have anything that will remind me of that bully and braggard." Dr Seene said. She paused momentarily and said:

"You may try placing a call to Dr Johnson. He is very likely to know since he is still in BGMC."

A call to Dr Johnson indeed provided the needed number. Doris scripted a short polite text message informing Dr Glen that she was informing him of her decision to "Let by-gone be by-gone."

"I have forgiven, and ask you to also forgive whatever wrongs that I may have done you." Doris wrote.

The response from Dr Glen was immediate and brief. It was a response that could only have come from someone of Dr Glen's temperament.

"Accepted with thanks!" Dr Glen did not spend more than two minutes before responding. It was as if she was waiting for the text message and had a ready-made response. It was a sign that he had begun to spend more time on his phone than on administration, ... or on Debbie. It was also a sign that he was still in good mental state of health, or at least relatively so.

But even with the apparent rebuff, Doris still made room for reconciliation and mutual forgiveness:

"Perhaps Dr Glen is too busy to go into further details. Perhaps he is as usual, still too arrogant in spite of events that ought to humble him or make him have a re-think about the non-permanency of any situation. Perhaps he meant well but did not wish to waste words. But whatever is the reason for the brevity and near-rebuff, I am happy that I have made an attempt at reconciliation with him." Doris muted in her simple accommodating language.

"At least any strong ill-will where persistent have been minimized. Certainly, on my part, any and all ill-will about Dr Glen and BGMC have been erased." Doris said. She then continued in a louder voice:

"Now that the clouds of malice and ill-will have cleared from my horizon, I can again see this great country for what it truly is: a land of endless opportunities, endless goodness and endless love. Where else but in America could I have had such great opportunities for meeting such great people from such diverse backgrounds? Where else but in America would I have such great opportunities of immigrating into with such relative ease and with my dignity intact? Where else but in this great land could I have been immediately welcome with open hands by a preponderant percentage of the population who are already very comfortable with their environment and social situations and who would still have been comfortable without my input?

"Even in the face of subtle and occasional overt bigotry by a few, where else but in America could an official policy be in place to enable my son Ron not to be brazenly chased out by the initial exclusive instincts of a Dr Swanson and deep-rooted bigots like him, without backlash from his Department or peers that obviously forced his oppressors to make redress? And where else but here could the baby of my house, my little Ron have the initial opportunity of getting into, in the first instance, and to be again reabsorbed for Residency when Portland Oregon manifested so much ingrained racial bias against him? I doff my hat for this country. No matter what anyone may say, no matter the initial shenanigans of the Glens and the Swansons, I see this country, with its diversity and evolving history as the freest and the best hope for mankind on planet Earth. And this is, if the small uninformed minority who still live in the past could learn to eschew bigotry and small-mindedness which ultimately lead to nowhere. I choose to see my new country defined by the likes of Dr Seene and Dr Shelia of this world and less of the old Dr Glen and old Dr Swanson each of who, happily has professed to have turned a new leaf. America, to my mind is truly God's Own Country. I can now proudly call It *My America*, as much as it is anyone else's America. And, in reciprocity, I will give my all to ensure a strengthening of this country's greatness. In whatever little way that I can, I will work to ensure that this goodness and the welcoming arms extended to me are vindicated and extended to others who are coming after me and who in their own little ways will also contribute to the growing greatness of this country." Doris said, as the tears filled her eyes out of emotions and out of joy.

As Doris spoke her thoughts also reached out amicably to her other work colleagues at BGMC.

"I also remember my erstwhile patient Ms. Laura Smith who was unwittingly goaded into lodging a completely frivolous and false complaint against me. She might have been completely misguided. I remember Debbie the amiable Dental Assistant who apparently could not help herself with Dr Glen. I do not forget Janet the Dental Assistant who became an Administrator. I have reserved feelings, yet tender words, for my young colleague Dr Anne Williams who stepped into the oversized shoes of Dr Glen by default. She might not deliberately have been trying to hurt or oust me. She might only have been trying to survive. The plot against me was certainly not of her making. She was perhaps merely an innocent beneficiary of bigotry and hate.

"I must have wronged many of these in some ways even perhaps without knowing it. And many of them have certainly wronged me either knowingly as in the case of Dr Glen, or unknowingly as in the case of Ms. Laura Smith. And as I remember these, I can see more clearly now beyond the fog of pervasive ill-will and injustices that had before now, weighed me down. Above all else I do not forget my great patient and life-long friend Lizzy, my amazing student-dentist patient and friend in New York. Lizzy it was who first showed me what dedicated friendship could be in New York.

I remember every face of the other staff of BGMC, the silent majority of these were amiable ordinary fellow staff who were helpless in the face of immorality and suppression. I can visualize the innocent faces of those otherwise hardworking staff who watched helplessly as immorality and maladministration slowly consumed a facility that was founded with the best of intentions. I am happy and relieved that sanity eventually returned to that fine institution." Doris said.

"Even now, I have a clear mental image of those good faces. I begin to see the fulfilment of those promises of America which I had hitherto missed. And those same promises already stare me in the face and ring gently in my ears. Yes, the promises are getting rapidly fulfilled and I cannot be more grateful for this moment." Doris said.

As she spoke, Doris' face lightened up and she remembered even more. She remembered those beautiful peaked mountains that dotted the landscape along the fringes of Lancaster and Rancho Cucamonga California. She remembered how she marveled at the beautiful clouds that appeared to touch the mountain tops as one viewed them from the valley. She remembered the other level of goodness, warmth and affection. She remembered Isogu his brother and Oyibo the latter's amiable wife, both epitomes of magnanimity and brotherly love.

"Again, I cannot ever forget those inanimate "sleeping passengers" who were awakened by a gentle arousal with the push of a button by little Nathan." Doris said. "Those are the beautiful memories that can only add to the fondness of the moment. Those are the other faces of unrequited love which only a fulfilment of the promise of America can fully portray. Yes, I can truly and proudly affirm that, though bigotry and chauvinism occasionally reared their ugly heads, and the frailty of man tended to suggest that we couldn't do better, that we have indeed done better, and that with our heads held high we can with gratitude to a benevolent nation of a very great people, proudly say that this is our America. This is certainly something close to the America of our dreams. It will not be long before lingering bigotry and whatever remains of malignant racism within the larger society will see the red card and realize that the time is up."

It was getting late in the evening even though the summer saving time with the distant rays of the sun still made 8.00 pm look like it was 4Pm. The beauty of the retreating summer sunlight added glamor and warmth to the joys which unexpected reconciliations alone could bring. And so, Doris needed to start preparing for the following day's work. She was very grateful that she did not any longer have to experience palpitations any time she thought of driving to her new work place. The latter feeling was once a regular feature of her days at BGMC.

The call from Dr Swanson to Ron, even when it was prompted by compulsion from the management of Oregon Medical Center, was certainly a development that portrayed great promise. Dr. Swanson could have chosen to remain stubborn. The fact of his apology to Ron was as promising as any great promise could be.

And from the Miami end, Dr. Glen if he chose to remain stubborn; if he truly harbored deep animus, could have chosen to ignore moves at reconciliation from Doris. His positive response, no matter how feeble and off-handed, was still a step in the right direction. It was a great pointer to the imminent fulfilment of the greater promise enunciated by Ron's Chief Residents Drs Shelia and Steve. With the latter and the likes of them, even with any, and all, who might still harbor bigotry and chauvinism, there was hope not just for the future but for the present.

The turn of events no doubt gave great optimism to Doris and Ron. Yes, they had suffered great emotional and perhaps physical hardships from misguided and completely unprovoked bigotry. But they had equally lived to see the reconciliation that followed. They had lived to witness the joys of the triumph of love and reconciliation over hate and bigotry. They had seen the materialization of a promise which was mused by two or three ordinary-day Americans who witnessed and were appalled by injustice and chauvinism. They had exhibited courage and patience. They had learnt to forgive and move on.

And, for Dr Seene and especially for Dr Shelia, their goodness which indeed reflected the goodness of millions of other good everyday Americans could only strengthen and empower them to continue to do good, to continue to propagate the tenets of humanity and inclusiveness and to continue to be beacons of hope for a better, more humane and more tolerant society which every other good American could look up to and feel truly proud.

Ron satisfactorily completed his Residency program in Internal Medicine from Columbia University New York. He had emerged top of his class and had won the top honors award for his set. He had maintained unbroken contact with Shelia who had long taken up consultancy positions in two top New York City Hospitals. On learning of Ron's top academic achievements Shelia had called to congratulate the once beleaguered junior Resident whom she had been an invaluable mentor to in Oregon.

"I told you that you were heading for excellence, Ron. I now feel vindicated and I am greatly happy for you. Congratulations, Ron. Now we can both agree that this is indeed your America." Shelia said.

"You are truly an Angel, Shelia. You flew in when I was at my lowest ebb. I can still hear the flapping of those angelic wings. I cannot thank you enough." A grateful Ron answered. Then in a low and emotion-laden voice he continued

"Yes, indeed Shelia, the present generation of Americans which you and I represent, are on the threshold of a great renaissance. A great promise that will transform the American society and its color relations for the better, stares us in the face. Gloom and sorrow had at one moment filled the eyes of my mother and me during my ordeal days in Portland Oregon. In exasperation and utter despondency each one of us, from some three thousand miles apart had asked the question: "Is this my America?" Yes, from three thousand miles apart from the Atlantic to the Pacific coasts, the same question was asked by mother and son respectively. Even you, with compassion and with all sincerity had feared for me. You compassionately and with candidness had in frustration stated: 'This is not your America'. I took note of that statement even as you assiduously worked to ensure that it would become *my America* too. From my mom and me, and indeed from my dad, the question posed a great challenge for which we had no immediate answer.   From the Pacific coast you provided the soothing balm. Mom's friend, one Dr Seene was there for mom at the Atlantic end. Though no immediate answer appeared to have come, the answer eventually in its full blossom did come. Bigotry, divisiveness, bias and even hate, appeared for a moment to triumph over mutual love and humanity. But it was only for a while. A minority but vocal band of purveyors of evil appeared to overwhelm the voices of the silent majority who would do unto others as they would love to see others do unto them. My family and I, deeply appreciate your kindness and encouragement, Shelia. You fully demonstrated that true humanity is color-blind. You fully portray the face of our true America and may God bless you." Ron said.

Mother, son and father met during Ron's visit to his parents in Miami. The family had congregated at the family home in Florida for the Thanksgiving Holidays. There was so much to be thankful for. Ron had passed his Board Certification Exams in Internal Medicine. Doris was doing very well in her new job. And Dege who always described himself as being laid-back in the scheme of things, still had that sense of fulfillment at providing the support base for the family as the good tidings unfolded.

Thanksgiving turkey was being cut, Doris readily remembered the common statement which she and Ron had at the height of their trials, simultaneously made from three thousand miles apart. "Is this my America? Each had asked."

It was one of those rare moments of togetherness for the now very busy family of medical professionals. Ron was particularly hilarious, having been away from home for rather protracted periods. After grace-before meals was said by Dege according to the Dege and Doris family tradition, Ron picked up a hard-roasted wing from the steaming Thanksgiving turkey. To the plate he added a slice of his favorite pizza from the rather odd pizza tray that was also laden with other goodies.

At the Thanksgiving party were three specially-invited guests. One came from a nearby neighborhood there in Miami Florida. One came from New York City. The third came from far away Portland in Oregon.

One was called Seene. The other was called Lizzy. The third, a most-sincere friend indeed, was called Shelia. All three were akin to the famed great "friends-in-need." All three were great "friends indeed". All three were the faces of the true America, the America that the Odyssey by Dege, Doris and Ron had travelled nine thousand miles in search of.

Ron cast a happy glance at his smiling mom and dad and involuntarily said: "I was told to my great dismay that this is not my America. It was one of the saddest days of my life. It initially really hurt. But I was encouraged to wade successfully through that reality. I would not wish my own children, when I have them, to similarly feel even for one moment that this is not their America. The hurt they will feel will be even worse than mine. It is therefore a duty that my generation owes our future children's generation, to ensure that nobody ever tells them that this country which we love so much, is not their America as much as it is for all other Americans. Today, with the likes of Shelia here with us, I feel fully confident that this latter goal will be fulfilled. In spite of the many tortuous paths that we have trodden I feel grateful and fulfilled. And, I thank God for the many good people in America."

As Ron spoke those concluding words, a streak of tears filled his eyes. But he quickly wiped those tears of joy as her Mom Doris moved close to him and patted him gently at the back.

Ron remembered his tortuous, tortured and most humiliating days in Oregon and how Shelia had come to his rescue with powerful humane words and sound advice. He equally happily remembered those words of remorse and apology no matter how labored, that came from his foremost tormentor Dr. Swanson. Doris remembered her tortured and marginalized days in BGMC and how Seene had provided sanity and the much-needed company. She also remembered the particularly-frightful day in the examination room in New York when, amidst a self-inflicted dilemma of a fractured denture, Lizzy's angelic presence and soothing words, provided a much-needed lifeline.

Doris beamed a smile of appreciation as she remembered the many trials and many acts of kindness which she and her son had been victims or beneficiaries of. And she knew that the trials were akin to the hottest fires that were needed for the making of the finest steel. She recognized that the good far-outweighed the bad in the American society. She was not given to flippancy. But Doris still looked up at her son and gleefully said:

"Yes, Ron. You are an American. I am happy that you have succeeded in disregarding and proving wrong any and all, who told you that this is *not your America*. This is your America. And the great majority of true and patriotic Americans around you acknowledge this. As an American too, it is also my America. It is your daddy Dege's America. It is our America, *the shining city on a hill* which we greatly love and owe total allegiance to! And we are eternally grateful to all those who through the generations and even today, have worked assiduously to make the inclusiveness possible. It is the benevolent and inclusive America of the great Founding Fathers. And, even with momentary apparent triumph of misguided bias and evil, and in spite of ignorance-inspired eruptions of bigotry and devilry by a vocal and bombastic few, the good herein outnumber the bad and the welcoming outnumber the bigots. And *from sea to shining sea*, the true America of the likes of Ms. Seene, Ms. Lizzy and Ms. Shelia, radiates to the world. And, the true America forever stands tall." Doris said, almost prayerfully.

Dege was sitting by Doris' side contemplating on which side to approach the giant roasted turkey from. He looked up amiably at his wife as the latter spoke. He had smiled all along as his darling wife of more than three decades spoke. He smiled more broadly when the latter mentioned his name during that memorable Thanksgiving grace before meals. The aroma of the big roasted turkey was already making the saliva to flow freely. Dege nodded his head in complete agreement with the prayers and without further waste of time he proceeded to *attack* the roasted big bird from the wing.

**************************** The End

Epilogue

THE GREATEST OF PEOPLE AND NATIONS

The greatest of peoples and nations can only be built and sustained by mutual love and understanding by members of all segments of the society.

Patriotism works best within the context of a just and equitable society. Internal divisions, rivalry and even mutual suspicions between groups are normal but they must never be allowed to degenerate into bigotry and hate. Love of neighbor as self must not be consigned to the Holy Books. They must start with me, with you and with all private individuals. Leadership by examples is key but must never be all decisive. Leaders are human who may falter and therefore may not always remain the yardsticks. We must aim at bequeathing a legacy of love, shunning of racial or religious bias and reasonable trust for fellow Americans to our children and grandchildren. It is the only way to ensure that America remains the envy of the world and all Americans continue to feel proud of their country.

The world flocks to America and there is a reason why. The salt and sugar of the Earth must not lose their unique taste or else they cease to attract. That Empires of old rose and crashed was never a story of a single day. Implosions often borne out of bigotry and injustice by a few but loud individuals often created the fault lines. Machinations from foreign invasions hardly succeeded in the presence of unanimity of purpose by citizens bound together by brotherly love.

Fault lines fueled by bigotry and hate may creep in like thieves at the dead of night. But they must never be allowed to take root or else they thrive. Citizenship of the greatest nation on Earth must remain a source of pride and a strong uniting force. A land that is the envy of all other lands may falter but must never fall.

The land that is looked upon for moral and material leadership must never abdicate its role.

What one glories in, is hardly ever fully appreciated until it is lost to bigotry and presumption.

"Not your America" should be replaced by "Love for all Americans" and that's the way to go.

Offices and public places should take the lead in manifestation of tolerance and mutual love.

Our children and grandchildren must embrace America and fellow Americans with hearty smiles and outstretched arms. The love and charming smiles on their faces must never, by acts of omission or commission be allowed to dim.

That way, present and future generations of Americans will continue to stand tall, patriotic and proud of their great heritage and beautiful country. That way too, the alluring wing from our roasted delicious Thanksgiving turkey will be more delicious for all.

BIBLIOGRAPHY

Andrea --- Nurse in Beaming-Grin Medical Center

BGMC --- Beaming-Grin Medical Center

Mr. Clifford --- ("Little Cliff") The C.E.O of Beaming-Grin Medical Center

Debbie --- Dental Assistant and friend to Dr. Glen

Dr. Burd --- Dentist in BGMC

Mr. Dan --- Dege's Assistant during presentations and exhibitions

Dege --- Dr Doris' husband

Dr Doris --- Dentist in BGMC; wife of Dege

Ms. Laura Smith --- Patient of Dr Doris at BGMC

Mezie --- Dr Seene's son and Ron's classmate and friend

Isogu --- Dege's brother in LA

Janet -- The office manager in BGMC

Jessica --- A Florida Dental Assistant subordinate staff;

Dr. Johnson --- The Jamaican-born young dentist at BGMC

Kate --- Ugoye's classmates at NYU College of Dentistry

Katelyn Sanders --- Front desk officer at BGMC

Kui --- Ron's classmate and friend in University of California

Lizzy --- One of Doris' patients' during her NYU exams

Nathan (Nnaa) --- Dege's young nephew in Los Angeles

Ms. Nancy Rogers --- Member of Board of BGMC

Oregon Hospital Center (OHC) ---The hospital where Ron started his Residency

Dr Peter Swanson … Ron's Attending Physician in Oregon Hospital Center

Professor David --- (Prof. D); Doris' teacher in New York University

Ron (Dr Ron Jacobs) --- Dege and Doris' son ("Baby of the House")

Tim --- Ron's classmate in University of California

Oyibo --- Dege's sister in Law in LA

Shelia --- Chief Resident in Internal Medicine Department at Oregon Hospital

Dr Steve --- New Chief Resident in Oregon Hospital

Ugoyeye --- Adulterated name for Ugoye by Prof D and Ugoye's classmates

Dr. Seene --- Dentist at Beaming-Grin; friend and confidant of Dr Doris

Tricia --- Ugoye's very smart classmate at NYU College of Dentistry

Ugoye --- Doris' classmate and friend at NYU College of Dentistry

Dr. Williams (Dr Anne Williams) --- The Doctor who succeeded Dr Doris in BGMC

Ms. Wilkinson --- Librarian in Astoria New York Library.

www.ingramcontent.com/pod-product-compliance
Lightning Source LLC
Chambersburg PA
CBHW021458240626
47154CB00002B/421